Deep Sky Void

A Cosmic Horror Novel

James Atkinson

James Atkinson Fiction

Cover Design by James Atkinson

Digital ISBN: 979-8-9887039-4-5

Print ISBN: 979-8-9887039-3-8

By The Author:

The Cold Black: A Collection of Terrors

Lake Life (short story)

Pound Of Flesh

Let's Be Friends!

Follow the author on these platforms:

Facebook – James Atkinson Fiction

X – James Atkinson

Instagram – author_james_atkinson

Slasher – James Atkinson

LinkedIn – James Atkinson

Tik Tok – James Atkinson / Author

Lemon8 – AuthorJamesAtkinson

Website:

www.authorjamesatkinson.com

Contents

One

Corey stretched, yawned, and downed the last swallow of cold coffee. Frowned at the empty paper cup. Fortunately, the coffee pot was less than twenty feet away. The screen of his IBM computer confirmed the usual: space was clear. Safe to make a refill run.

He also felt the urge. His only vice. Well, the only one that was illegal.

His friend and co-worker Max dozed over his keyboard, an empty paper cup next to his elbow. The caffeine hadn't helped the poor guy. A nasally snore rumbled from his gaping mouth, proof he was down and out. Corey karate-chopped Max's arm and his friend almost face-planted the keyboard.

"What the hell, man?" Max whined, wiping his soggy chin. "So uncool."

"Let's take a walk." Corey scanned the skeleton crew of two other co-workers to make sure no one was listening. Both wore earphones. Lionel, head bobbing and shoulders swaying, was probably listening to his Michael Jackson *Thriller* cassette for the four-thousandth time, and Aaron was listening to one of his favorite metal bands: Metallica, Iron Maiden, Megadeth. Or maybe that new group everyone on MTV couldn't stop talking about, Guns N' Roses.

Like the skies, all was clear.

Max knew what this meant. The two slipped out a side door that opened beneath a canopy. This was the smoking area. Simon hated cigarettes—his mother died from lung cancer—and refused to allow smoking in the building. Corey and Max smoked cigarettes, but they preferred the left-handed variety. The rear corner of the one-story nondescript building was the darkest spot on the property. Away from the parking lot lights, and away from the flood lights on the front of the building on opposite sides of the main entry. Corey tugged a plastic baggie out of his back pocket, unrolling the treasure snuggled inside. He torched the tip, smoke catching in the light breeze as he inhaled, and held his breath before passing the joint to Max. Corey slowly exhaled, his head lighter, suddenly relaxed. Three nice hits each and the joint disappeared back inside the baggie. A cigarette, a real one this time, helped mask the marijuana scent. Max returned to his workstation while Corey made a pit stop at the coffee pot.

Corey blew on the steaming liquid as he settled back at his computer. The buzz had him mellow, but it did nothing to dull his awe of the room. He still marveled at the sheer amount of technology, especially the massive wall of TV monitors that stretched from the floor to the fifty-foot ceiling and eighty feet across, like a movie theater screen. The litany of computers and monitors lining rows of desks that ran parallel to one another, six rows in all. The five-thousand-square-foot server room off to the right, packed to capacity, holding powerful computing equipment second only to NASA.

Deep Sky was still in its virgin years, a start-up run by the owner, Simon Eigenbrook. Simon was a brilliant, passionate former astronaut who chose to part ways with NASA after he was quietly and without explanation passed over for the ultimately tragic Space Shuttle *Challenger* mission in '86. After watching the shuttle explode, he had decided maybe the time to move on was upon him. Simon relaunched a new career by constructing his own state-of-the-art facility named Deep Sky. Simon paired his lifelong dream of space discovery with a relentless pursuit of galactic study and observation. He financed the initial work out of his own pockets, but his hard-work, inside (he called it *politicking*) ties, and tireless badgering of NASA brass landed him a substantial contract that allowed expansion of the facilities, equipment, and staff. Corey was lucky enough to get a foot in the door at that opportune time of growth.

At 2.a.m., most people in the world were asleep, but Corey was a night owl. Always had been. It was the reason he applied for this job: Celestial Analyst. Third shift hours monitoring and mapping space. His interest had been peaked from the first sentence of the job description: *Possess a passion and excitement for space exploration?* He'd answered that question with an enthusiastic affirmative, and applied on the spot. When Deep Sky had called him in for an interview, he'd been shocked. He had just graduated with a Master's in Space Studies from Gulf Coast Tech, and had not been among the top three percent of his class. With no resumé to speak of and a subpar GPA, he'd assumed Deep Sky would toss his application and move on to the next, more qualified candidate. Not only had he been asked to come in for an interview, but he had been called in for three more evaluations before finally meeting with Simon Eigenbrook. He had passed the litany of tests and questions, receiving a personal invite to join the team from Simon himself. It had been a dream come true.

Almost two years later, Corey was still starstruck—no pun intended—with his job. As a kid, he had been mesmerized by space. He used to love climbing out the window to lie on his trampoline, staring at the stars. Wondering why some twinkled like Christmas lights and some remained boringly solid. What held the stars in place? How were planets formed? Was there anything beyond what we could see? Was there life on other planets? The list had gone on and on.

He now knew the answer to some of those questions, but new mysteries arose daily. Space was an ever expanding enigma. The more mankind learned, the less was known.

He took a sip, and quickly ran his tongue over his scorched lip. Needed to cool a little more. As Corey set the cup to the side, a pixelated mass slipped onto the screen. It looked like the rocks in the old Atari game he used to play, *Asteroid.*

He squinted, confused, thinking maybe the pot was more potent than he realized. Maybe he should've limited himself to two hits.

The mass slid along the screen, leaving a faint effervescent trail in its wake. The satellite responsible for sending him this image wasn't capable of providing data about the exact size of the anomaly. It simply provided the unscaled image, and it was quite large. About the size of an average single-story house.

"Max," Corey called over his shoulder. Max was asleep again, mouth open, a bubble of drool forming on his lip. "Max!"

Max jumped awake, fingers instantly tapping the keyboard as though he had been hard at work. "Yeah?"

"Check this out." Corey hit a key and the image on his small computer screen leaped to the massive wall monitor.

Max was quiet for a second, then: "What the hell is *that*?"

"Go to Sector Eight. See if it shows up there." Deep Sky were the experts at space mapping. Contracted by NASA almost three years ago, the company's goal was to have all of the documented space charted by the year 2000. Every star, every planet, every black hole, every supernova. Of course, NASA was constantly pushing their scientists to create more powerful telescopes to see beyond our galaxy, and ambitious plans to build a space station in Earth's lower orbit sometime in the near future would only accelerate exploration of the furthest regions of the cosmos. Expert opinions on the true depth and width of space varied from trillions of miles to infinity. Corey hoped for infinity. That was the true definition of job security.

"Not in Sector Eight, but it is in Sector Seven, and it's hauling ass."

Corey picked up the phone that dialed directly to Simon. Before he could press one to initiate the call, the mass on his screen disappeared.

"What the—?" Corey asked, looking around at Max.

Max punched keys and checked results, punched keys and checked again. "It's gone."

Impossible. "Check again. All sectors surrounding seven."

Corey held the phone to his ear, finger hovering above the call button while Max banged away behind him. No way something that large disappeared. The satellite that captured the image was old but still a technological marvel that could detect a meteor the size of a baseball. A rock that big couldn't vanish into thin air. It would leave a trail, albeit faint.

When NASA hired Deep Sky to work on mapping the solar system, the purpose was multi-layered and complex. Understanding our galaxy and everything in it was imperative to space exploration. Launching a space shuttle into the unreachable was dangerous enough without doing so blind. Charting every aspect of space was like mapping planet Earth. It provided a sense of direction and purpose.

With the United States government handing NASA blank checks, the word on the street was that space exploration was only part of the agenda. Meteor fragments and space stones had been discovered many times in the past, but when a rock the size of a Ford Mustang crashed on farmland in North Dakota twelve years ago, guys in black suits showed up and took the rock from the farmer "in the interests of national security." Said rock was analyzed and scientists found extremely valuable minerals with amazing capabilities and uses. Allegedly, the rock was estimated to be worth over ten million dollars.

Finding and tracking meteors and asteroids was now a crucial part of daily work assignments. When a meteor crashed on a distant planet, where was the location? When an asteroid entered our solar system, where was its origin and where was it headed? The brightest minds in astrophysics were working behind the scenes to formulate a plan to harvest space minerals that weren't even registered on the periodic table. It was believed to be a trillion-dollar-a-year endeavor. The U.S. government wanted to ensure they were ahead of Russia, China, and Europe in the race for space mining. They weren't interested in sharing a single piece of that celestial money-making pie.

Another aspect of Deep Sky's research was, in Corey's opinion, the biggest of them all. Life beyond planet Earth. Were alien's real? Was there life on other, undiscovered planets? Were they like humans or more advanced, intellectually and physically?

"Nothing," Max called out. "Not a thing. There one minute, gone the next. Like they threw the invisibility cloak button or something."

Except it wasn't a spaceship that showed up on radar. It was a rock. As far as Corey knew, rocks weren't equipped with invisibility cloaks or any other technology.

"Maybe it was a glitch," Corey said, spinning in his leather chair to face Max. Not really believing it. "A phantom in the system."

Max shrugged. "I mean, it's computers and they act herkie-jerkie all the time. So, yeah, it was probably just a ghost in the machine."

Corey nodded. Sure. That explained it.

A ghost in the machine.

Two

Dave Evans slowed to a walk.

Waves crashed against a rocky outcropping while the wind chilled the sweat on his hairless head. He placed his hands on his deeply tanned knees and concentrated on catching his breath. A crab scurried sideways along the water's edge until an anxious wave swept it out to sea. A dozen seagulls squawked from their perch on the slick rocks. They, too, were here for the show.

Dave was an early morning jog kind of guy, a habit formed in his middle school days. Playing soccer required it. At first, he jogged because it was mandatory in order to play the mid-field position. Stamina, toughness, relentlessness, all the soccer slogans. By the time he arrived at the University of Nebraska, it had become a habit. Everyday. Rain, snow, or shine. He wasn't aware of its calming effect until after college. The sound of his own breathing, thudding heartbeat, rubber soles smacking the pavement—or the muted thump of bare feet in sand. Time alone to center himself. He'd tried jogging with his Sony Walkman but the noise was a distraction rather than the intended adrenaline rush. He needed the silence. Serenity. That was Dave's adrenaline rush.

Early morning runs also taught him to appreciate the sunrise. It became a speechless thrill. The slow and methodical brightening of the day. The brilliant splash of colors across the sky on clear mornings, or the grey doom that sat claustrophobically low on stormy days. It was all magical to Dave.

He dropped down into the sand, staring out across the Gulf, enjoying the peace and quiet that came with the early pre-dawn hour. By ten a.m. Riptide Island would become a madhouse as park attendees flooded out of their air-conditioned rooms and villas to bask in the sun and enjoy all the thrills offered by the water park.

Florida was out of sight, but there. Beyond the ocean horizon, a blazing golden coin took its first peak across the western hemisphere, its brilliant glare a sign the day had begun. The virgin-yellow rays rippled across the uneasy water as it ebbed and flowed.

Out the corner of his eye, Dave caught movement to the west. He turned to locate the airplane—*what else could it be?*—but found a fireball instead. Streaking toward the ocean, a smoky tail trailing behind it for miles. It was hard to get an accurate sense of dimensions because of the distance but Dave guessed it was pretty big.

He leaped to his feet, thinking it was a crashing plane. Not a jetliner, but a small aircraft, like a Cessna. If it was, the pilot and passengers were already dead and the plunge into the ocean was nothing more than a formality. He ruled out that idea immediately. This was a falling star, or a meteor. Something falling from space. Scorched by its entrance into the atmosphere.

He had no idea. Cool thing to watch though. It slammed into the ocean and a magnificent geyser bloomed at least one hundred feet in the air. Dave stood and waited, slightly fearful of what was next. He wasn't a seismologist, but it seemed like the impact should have at least caused a noticeable height increase in the waves.

Nothing changed for fifteen minutes. The waves continued to roll in like they had since he'd arrived at this spot to rest. The meteorite must have been far enough away that the ocean ate the impact and the distance consumed the remaining energy.

Dave wiped the sand from his black Umbro shorts, and jogged back to the Evans Family Villa, so said the personalized placard on the room door. Penny was awake, lying in bed reading *Cosmopolitan*.

"How was the run?" Her eyes never left the pages.

"Nice. But already an oven out there." Dave filled a glass with ice and water. "Saw the coolest thing. A meteor crashed into the ocean. Thing was nothing but a fireball. Wish the kids could've seen that."

Penny sat up and stretched. Her messy blonde hair spilled over her delicate, tanned shoulders. The white tank top she wore to bed was twisted and showed an ample amount of flesh, but Jessica and Van would be up anytime now. No time for hanky-panky.

"I see you," Penny said with a deviant, sleepy smile. "Kids'll be up soon."

"I know, just looking."

She pulled the shoulder strap aside, flashing him.

Dave dove his six-foot, 185-pound frame across the bed, landing on her. Penny's laugh was as contagious as the flu, and Dave caught it. He tickled her while she beat him with a pillow.

"Stop," Penny cried. "Stop before I pee myself."

Before Dave pulled away, Van was on top of him, play fighting. At eight-years-old, the kid was a bolt of electricity. Wide open from first light, all day, every day. At nine p.m., when bedtime arrived, he dropped like a rock. Played hard, slept harder.

Dave twisted to his back, got his hands under the boys arms, and tickled through Van's ever-present, faded *Ghostbusters* pajamas. Van screamed with laughter, tried to squirm away. Jessica jumped into the bed and helped dad deliver more fatal fingers to the ribs.

Several years ago, after Molly, this sort of laughter was impossible to find in the family. It took a while to smile again. Took longer to laugh. Each of them had to rediscover joy.

Dave still felt a pang of guilt when he laughed; he imagined he always would. Part of the grieving process. Or so the psychiatrist said.

"Okay, okay," Penny said, untangling herself from the twisted sheets and bodies. "Kids, get showers. After you put on your swimwear, I'll lather you down in sunscreen. We have a busy itinerary. Today is going to be epic."

Since the park was closing at five to prepare for the night's festivities, they were returning to the villa to rest for a few hours before dressing in costumes for the Riptide Rapids Haunted Halloween Celebration taking place after dark. The travel agent who booked this trip said the entire park transformed into a haunted carnival. Characters like Jason from *Friday The 13th*, Freddy from *A Nightmare On Elm Street*, Michael from *Halloween*, Pinhead from *Hellraiser*, and many others would roam the park scaring visitors. The park also offered kid-friendly ghosts and goblins and a wide variety of cartoon characters to maintain a mostly PG status. Van was excited to wear his *Ghostbusters* costume but not so excited about the inclusion of the scarier monsters. Jessica wasn't convinced it would be scary, but she was ready for it all.

Dave lay stretched across the bed, staring at the ceiling fan. Jessica and Van argued about who would get in the shower first. Jessica, being the oldest, won. Penny sang *But You Know I Love You* by Dolly Parton in the master bathroom shower. She had been the lead singer in a country band before everything happened with Molly. Damn good at it, too. The band had mostly played covers, but they had started writing originals and one received rush hour airtime. The crowds at the shows had started increasing in size as the band's popularity grew.

The writing had been on the proverbial wall: a record deal was going to happen at some point. Dave had been disappointed that she gave up on her dream, and could only imagine how painful that must've been for her. She had downplayed the decision to quit, even to Dr. Willis, citing her family was more important, but Dave knew she missed performing.

There was a time when Dave was not appreciative of his family. Not truly. He had taken so much for granted: his beautiful, talented wife, his children, life stability, a great job, nice house, money in the bank, good health. After Molly, he had learned that life was as thin as onion skin and just as fragile. It had been an eye-opening, even if painful, lesson.

Now, lying on the bed, he took it all in. Savoring the singing and the arguing. Thankful.

When he heard Penny shut the shower off, he hopped in. Listening to her switch to her favorite singer, Barbara Mandrell, while she blow-dried her hair, Dave smiled. Penny had been right: today *was* going to be epic.

Three

Leon pumped gas into the 39' Sea Ranger while his helper, Scuba, dropped fishing rods into the rod holders. The ice boxes were full, bait was cut, tackle was stored, coolers were full of beer and water, and the first aid kit overflowed with motion sickness medicine. The skies were a clean, polished blue, winds at fifteen knots out of the northeast, seas two to three feet. A perfect day for deep sea fishing.

"Check that out," Scuba called, pointing in the distance.

"I'll be damned," Leon said, marveling at the flaming ball rocketing towards the ocean. It slammed into the water and disappeared in an eruption of salt water.

"What was it?" Scuba asked, already back to work.

"Prolly just a space rock. Meteor or something. Happens from time to time."

Leon heard laughter and feet on decking boards and knew today's appointment had arrived. Six guys who threw money in a pot to book a day of reprieve from screaming children and ill-tempered wives. Leon heard the stories on just about every trip out. Made him glad he wasn't married. Though Julie was trying hard to change that.

"Good morning, gentlemen," Leon said, smiling big to show off his not-so-new-but-still-gleaming dentures. He took a quick study of each male walking toward him: tall and lanky carried himself like a clumsy person; average height and chubby appeared to be the gregarious one; athletic and tanned was the alpha; fair-skinned with glasses looked like he was ready to hurl and he hadn't even set foot on the boat yet; grey haired and bearded was the most experienced at fishing; and last but not least was soft-faced and smooth hands who no doubt worked in a cozy office and received tetanus shots for paper cuts.

This should be fun.

Leon clapped his hands, rubbed the calloused palms together. "Okay, this is my boat *Riptide Rebel* and that is my crew mate, Scuba. Like the diver, not the dog in those cartoons." All the guys laughed at this well-worn, scripted joke. Which was a good start. "I'm your captain, Leon Thibodeaux. Used to run shrimp boats off the Louisiana coast six months at a time. Over twenty years I been trolling these gulf waters. You're in good hands. Now climb in and let's go catch some fish."

Leon's enthusiasm was infectious. The guys high-fived, hollered, and climbed aboard. Once situated, Leon pulled out a sheet of stickers with names written in marker. "Which one of you is Neil?" Neil—short and chubby—raised his hand and Leon handed him a sticker to place on his person for easy identification. Five more names were called out and soon everyone was badged. Leon was pleased to see he went six-for-six in his personal game of *Who's Who.*

"Alrighty!" Leon exclaimed. He climbed a short ladder to the helm, and fired up the high-hour-but-still-going Volvo inboard. "Scuba, pull those lines!"

This was always a magical moment for Leon. Cruising out of the marina, a wide-open sea spread so far it met the horizon a million miles away. Scary to most, but like home to Leon. Off to his right, the faint dot of the ferry appeared as it headed for the water park. Loaded with tourists ready to spend a few days enjoying the most thrilling water park adventures ever built.

Leon admired the sheer size and magnificence of Riptide Rapids. Water cascaded down dozens of colorful slides, some of them climbing as high as five stories. Slides inside of tubes, others just a bumpy board. Lazy rivers that cut through scenic island vegetation. On the tracks of Adrenaline Adventure, an empty coaster car performed a safety test run through a fake exploding volcano. Faint smoke billowed from the Riptide Island Jungle Journey train as the conductor tested the engine, even tooted the whistle. Dozens of workers in matching canary yellow shirts and khaki's bustled around the park performing their job duties to ready for the day.

Once *Riptide Rebel* was clear of the No Wake Zone, Leon pushed the throttle and the boat surged forward, bow pointed northwest. Leon double-checked the compass but didn't need to. He knew where he was headed. It was a great fishing spot, guaranteed to keep these boys reeling until their damn arms gave out. Grouper, wahoo, cobia. Leon even caught tuna several weeks before. When they returned later that evening, the beer and bait cooler would be empty and the fish box would be full.

Glen, the tall, lanky fellow clumsily made his way up the ladder, sea legs a trifle dorky, and stood next to Leon, a goofy look on his face.

"Everything okay?" Leon asked, voice elevated to fight through the wind and motor growl.

"Everything is perfect," Glen answered, fidgeting. "Just wondering, how far out are we going?"

"Around sixty miles. There's a spot I like to hit this time of year where the fish bite faster than you can bait a hook."

"My man!" Glen clapped Leon on the shoulder and stumbled back to his friends.

Leon watched him relay the news. Everyone laughed and clapped. Except Philip, the green-faced water virgin. Leon opened the compartment over his head and handed Scuba the first aid kit. "Give a few packs of TumEZ to Philip. I don't want him spray painting my boat with breakfast."

Scuba guffawed and did as instructed. Philip downed two pills like his life depended on it. Which it did; Leon would hate to toss him overboard.

The ride out was uneventful, just the way Leon liked it. The sun drew higher in the sky pushing the temperature up with it and the breeze picked up out in the open water. Three-hours later, Leon killed the engine.

'We're here fellas," he called to the guys below, flashing his dentures again.

Leon pulled a Panasonic radio/cassette player out of the overhead compartment, pressed the PLAY button, and eased the volume down on Elvis' soulful voice. Leon was an Elvis fanatic. Been to Graceland fourteen times. Had all his records. Still had the ticket stubs from the six concerts he attended to see The King. Elvis died the same year Leon's marriage to Lorraine ended. He still got a lump in his throat thinking about Elvis' tragic fate. The marriage, not so much.

"Ah shit," someone cried out from the bow.

Leon's attention snapped from the radio to the sight of Ray, the jock, holding up his thumb with a hook piercing the flesh. Dribbles of blood splattered on the somewhat clean white fiberglass floor of the boat. "Hold still," Leon called, one finger in the air. He grabbed the first aid kit Scuba had left abandoned on the console, and a pair of needle nose pliers with a wire cutter built-in. Ray held his arm out while Leon snipped the tip off the hook and slowly worked the rest out. He handed Ray a bandage. "Are you current on tetanus shots? This hook is marinated in fish guts."

"Haven't had one since I stepped on a sharp piece of rusted tin as a kid. Split my fucking toe to the bone."

"When we get back this evening, I would recommend stopping by Urgent Care to see Dr. Lyla. She'll give you the shot. Not sure what it costs, but it's better than a hospital stay for tetanus poisoning. That's a sickness you want no part of."

"Roger that."

Scuba finished handing out rods to the rest of the fishermen while Leon tied a new hook on Ray's line. Mike, the gray-haired and bearded gentleman whom Leon had suspected was experienced at deep sea fishing, was the first one to cast a line. His throw was smooth as silk, and the line flew out thirty feet before plopping into the water like an Olympic diver. He cranked the reel two full rotations, moved to slide the handle into the rod holder on the side of the boat when the tip bowed, jiggled, then bowed further. He jerked the rod, cranked the handle. The rod bowed in half.

"Give 'em some slack," Leon called, moving to Mike's side. Whatever was on the hook was a big bastard.

Mike gave the fish room to run, then pulled on it again. He grunted with effort, fat beads of sweat dotting his forehead. He reared back, cranked the handle, leaned forward, repeated.

The line suddenly went slack. Mike looked at Leon, his brow furrowed. "I think I lost it."

The ocean erupted around them. Thousands of fish splashed near the surface, the water spraying like grease in a hot griddle. Dolphins leaped out of the water in dizzying displays of fear, squeaking their signature cry of panic.

Something bumped the bottom of the boat.

"What's going on?" Philip asked, his formerly green face now bleached.

"Not sure," Leon answered, leaning over the side of the boat to try to catch a glimpse of the source. *Whale? Shark?* "Something scared the fish."

Another thump caused the boat to rise a foot as if riding a wave. Except there were no waves at the moment. "Holy shit," Glen said, dropping to his knees and looping his arm around the railing.

"Everyone be quiet," Leon instructed. In his twenty years of fishing and trolling ocean waters, he'd never experienced anything like this. He'd seen small pods of frightened fish being attacked by sharks. But never this many. Never this frantic. The fish were bouncing off the surface of the ocean.

A six-foot swordfish sailed into the boat, its spear-tipped nose impaling Mike through his side. The force and size of the fish drove Mike to the floor. The swordfish flopped around, spinning a screaming Mike in circles as blood splattered and streamed toward the floor drain. Leon yelled to Ralph and Wesley to hold the fish still. Ralph dropped on top of the squirming thing, using his body weight to reduce the severity of the flopping while Wesley held the fishes tail to further minimize movement. Scuba handed Leon a hatchet from the tool bin. Leon went to his knees, thankfully found Mike unconscious, and chopped the spear-shaped nose. After three whacks, the appendage severed from the snout. Ralph and Wesley grunted as they dragged the swordfish to the edge of the boat and heaved it overboard.

"I need to disinfect the wound," Leon said to Scuba, checking and finding a pulse on Mike's neck. "Get my bottle of Rot Gut."

Scuba hurried to the console, returned with a full bottle of whiskey.

"You're not going to try to remove that, are you?" Glen asked, high and panicked.

"No," Leon answered, pouring the whiskey over the wound. Mike gasped awake, then passed out again. "I don't have any sterile knives to perform some half-assed ocean surgery. I'm just trying to decrease the chances of major infection until we get back to shore."

Another thump against the bottom of the boat pushed Leon to his feet. "You guys watch him. Keep him from rolling around on the floor and keep him calm if he wakes up. We're heading back."

The engines fired instantly, but when Leon pushed the throttle, nothing happened. The boat refused to move. The engine revved, but the boat bobbed in the light current instead of charging toward the island. "Scuba, check the engines. I have no forward thrust."

Scuba disappeared below deck. Came back. "I can't see an issue. Everything looks fine."

"Something is very much not fine, Scuba. We're not moving."

"I'll have to go in the water to check," Scuba said. "Let me get my suit."

"Hold on Scuba," Leon said. "Something is in the water. You can't go in there."

Leon had never seen Scuba scared before, but, at that moment, the seasoned pro looked mortified. Yet: "I have no choice, boss. Gotta check or we'll be stuck out here."

Scuba was right, of course. Leon hated to admit it. Putting his best friend in harm's way was fucked up at best but he saw no other way.

"Okay, but make it quick. In and out. Got it?"

Scuba nodded, rushed below deck.

Leon leaned over the edge of the boat, and tried looking past the commotion to see what lurked below. What was driving these fish crazy? Too much was happening on the surface.

Scuba reappeared, tugged his mask on, and dumped backwards into the ocean without hesitation. He cut through the schools of floundering fish and disappeared from sight. The seconds squeezed Leon's chest like a medieval torture device.

Scuba had been with him for over fifteen years. A boy without home had become a man of the sea, and Leon's best friend—besides Julie, that was. Scuba the boy had shown up on the dock's of Louisana's Gulf shores one day hungry and begging for a job. Leon had told him to get lost, even though he needed a helper. He hadn't known the kid and trust had not been Leon's strong suit. For three days, Scuba returned and asked for a job. Leon, seeing his desperation and internally surprised by his persistence, had relented. He had given Scuba one shot.

"Fuck up, and you're done," Leon had warned him.

Scuba had smiled, teeth caked with years of food. "Yessir."

Scuba had not fucked it up. In fact, he was the best hire Leon ever made. And here he was, risking his life for Leon and these six strangers.

Scuba popped out of the water like a cork, tugged his mask up. "I don't see anything," he yelled over the cacophony caused by the frightened fish. "The propellers are clean. It should—"

Scuba was snatched under mid-sentence. One blink there, next blink gone.

"Scuba!" Leon yelled, catching himself from jumping overboard. Animal instinct of a parent. Protect your child.

Scuba lunged out of the water, top half of his body clearing the surface, arms flailing at the sky, mouth spewing salt water as he tried to scream, before crashing and splashing and vanishing again.

Leon shouted at Philip, who gawked, frozen in place. "Hand me a fucking life jacket!"

Philip never acknowledged Leon. Fear had him its cold, iron-clad grip and he was too weak to escape.

Ray reacted in a flash. He snatched the life ring buoy from its hook near the bow and hurled it into the water where Scuba had gone under, keeping a tight hold on the rope, ready to haul him in if he resurfaced.

One arm shot out of the water like a bullet, hooked the ring. Ray yanked on the rope, but whatever had Scuba was more powerful than the jock from Virginia. The rope was drawn out of Ray's hand until he let go after his palms flayed open. Scuba and the buoy went down and, this time, failed to come up again.

For the first time in his fishing career, Leon felt genuine fear. Not just from the thousands of fish seizing around the boat or the man lying in a pool of blood with a spear impaling his torso, or Scuba.

Leon wiped the tears streaming down his face. "I'm calling for help."

Leon cried into the mike of the radio. "Mayday, mayday. This is Leon Thibodeaux. I am the captain of a charter boat for Riptide Rapids Waterpark. I have six others onboard with me, one of which is injured badly, and one man overboard. We are stranded. I say again, we are stranded. We are about seventy miles northwest of Riptide Island which puts us about one hundred fifty miles southwest of Miami, Florida. We need a rescue crew, and tow boat. I repeat, we need a rescue crew and a tow boat. Acknowledge."

The speaker crackled white noise. Leon pressed the button on the mike and repeated the emergency request. His stomach clenched when the plea for help went without response.

We are in deep shit now.

Leon loaded the flare gun, raised it to shoot, but was knocked off his feet when something collided with the boat. The flare gun flew overboard and disappeared in the churning water. A cry from the bow of the boat preceded a loud splash. Phillip had gone overboard.

Leon scrambled to his feet, hooked an arm over the railing to steady himself in order to locate Phillip. He was swimming back toward the boat, whimpering. Suddenly, he was yanked under the chaotic sea. He resurfaced, eyes terror-wide, spitting water and sucking air. Before he could begin swimming again, he was snatched under. This time he didn't resurface.

"We're gonna die," Glen yelled, arm still locked around the safety railing.

The ocean exploded on the starboard side of the boat, spraying thirty feet in the air. Leon barely had time to register the cause of the eruption. His brain refused to concede the damnation hidden inside the plume of salt water. It had to have been spat from the bowels of Hell.

If he'd had the time, Leon would've prayed. Long and slow, with all his heart. As it were, he had just enough time to scream before the world went black.

Four

The walkie talkie crackled, cleared as a female voice spoke.

"Sixty-five, this is twenty. What's your location?"

Sixty-five was park lingo for Jared's handle. Each maintenance employee had a number. Twenty was Cindy, the glue that held the whole operation together. The walkie was alive with a constant surge of calls and complaints, same as every other day. Overseeing a water park this size with technology that didn't exist prior to building some of these attractions was taxing on the maintenance department. There wasn't an Acme Hardware store nearby, and even if there was, it wouldn't carry parts that were custom-made for this place. From the start of first shift at six a.m. to the park closing at ten p.m., the team of twenty-five workers barely had time to take a break. Most of the guys and girls employed for maintenance on Riptide Island were graduates of some of the most prestigious tech and mechanical schools in the United States. A few others, like Jared for instance, were hired because of their proven track record to simply make shit work. The MacGyver effect. Springs out of ball-point pens, paper clips, and such.

Jared likened it to common sense. Some people had it, some people needed books to close the gap.

Like now. College boy Brandon Peters was ransacking his brain to figure out how to stop the hydraulic leak in a faulty rubber hose. The hose was cracked because someone overtightened the hose clamp, and the maintenance department was currently out of these three-inch hoses. The Order Acknowledgement said fifty hoses were shipping the following week from Industrial Fittings and Fabrication in Michigan, but Jared had no trust in that date. The parts had been backordered on the original Purchase Order and were now four weeks late.

Jared knew the solution to the problem but thought maybe it was best to let the college grad flounder a bit longer while he answered Cindy.

"Sixty-five here," Jared said into his walkie. "Down at The Ripper with Brandon. What's up?"

"Got a call from Freddie in the arcade. The *Pac-Man* machine is eating quarters but not allowing anyone to play. Over."

"Tell Freddie to put an out-of-order sign on it and I'll be there later to check it out." Jared clipped the walkie back to his belt and pushed Brandon out of the way. He could only watch this kind of stupidity for so long.

But Cindy wasn't done. "Sorry, no-can-do. That machine is the number one money maker in the arcade. People line up waiting their turn. If it's down, we lose money. So Quinten wants you to double-time over there and fix it ASAP. Over." Quinten was the maintenance director and a former member of the Army. Everything he said had some sort of military reference. Like he was still a drill sergeant.

Jared sighed, and unclipped the walkie. "Ten-four. I'll 'double-time' it right now. Over."

Jared crouched, pointed at the hose. "Brandon, this is not rocket science. Once the coaster returns from its current run, tell Sam to hold the next run for ten minutes. Remove the clamp, cut an inch from the cracked end, lube the hose, slide it back on the nipple, tighten the clamp. No more leaks."

Brandon smiled. "Look at you with the dirty talk."

Jared rolled his eyes. "You got it?"

"All day everyday, cool breeze. That's why you get paid the big bucks."

Jared shook his head. If Brandon only knew how little he made. "Just don't over tighten the clamp like the last dingbat. Snug it, and stop."

"Groovy."

Brandon was from California. A transplant looking for the right soil in which to grow. He was smart but you wouldn't know it most of the time. He was too busy trying to pass himself off as a surfer bum.

Jared double-timed it to the arcade located on the opposite side of the park via the underground tunnels. Though conditioned, his shirt was soaked with sweat by the time he climbed the two flights of stairs that put him inside a small, inconspicuous shed that stayed locked and hid the stairwell—and subsequent tunnels—from civilian sight. Another hundred yards and Jared stepped inside the rambunctious, but cooler climate of the arcade.

"Took you long enough," Freddie said. "Already had fifteen kids complain."

"The arcade is not the only attraction on the island, Freddie."

Riptide Galleria reminded Jared of the arcade at The Pavilion in his hometown of Myrtle Beach, South Carolina. Blinking lights, electronic voices and game noises, crowded from sunrise to sunset, hands slapping plastic buttons, kids yelling at the machine after losing, the endless tinkle of quarters dropping into the metal bin of the change machine, loud music over the speakers. When Jared first arrived on the island, he had wondered why have an arcade when there were dozens of attractions for kids to enjoy. He soon learned that Riptide Rapids and its wide variety of rides did not appeal to all kids. The ones that frequented the galleria were mostly social rejects. Black t-shirts, earrings, smelling like sweat and cigarettes, awkward, socially inept. Jared understood their plight. He had once been a reject himself.

After his mom split, Jared had lived in a depressed, run-down trailer park in Myrtle Beach with his dad. Half of the trailers had been abandoned. One had been a blackened husk from a fire that claimed the lives of five crackheads before his family moved into the park. Most of the residents had been drug addicts. The park had smelled like marijuana pretty much twenty-four-seven. Police had been regular visitors, hung out in the park more than the donut shops. Very few days had gone by without a domestic disturbance or someone being picked up for murder or someone overdosing.

When he saw those kids, he saw himself.

One such boy, about fourteen years of age, was standing in front of the *Pac-Man* machine, staring at the OUT-OF-ORDER sign. His unruly hair was greasy black, complexion pale, cheeks alive with puss-filled acne, arms and legs thin and knobby. Jared wasn't sure if he couldn't read, or simply couldn't comprehend.

"You okay?" Jared asked, setting his worn, oil-stained tool bag down beside the machine.

The kid looked at him like he was an alien. Jared noticed the wide pupils and dodgy eyes. High as a kite. "The little yellow guy is hungry. He needs to eat. Why won't you let him eat?"

Where are his parents? Jared glanced around the arcade, saw only more kids roaming through the machines with a fistful of quarters. "Run along, kid. Little yellow guy will be eating soon."

The kid looked at the sign, and back to Jared. He smiled, shrugged, and disappeared into the maze of machines.

Jared pulled a screwdriver and removed the fasteners from the front panel. He decided to try a hard reset first before removing parts. Like anything electronic, sometimes it just needed to start over. He waited five minutes for the game to fully come back on, then dropped a quarter in the slot, hit the ONE PLAYER button, and watched the little yellow guy streak across the screen. After the initial start-up video was done, Jared let the hungry guy munch away.

The kid returned as Jared packed up his tools.

"Can the yellow guy eat now?"

"It's a buffet kid. He can eat all he wants."

Jared stopped at the front counter where Freddie leaned, picking at his fingernails. At six-six, Freddie could've been a basketball player, but he was as athletic as a cinderblock. Gangly was the word that popped into Jared's head every time he saw the guy. His hair always stood up in the back, and he looked ill-fitted for the canary-yellow shirt and khaki shorts. His ghostly white legs suggested Freddie was allergic to the sun.

"Fixed?" Freddie asked.

"A kid's already on it."

"Number one money maker. The only machine in the building I have to empty at least half-a-dozen times a day."

"So I heard," Jared said. "Listen, the kid that's on it right now."

"What about him?" Freddie continued picking at his nails, uninterested.

"He's like, fourteen, and looks to be high on something."

Freddie stopped picking, dark eyes rising to meet Jared's. "Yeah? And?"

Jared cocked his head to one side, making sure to enunciate each word. "The. Kid. Is. Fourteen. It's dangerous and a liability to the park. What if he passes out while playing a game? Hits his head on the corner of *Frogger*. In *your* arcade."

"I'm not his babysitter," Freddie whined.

"You are when they walk into this building," Jared said, smacking the counter hard enough to make Freddie jump.

Freddie called to Jared but he wasn't listening. Jared was hypersensitive to kids doing drugs. He had witnessed a girl overdose at a party when he was a teenager. She died three days later. He credited that incident as the single most important moment of his life. The catalyst behind him getting off drugs, becoming more responsible.

He walked into Cindy's office and sat down in a chair in front of her desk. She was on the phone, one finger wrapped by the coiled telephone cable like a mummy. She nodded at him, shot a quick smile, and finished the conversation.

Jared had never made a move on Cindy, but he secretly had a crush on her. Sandy blonde hair with the perfect poof in her bangs, striking green eyes enhanced just enough with makeup, playful lips, five-foot-eight, and one hundred fifteen pounds. Better yet, she was easy to talk to, funny and vivacious. Perfect.

Cindy dropped the phone in its cradle. Brushed her hair away from her neck, straightened her blouse. "How's *Pac-Man?*"

"Little guy's hungry and eating." Jared tried to hide the butterflies that were surely fluttering from his lips. Happened every time she looked at him. Like she was reading him, his thoughts, his secret infatuation.

Her forehead wrinkled along with her cute, slightly pug, freckle-sprinkled nose. "Okay. Does that mean it's fixed?"

"Yes," Jared said. "Freddie's happy for the time being."

"Won't last long," Cindy said through a sigh, now fidgeting with her earring. "We'll take it for now."

"I'm here out of concern."

"For who? Freddie?"

"No. There is a kid in the arcade who looks high as the clouds. He can't be more than fourteen or fifteen."

Cindy's fingers drummed the desk. Her way of thinking. "Did you see the kid's parents?"

"No. I didn't see any parents."

"Write down a physical description. I'll call Moe and have him get one of his guys to keep an eye on the kid. Once we identify where he's staying, we'll call the parents in."

"Good."

Cindy handed Jared a pad and pen. "The last thing we need is someone dying on the island."

Five

Riptide Island was home to Riptide Rapids, a 350-acre waterpark attraction with the best water slides, chutes, splash pads, swimming pools, wave pools, and sunbathing areas in the world. But it was more than a waterpark. With four rollercoasters, a vertical plunge that dropped riders eighty feet in the blink of an eye, a lazy river, a swinging pirate ship, a thirty-story observation tower with breathtaking scenery of the island and ocean, a jungle-touring train, two putt-putt courses, swimming with the dolphins, fishing charters, game rooms, a carousel, a dedicated kids section with bumper cars and swings, tilt-a-whirls and aquatic-themed rides, along with over fifty shops, restaurants, memorabilia cabanas, candy huts, ice cream parlors, and luxurious five-star hotel accommodations, Riptide Rapids was an entertainment juggernaut second to none..

Larry Taylor had expected it to fail. From day one. The park was on an island. In the middle of the ocean. Remote and isolated. Who would come here?

He had been wrong. And was glad of it. His job as Park Director relied upon Riptide's success.

His early opinion of the park had been mostly shaped by the challenges and failures during development and construction. According to geologists, the island had initially formed over time from volcanic activity. Further analysis confirmed a meteorite had struck the still-forming landmass causing a modification to its progress. Over the course of millions of years, the land mass expanded and formed around the meteor via sedated lava flow, atmospheric changes, and marine life. Once the volcano became dormant, plant life flourished. Thousands of years of growth resulted in an island that many considered uninhabitable due to its savage jungle, ferocious wildlife, and suspect structural integrity.

When Tim Plank, a premier land developer in America, approached Kim West at Grandiose Capital Investment Corporation in search of investors for his ideas for a destination attraction on the island, she had responded with a hard no. She'd thought the idea was preposterous. But Tim had been undeterred—an indisputable trait of the successful. He hired a firm out of Knoxville to design storyboards to present to Kim and the powers that be at Grandiose. The design team harnessed his vision, creating rough drawings for him to use to refine his approach. They devised six-story boards and a park map with bright color concepts, exciting attraction proposals, resort schemes and themes, and a list of potential attractions that had never existed before. It had been a bold daydream.

Kim West had not only been impressed with the idea, she wanted Grandiose to fund the whole endeavor. She hadn't wanted to share the idea with other investors.

That's where the problems started. Like the project was cursed from the start.

A land surveyor was bitten by a Bushmaster while reviewing the island. He and four others had arrived on the island by a boat chartered in Key West. The boat had been equipped with quad 250s but the surveyor died before they reached a hospital. His co-workers said he appeared to choke to death.

A year later, Tim died in a car accident just before construction began. Brakes malfunctioned two miles from his house as he rounded a sharp curve in the middle of the night. Car hit a tree head on. Tim was killed instantly.

The next accident occurred when a barge transporting heavy equipment to the island to begin clearing and grading the land for construction sank just off the coast of Florida, killing six crewmen and losing fifteen million dollars in equipment.

During the site work, one of the bulldozer operators decided to explore the island after his shift ended. His co-workers warned him not to go, but he went anyway. He was never seen again.

Accidents happened on most job sites, big and small, but the construction on Riptide Island experienced a high number of injuries and fatalities. Grandiose blew it off as occupational hazards. The job was too big to fail. Too much money had already been spent. Advertising had already started. Pre-sales were being announced. Summer of '88 had been chosen as the grand opening, just in time for Independence Day.

Ticket sales had eclipsed the wildest imaginings of the board members. The park opened to huge fanfare and had not relented in the year and half it had been in operation.

Larry sipped his coffee while he stared out the large window of his office that faced the park. His office building sat on a ridge that provided a nice view of a portion of Riptide Rapids. Everyday he battled anxiety, and today was no different. At some point, the curse on this island was bound to creep from its dark lair to strike again. Larry hoped he was wrong, but deep down inside he knew it was only a matter of time.

Sometimes he considered quitting. Hopping on the ferry, returning to the mainland, handing his keys to the captain of the ship, and heading to his empty home in Pittsburgh. Let someone else deal with the aftermath of some freak accident that killed a child or severely injured a mother or father.

It was not a question of if.

It was a question of when.

Six

Pete Palmer turned the page, pushed his sunglasses up. He was reading *Phantoms* by Dean Koontz and damn it was scary. He had no idea what happened in Snowfield, but he'd be getting the hell out of there if it were him.

"Look at this dork," a boy said to his friend as they walked past, pointing at Pete. Five foot tall, stocky frame, buzzed light brown hair with a curly, dyed-red rat-tail hanging over his t-shirt collar, red cheeks. The kid presented all the traits of a high school bully: angry eyes, self-hate in his stride, probably abused in one way or another by his dad and/or mom.

The taloned claws of dread clinched Pete's guts. He was often the subject of hateful remarks at school. And though he tried to take it all in stride, pretending the words failed to hurt—sticks and stones, after all—or even penetrate, when alone those comments turned to angry hornets that stung reckless abandon Books and music were his only reprieve. Taking him away to worlds where no one laughed, made fun, or ridiculed him. Much-needed places of serenity.

`Pete watched the asshole saunter around the pool making fun of other kids. Even puffed out his cheeks to imitate an overweight parent. He tossed a lewd comment at a pretty girl sitting on the edge of the pool with her feet in the water, and was chased away by her muscular boyfriend.

Pete smiled—what goes around, comes around—and went back to his book. A blade of sunlight washed over his feet and he readjusted his lounge chair to hide beneath the canopy of shade better.

Pete was a loner. A dork, as the bully suggested. And he was okay with that. He had a few like-minded friends, guys who liked comic books, *Dungeons & Dragons,* read a lot, and played instruments in their little makeshift metal band. Otherwise, he kept to himself. One classmate asked him why he was so shy. He had shrugged and walked on, but the truth was deeper than that. He wasn't shy at all. In fact, he would talk the ears off an elephant once he was comfortable. He was eccentric, liked what he liked, and most of his classmates liked other things: football games, pep rallies, hanging out at the mall, going to the skating rink, riding the strip, sitting in vacant parking lots listening to the four twelve-inch subwoofers rattle the fenders on their low-rider trucks, underage drinking at parties usually hosted by rich kid and star quarterback Mark Larimore. None of which appealed to Pete.

This vacation for instance. A complete waste of money and time. His parents had been determined to come to this sweatbox for one reason. To get Pete out of the house. Or at least, that was how they presented it. And there was a shred of truth in that admission, but they really wanted to come here themselves. Most adults were just big kids who were required to act like adults because other adults would frown upon them acting like kids. Even while secretly wishing they themselves could let the inhibitions go and Just Be Free. Get it?

Pete certainly could. Even at the green age of sixteen.

"Pete, why must you wear that shirt out here?" Pete's mom, Darlene, asked, hands on hips, disapproval all over her face.

Pete loved the shirt. Saw nothing wrong with a smiley face with a bullet hole in the forehead, blood dripping down smiley's face, and the phrase *Have A Nice Day* printed across the bottom. "What's wrong with my shirt?"

"It's ... indecent. And brash."

"I'm a drummer in a metal band, Mom. I like brash."

"Why don't you hop in the pool and cool off?" She untangled her beach towel from the chair she was using and dried her long, red hair. "Your cheeks are flush."

She meant well. Dad, too. They were normal. Boring even. His dad was an insurance salesman for Planet Life, and his mom was a registered nurse for Doctor Bennell, a family physician. They were in a bowling league together. Watched *Wheel Of Fortune* and *Jeopardy* religiously. They probably wondered—privately, of course—what happened to him. Two positives shouldn't make a negative. "I'm good, Mom. I'll go in a few minutes."

"Pete," she sighed. "I know we just arrived yesterday, but you haven't done anything but lay by the pool in the shade and read. We paid good money to come here, and we did it to get you out of the house. I want you to get up, and get in the water. That's an order."

It was Pete's turn to huff. But to avoid making a scene, he stabbed the bookmark between the current open pages—Jenny and Lisa would have to navigate the dead quiet of Snowfield alone for awhile—and slid the book under his chair. "Okay, okay. I'll go. But you know I don't like swimming."

"I know. Just try to act like you do. The park will close in a little while and we'll head back to the hotel for a bit of r and r before tonight. I know that's what you really came for."

She was right. The Haunted Island Festival was the only reason Pete hadn't thrown a fit when they told him about this trip. Halloween was his favorite holiday; even better than Christmas. The idea of converting a family-friendly island by day into a haunted attraction by night was too good to miss. "Alright. I'll go in until it's time to head back to the room. Sound good?"

Darlene kissed him on the cheek. "Thank you."

Pete slipped into the water, secretly enjoying the coolness. He'd never tell Mom though. She'd go on forever about how she told him so. He waded past splashing swimmers to the opposite side of the pool. He leaned on the edge and watched the smaller kids running around the splash pad section twenty yards away, sliding through wet tubes made of bright colors, standing below a huge bucket that dumped gallons of water every few minutes, laughing and squealing.

"Looks fun, huh?"

Pete jerked toward the unfamiliar female voice to find an equally awkward girl smiling at him. Awkward but gorgeous. Jet black hair pulled into a pony-tail—no bob in the front like all the preppy girls at his school. Skin unblemished by the sun, as milky and pale as a vampire. Skinny but not anorexic. Eyes the color of the pool water; transparent blue and shimmery. Black bikini top barely covering swollen breasts which required great restraint not to stare at.

"Um." Pete fumbled for words like a desperate blind man searching for his walking stick. Girls at his school usually didn't speak. The one's that did, well, nothing to get worked up about. He blinked to hit the reset button. On the other side of that dark flicker, she waited patiently. Like this happened all the time. Maybe it did. "Um, yeah, um, it does. We don't have anything like that where I'm from. Looks cool."

"And where's that?" She pushed through the water to place her arms on the edge next to his. One elbow brushed his and he received a shock of electricity. Corny, but true.

He lost his train of thought. "Where's what?"

She laughed. Enjoying his anxiety. Chewed on it like bubble gum. "Where are you from?"

"Oh, yeah, um, I'm from Tennessee. Milan. Hole in the wall." He glanced towards the kids playing again. More so to untie his tongue and his brain than anything else. "Um, what about you?"

"Georgia. Augusta. Not a hole in the wall. Still lame though. If you follow golf you've probably heard of it."

"I know nothing about golf. Lamest sport ever, in my humble opinion. My dad plays every now and then. Always asks me to go. Gets the same answer every time. No."

She stared at him, those glassy blue icebergs capsizing him as surely as the *Titanic*. "I'm Nola." Her wet hand rose and waited to shake, water dripping from her delicate fingertips. Nails painted black.

Pete shook it. Noting the electricity again. "Pete."

"You going to the haunted island tonight, Pete?"

"Yes. It's the only thing about this place that's not lame." He added, "Hopefully."

Nola nodded in agreement. "You're in Driftwood Haven, right?"

"How'd you know that?"

"I'm there, too. I saw you checking in yesterday."

Ah! "What floor are you on?"

"Third. You?"

"Sixth."

"Well," Nola said, her voice slinky, "maybe we should meet up in the lobby at dark and we can explore the haunted island together. What say you?"

Pete glanced back across the pool. His mom was watching the two of them from her chair. Pleased, no doubt. "I say that's a great idea."

"Will your parents let you go around without them?"

“I don’t think they’ll mind at all actually.”

“Cool. It’s a date then.” Nola turned her attention back to the kids at the splash pad.

Pete stood there stunned by the turn of events. Suddenly, this was looking like the best day of his life.

Seven

Julie tried to swallow her frustration. No reason to take it out on customers. This problem was born out of poor management. The rest of the park received all the help needed while she floundered in desolation. Whenever she mentioned it to Larry Taylor, the Director Of Park Services, he would aw-shucks his way through excuse after excuse of why resources were plentiful everywhere else, but none were available for the fishing expedition attraction. Never addressing the shortage of help. Never.

When she pointed out the imbalance of other attractions having too many workers while she had a total of three, Larry would laugh it off, and roll into the next part of his rehearsed bullshit speech about budget numbers and fiscal responsibilities and supply versus demand and yada yada yada. The only thing those conversations managed to do was piss her off even more.

She knew what it was about. She was just a lowly receptionist with a lowly GED. Still carrying the smear of not graduating high school after getting knocked up during half-time of the local South versus West varsity football game. By the dad of her best friend who chose to take sixteen-year-old virgin Julie in the backseat of his faux-paneled Griswald Family station wagon instead of his wife who was waiting at home, no less. What a stink that had been. Ruined her friendship with

Betty. Ruined her home life with her parents who became angry and bitter for having to help raise a newborn, possibly contributing to her mother getting sick. Ruined the rest of high school; prom was out, volleyball was out, graduation was out. Ruined future relationships. All for a measly backseat grunt and squirt.

Leon was viewed with the same disdain. A redneck boat captain who smelled like fish and stale sweat, with more grease under his nails than on the high-hour engine the powers-that-be refused to replace. More budget bullshit.

The incessant ringing phone dragged Julie from her mental bitch-fest. She groaned, but answered pleasant enough. “Riptide Fishing Charter, this is Julie. How can I help you?”

Julie took the name and number, checked her calendar for bookings during the week of Thanksgiving—pissed all over again that they were working Thanksgiving Day— confirmed Leon had an opening the Friday after, and confirmed the reservation. She hung the phone up a little more aggressively than intended, but shrugged it off. *Whatever.*

She glanced up at the oval clock on the wall, happy to see it was almost three-thirty. The park would be closing in an hour.

Julie jumped out of her chair. “Oh, my.”

She’d been so busy, she’d forgotten about the amended schedule. Leon was supposed to have been back by now. Larry made that crystal clear. No patrons were allowed on park grounds from five until nine to allow staff to prepare for the Halloween festivities. Shutting the park down at four-thirty allowed time for staff to clear the park before locking the gates.

Julie grabbed the binoculars out of her desk drawer and rushed outside, wincing at the suffocating heat that dowsed her like a steaming winter soup. From the dock, she had a clear view of the ocean. She adjusted the dial to focus the lens. Slowly panning right, she searched the horizon until she was facing east and away from the direction he always went. She ran back inside, and tried the crappy CB radio.

"Leon, you read?"

White noise responded.

"Leon, Julie here. You read? Over."

Panic set in. Leon was always back on time. The radio was hit and miss, but she'd never needed it for emergencies. There had never *been* an emergency. But if they weren't back by five at the latest, Larry would flip unless they had a damn good excuse.

Maybe that over-worked inboard finally threw a piston, she thought. That was about what it would take to get it replaced.

She tried again. "Leon, you copy? This is Julie. I need you to answer if you read."

More crackle and pop. She ran out to the dock again, took a deep breath, raised the binoculars. A slow scan revealed an empty ocean. As far as the eye could see. She moved left again, a triple check, to find more of noth—

A speck appeared. Julie walked sideways to the end of the dock as if ten more feet would help her see better. She thumbed the dial to clear the image. It went blurry for a moment but came back to a clean resolution. The speck was a boat. Leon's? Who else could it be? But she had no definitive proof. Could possibly be another fishing boat. Wouldn't be the first time a charter from Florida or Alabama had come this far.

Julie watched and waited. The minutes ticked by at a snail's pace. Her bare feet tapped the weathered deck boards until, finally, she could see enough of the boat to confirm or deny it to be Leon. Her body went slack with relief. It was Leon. He was safe. It would be close to five before they returned. Regardless of the reason for the tardiness, Larry would probably shit a gold grenade.

Julie hurried back toward the office, intent on tidying up. Halfway down the dock, a sharp and brittle pain jabbed the bottom of her foot. She stopped to raise her leg, already knowing the problem: the ragged tip of a splinter was lodged underneath the thin skin. Blood dripped on the deck boards as she hopped on one leg through the open office door to her chair. The phone was ringing but she let the answering machine pick it up. She'd return the calls tomorrow.

Julie knew better than to run down the dock barefoot. Scuba had gotten a splinter in his foot several months before that got infected with a thimble-sized puss pocket. Doc had to clean it out and give him antibiotics.

Julie opened the top drawer on the right side of her desk where she kept extra napkins from lunch. She let the napkins soak up the blood while she opened the pen drawer to retrieve her box cutter. A cigarette lighter sterilized the blade. The thin silver turned black then red before she considered it sanitary. The splinter was damn near big as a small pencil. A chunk of rough wood stuck out beyond the flesh about a quarter-inch. She pressed the blade into the wood fibers like a hook and pushed down to maintain leverage while slowly pulling the splinter out. Fiery pricks like a dozen wasp stings caused her foot to tremble, but she grimaced and bore the discomfort. The splinter dropped to the floor once it was out and she collapsed back in the chair as the pain instantly diminished to a dull throb.

Julie sighed, and pulled a first aid kit from the bottom drawer. Mercurochrome burned like a bitch, but she blew on it until the worst abated. She wrapped her foot with gauze and strapped it down with hospital tape, then gingerly slipped into her dirty Reebok's. A thud outside caused her to leap out of the chair, hissing when she put too much weight on the painful heel.

Riptide Rebel was at the end of the dock. Scuba climbed off, grabbed the rear rope from one of the guys onboard and tied it around the stainless steel cleat. Another guy tossed him another rope from the front of the boat and Scuba looped it around another cleat, securing the boat against the eternal tide. Then Scuba went ramrod still, facing the boat, his back to Julie.

Odd, she thought.

There was so much to do when they returned to shore that usually Scuba was running around like a chicken with his head cut off, Leon barking orders. But Leon was standing at the helm. Dirty calloused hands on the wheel. Staring straight ahead through the grimy, saltwater-splashed windshield. The guys that booked the trip had stopped moving as well. The entire party, dead-still.

A tide of pinguid unease rolled down her spine from the nape of her neck to the small of her back. Gooseflesh erupted beneath her scalp, made her head itchy.

"What the hell?" she whispered, leaning forward and squinting. Wondering, also, why their hands started dramatically shaking. All of them. In unison. Julie's mother—*God rest her soul*—had been diagnosed with Parkinson's when she was forty-three-years old. By the time she was sixty, she could hardly talk and needed a wheelchair to get around. What Julie remembered most about her condition was how her twisted hands and knuckles would ceaselessly bang against the side wall of the wheelchair as her body trembled from the disease. Julie got used to it but at first she had imagined that was what it would sound like if a corpse knocked against a coffin lid as it was being lowered into the grave.

Julie was about to move to the door when the shaking hands abruptly stopped and they all started moving again. The six guys who chartered the boat climbed out and walked gracelessly down the dock toward the office Julie now stood inside, puzzled scowl etched across her face. One of the guys, shorter and older, wore a tattered, bloody shirt. The other five were also bloody, but it was *smeared* blood. As if they had administered aid to their friend in the torn shirt. Julie could see a massive wound through the tear in his shirt to the guy's abdomen. It was scabbed over, but his saturated shirt indicated he bled a lot. Strangely, the guy walked along with his friends as if nothing was wrong, face devoid of pain. Hell, devoid of anything, if Julie was being honest.

The six of them halted. The tallest of the group looked down, then squatted slowly. Julie couldn't see what he was doing because of her vantage point. She leaned forward to try to get a better view, but he rose, licking one of his fingers as if tasting something. After a moment, the six of them continued past her office.

She waited until they were out of sight before leaving the office and heading down to Leon and Scuba. She inspected the decking where the tall guy had stooped, but saw nothing except her blood droppings from the splinter.

Scuba returned the rods and reels to the storage shed. A normal ritual, but Julie noticed something not so normal about Scuba: he lacked emotion. He was an unusual character in that regard. Always happy. Always. Even if Leon barked at him, he'd smile, yell "Yessir, boss" and go about doing his business. He carried a light inside most people simply lacked. Some inner appreciation for everything. Julie had never seen him mad or upset. She'd never even seen him sick. He was the most reliable employee she had ever hired.

To see his scrubby face now mute and flat was completely out of character.

"Hey Scuba," Julie called as she moved closer. She could still feel the pain in her foot, but it was barely registering.

"Hi ... Julie."

She stopped, maintaining a slight distance. Something was wrong.

Scuba had paused for an iota. In his movements and salutation. Like he had to remember her name. His expression never changed.

Julie wanted to turn around and go back to hide in the office, but this was Scuba and Leon. They must be acting weird because of the guy with the torn, bloody shirt. Obviously, there was a terrible accident.

They're all in shock, Julie thought, and exhaled a tense breath. Of course. Made sense now.

She stopped at the edge of the boat, looked down on Leon as he stowed away life jackets. "Everything okay? Why was that guy's shirt bloody?"

Leon paused, remained still for ten seconds. Finally, "He had an accident. Looks worse than it is. Scared us all pretty bad though. Never had anything like that happen on my boat before."

Yep, in shock. Even his voice is weird. "He gonna be okay?"

Leon turned to face her, an odd smile stretching his lips further than she ever remembered, his new dentures twinkling. Julie thought she saw his eyes flash with a weird light, but the was just the harsh sunlight. Leon was not a handsome man. Too much time spent in the sun had his face and arms the texture of rawhide. His wiry grey hair puffed out around that damn filthy *Old Milwaukee* hat he refused to wash or, better yet, burn. His idea of fashion was overalls and rain boots. But that smile was diabolical. Totally unlike Leon. It gave Julie the heebie-jeebies's. "Oh, yes. He is going to be just fine. Better than new in a day or so."

Julie nodded, her inner voice babbling red alert warnings. Julie again dismissed the idea. This was Leon. The kindest man she'd ever known. He was as dangerous as a butterfly. The shock had him off-kilter. "Okay. Well, I'm going to lock up and head back to the cabin to get ready for tonight. You guys need to hurry. Don't want Larry busting our chops about being late."

"Do not worry about Larry," Leon said, locking the drawers and doors that held his gear. "I am sure he and I can come to an understanding."

"You okay?" Julie asked as she turned to head back to the office. "You're acting ... odd."

Leon paused, that lunatic grin stretching from ear to ear again. "I am fine. Never been better."

Eight

Dave stepped up to the admission's kiosk. The plexiglass partition reflected the sun into his eyes, making it hard to see the woman inside. Typing paper was taped to one side of the plexiglass and read:

Closing At 4:30

10/30 - 10/31

"Can I help you?" The woman called through the hole in the partition.

"Yes, I have four," Dave said, huddling his family closer.

"Can I see your badges please?"

All four dramatically tugged on the color-coded, numbered badges hanging on lanyards around their necks to show they were indeed eligible for this attraction.

"Okay, you can go, but be aware, we close early today so you will not get the full forty-five-minute experience. Enjoy your visit to Riptide Dolphin Run."

Van ran ahead, ducking under the stanchions until he was in line. With the attraction closing early, the line was short. Jessica followed Van but Dave and Penny chose to weave back and forth until they joined the kids.

"I heard," Van said to Jessica, wide-eyed and jacked up on adrenaline, "they let you *ride* the dolphins. Not just swim with them."

"I know," Jessica said, failing to hide her own excitement. "Liz came here last year when they first opened, and she did it. Said it was the most amazing thing ever."

Seeing the kids so happy was like an elixir for Dave's soul. Healing from trauma always took time, and the pain never went away, but life had a way of continuing forward, presenting opportunities to find some measure of peace. Nurturing that serenity, accepting its growth, maintaining a healthy outlook on the day-to-day, was an individual choice. Some people chose to wallow in the misery, and, for them, peace was unattainable. Heartbroken and torn and content to remain that way. Dave wondered early on after Molly's passing how the future would look. Would life ever regain its equilibrium? At some point, he realized that was up to him. It was up to Penny. The paths were clear: provide nourishment to the healing, or feed the hurt. Together, they made a verbal choice. For their children. For their lives.

The family in front of them followed an attendant through a door in a wall that acted as a sight screen to keep those in line from seeing what was happening in the attraction. Or, in park lingo, building the anticipation. Screams of excitement and laughter found a way around the sight screen, further fueling the desire to get inside.

The young female attendant returned and opened the gate. Her name badge declared her to be Mona. "Follow me please."

Van was on Mona's heels, chatting with her like she was a life-long friend. Jessica walked beside him, rolling her eyes. On the other side of the sight screen were six of the largest rectangular swimming pools Dave had ever seen. Olympic-sized if he were to guess. About twenty feet separated each pool from the next. All ran parallel to each other. Near the entrance, at the pool's edge, there was a small "holding tank" that resembled a jacuzzi and was separated from the dolphins' swimming area. In each of the occupied pools, about half a dozen people waited inside these jacuzzis. Dave assumed this was to separate the waiting patrons from the animals.

A tall wooden privacy fence surrounded the pools, painted the color of sand to blend with the surroundings. Palm trees lined the fence, and the illusion of openness was quite convincing. A brisk ocean wind pushed the palm fronds side to side. A one-story mirror-paned building sat beyond the first pool, and a smaller stucco structure was next to it. Each pool had its own lifeguard watching and waiting to assist if needed.

Mona led them to the third holding tank from right, instructing each one to watch the slippery steps when climbing down. Dave pushed his sunglasses higher on his nose to block out as much of the blinding pool glare as possible. Van and Jessica moved straight to the edge of the holding tank, watching the water for signs of the porpoise.

Someone screamed, drawing Dave's attention. Water surged from the farthest pool, and the people in the holding tank scrambled to get out. An older woman wearing a visor and a one-piece slipped, and Dave winced as her face slammed against the pool's edge, the sharp crack followed by a spray of blood. Mona and several lifeguards rushed to her side as the excited chatter quickly turned into frantic shouting.

Patrons spilled out of the other holding tanks to run and gawk. More park employees responded to the disturbance, trying to help resolve the problem—whatever it was—and keep the crowd at bay.

"Stay here," Dave said to Penny. He could no longer see due to the wall of people blocking the view. "I'll be right back."

Dave climbed out, mindful of the steps. He pushed through the thickening crowd to get to the front. A few people were crying, and Dave saw why. The woman who face-planted was on her back next to the pool and a fit, heavily tanned lifeguard was providing CPR. He pumped away at her chest while counting out loud, then moved to blow into her bloody lips. Her nose and the area between her eyebrows—the gabrella, Dave thought it was called—was crushed. Like she'd been smashed in the face with a sledgehammer. Three women and two little boys Dave assumed to be family, stood to the side, sobbing violently. Everyone's attention was centered on the woman who was dead or dying, but activity from the pool drew Dave to weave his way to the pool's edge. There was so much wave action the water was sloshing onto the concrete deck. The female dolphin trainer had climbed out and was making hand motions like sign language. Communicating with the dolphin. But nothing worked. The animal was in hysterics. Flailing, darting from one side to the other. Someone shouted and all the trainers climbed out of the troubled waters, frantically hand signaling and yelling to get the creature's attention. Dave waved at Penny, jabbed a finger at the stucco building.

Get them away from the pool.

She nodded and hustled the kids out of the holding tank.

Dave jogged to one of the trainers. She was old enough to have grey hair, but she was thin and fit and obviously spent lots of time in the sun. "What's wrong with them?"

"I don't know," she answered, tense. "I've never seen this before, and I've been doing this a long time. Something has scared them, but this is a self-contained system. No way for something *to* scare them. Strange as hell."

Dave looked around, a question forming. "Do the dolphins stay in the pools all the time?"

"No, they live in tanks inside that glass building."

"How do you get them there from here?"

"Through underground chutes attached to each pool."

"Maybe you should try getting them to swim the chutes back to the building. Maybe they would feel safe and stop this racket."

She faced him for the first time, but he couldn't see her eyes behind the mirrored Brett Hart sunglasses. The way she paused told Dave she had been so preoccupied with calming them down, she hadn't thought of moving them inside. "Good idea. We can try it."

She turned to the trainer of the pool next to hers. "Hannah! Let's open each chute one at a time and see if they'll swim back inside!"

Hannah had the same eureka moment, and nodded vigorously.

The woman moved to a control panel mounted underneath the lifeguard tower. Her palm slapped a button Dave couldn't see. The dolphin spun in circles a few more times, then disappeared. The water began to calm instantly.

Dave gave her a thumbs up, and she slapped the button again to close the door.

Hannah ran to the lifeguard tower next to her pool and repeated the process. Eight minutes later, all the pools were empty. The trainers ran inside. The woman yelled "Thanks" and followed her co-workers.

When Dave returned to check on the woman receiving CPR, he found raw grief. The lifeguard was on his knees, tan face white as a ghost, body language of despair, eyes lost to horror. The family held the deceased woman in their arms, their bodies wracked by pain. These people had come here for a good time and now one of them was leaving in a body bag.

For a moment, Dave was transported back in time. To the coroner's office. He and Penny holding the limp body of their daughter. Trying to scream but the shattered remains of their broken hearts somehow prevented the release of the immense pressure. Dave cinched his eyelids tight to stop the memory from taking hold of the day. Torturing himself was better suited for nighttime.

When Dave opened his eyes, three paramedics rushed through the entryway pushing a gurney, toting ALS bags. They needed the gurney, but not the bags. Too late for that.

Dave skirted the gawkers and went to his family who cowered against the stucco building. Alone and scared.

"What happened?" Penny asked after he hugged her.

"The dolphins went berserk," Dave said, lifting a visibly shaken Van into his arms. "The trainers don't know why. That lady slipped while trying to get out and smashed her face on the pool." With Van in his arms and Jessica standing at Penny's side, Dave chose not to say the words out loud. He mouthed to Penny, "*She died.*"

Penny gasped and covered her mouth, tears spilling through her fingers.

"Why did the dolphin's go crazy, daddy?" Jessica asked.

Dave wondered the same thing. In the ocean, it was logical to think that dolphins would panic if a predator got too close. They were docile creatures with no good way to defend themselves against, say, a shark.

But in a controlled environment like the one the animals currently inhabited, with no contact with the ocean or the dangers within, it seemed highly unlikely that a possible shark patrolling the ocean waters some eight hundred yards away would illicit such an alarming response. Dave had to think this was something else. But damned if he knew what.

"I'm not sure sweetie," Dave said pulling Jessica to him with his other hand.

"That was really scary," Jessica said quietly.

No argument here.

Nine

Riptide Island's goal was to be family friendly. Part of this commitment was to be holiday friendly, as well. July Fourth had been celebrated with a patriotic showing that sent patrons to their rooms swollen with American pride.

Christmas had been a big ordeal in the park's inaugural year. For the whole month of December, Riptide Island had become The North Pole. Miles of Christmas lights had been strung, over one hundred fake balsam fir trees had been placed around the walkways and thoroughfares and on top of shops and even a few rides. Santa—albeit three different guys working shifts—roamed the park from dusk til dawn, taking pictures by the thousands. Dozens of elves prattled busily around the park, dispensing candy to kids and parents, handing out surprise gifts, and line dancing in the town square. A real-life reindeer had been brought in and the kids loved her. For the families that stayed on the island Christmas Day, the park had prepared a special feast in its entertainment pavilion. Free of charge. Bringing a little bit of home to the balmy coastal shores. It had also been a chance for families from different parts of the country—and world—to meet and mingle. After lunch, the park handed out presents to excited children.

But as fun as those two holidays were, Jared loved the Haunted Island transformation the most. Last year went well, but this year,

Larry was sparing no expense. The Riptide Convention Center, a fifteen thousand square foot building normally used for various specialty shows was now The Haunted Asylum.

Jared walked through the attraction with Cindy, amazed at the sheer scale and authenticity of each set piece. *The Nightmare on Sanitarium Street* section, a terrifying tip-of-the-hat to *The Nightmare On Elm Street* with a crazy twist resembled the alley scene in the first movie, but with prison cells. They were almost at the end of the street when Freddy Krueger burst from around the corner and Cindy jumped so high Jared caught her. She was light enough to carry for miles, but Jared eased her back to her feet as Rusty, a.k.a. Freddy, laughed so hard he had to pat his knee.

"Yeah, yeah," Cindy said, face slightly flushed. "Laugh it up, asshole. Just wait. I'll get you."

Rusty's laughter followed Jared and Cindy out of the building.

"Asshole," Cindy said again, but she was smiling, her complexion back to normal.

Jared wanted to laugh but decided to play it safe. No need to poke the bear. "So," he cleared his throat, "you're heading out to find Moe?"

"Yes," Cindy nodded, slowed to a stop. When she looked at him, the background went blurry. "Thanks."

"For what?"

"Catching me," she said, giggled. "Never been carried like that before."

I'll carry you anywhere you want to go. It was what he wanted to say, and almost spit it out. Instead, he went with the feeble: "Anytime."

Cindy walked away to find Moe. Jared waited, hoping for a quick look back. Even a glimpse was sufficient. She dropped her head and for a brief moment, he thought she was going to leave him disappointed.

But her head swiveled, and she smiled with a magic that Jared felt in his chest. He winked, and turned away, then remembered. "Hey."

Cindy slowed. "Yeah?"

"Don't forget to remind Moe about the kid at the arcade."

"Yeah, yeah," she said, waving him off. "Moe's on it."

"The only thing Moe's on is the triple pack of hot dogs from Pop's," Jared called back. It was meant to be a joke, and Cindy laughed, but it was also the truth. Moe loved to eat. No secret there. And Pop's had the best hot dogs in the world. No secret there, either.

Jared used his grand master key to enter the rear door of the momentarily shuttered Riptide Island Memorabilia Cabana, one of eighteen in the park. The small building served dual roles of selling various items—t-shirts, stamped golf balls, pens, teddy bears, etc. —for keepsakes, and acted as a front for tunnel access. Jared entered another locked door to a storage room with an elevator. He pressed the DOWN button and waited.

The elevator door dinged when it slid open and Jared stepped inside, punched the glowing DOWN button again. He stepped out into a bustling tunnel corridor. Park employees working the main areas were now horror characters. Some dressed as known villains while some wore everyday costumes with a gory variation. Barb, the counter saleswoman working the memorabilia shop, hurried past him wearing a nursing outfit splattered with blood. She was on her way to make-up to have a fake noose tied around her neck and a raw, bloody lesion applied to her throat just below the jaw.

Park employees working the kid-friendly section were dressed in less frightening costumes. A princess sauntered past as well as a unicorn. Scooby Doo pushed through the crowd, in a hurry for a snack before the night began.

Jared's maintenance crew labored behind the scenes but were still required to wear costumes. Larry wanted everyone to look the part, "just in case." Some of his guys balked initially; keeping the park running smoothly was hassle enough. Jared's solution was simplicity. All maintenance workers were told to wear overalls, work boots, and painted faces. A few were still not overjoyed by the idea, but they all agreed to make it work.

Jared weaved through a convoy of demon fairies, rabid rabbits, zombies, a Frankenstein, several vampires, and a slew of superheroes before he slipped through the metal door leading into his maintenance shop. One of the largest rooms below the park, the 8,000-square-foot space served as the hub for park services. Fernando Indigo ran th welding and fabrication area in the back corner. Fernando once welded beams on skyscrapers but he got injured when he fell forty feet and broke both legs and both arms in multiple places. After surgery and rehab, he decided to change to a job where his legs—now braced with steel pins—and feet stayed on solid ground.

3,000 square feet of the place was taken by storage racks. Jared thought it looked like an auto parts store.

The rest of the shop was open space with several workstations. A caged tool pit held one of the corners by the workstations. Whenever one of the workers needed a tool, they had to sign it out and back in when finished. When the park first opened, there had been no tool cage. An employee with sticky fingers changed that. As knuckleheads generally do.

Jared sat behind his desk, leafed through tomorrow's work orders. Of which there were always dozens. Riptide Island Discovery, a quaint little shop that sold odd artifacts found on the island during the construction process, needed the back door panic device repaired; NOT LATCHING was written on the work order. Riptide Rapids needed a repair on one of the water pumps responsible for the water rapids in turn four. Riptide Grill needed someone to look at an electrical outlet; NO WORK was handwritten in the comments section of the paper.

Jared heard footsteps approaching from behind and turned to find one of his guys half-walking, half-limping toward him. He thought it was Wesley, but it was hard to tell. His face was chewed up and leaking, mouth open and bubbling white foam. Eyes rolled in the back of his head.

Any other day, Jared would've fallen for the disguise. "Is that you, Wes?"

The undead stopped, held stance, then started laughing, white foaming splattering the polished concrete floor. "Aw, man, how'd you know?"

"Lucky guess," Jared said, tossing the work orders back on his cluttered desk. "What is that foam coming out of your mouth?"

"Antacid tablets." Wes spit the rest into the trash can, went to the water fountain to rinse the rest out. "Tastes like shit, but it works."

"Where is everyone?" They should all be down here. The agenda for tonight and tomorrow night was simply hang tight, be available if needed. After running around the park all day in the stifling heat, the maintenance crew was tired and ready for rest. By only having to respond to emergencies, Jared hoped to keep everyone somewhat fresh for tomorrow. On November first, a relief crew would take over for a week to allow his guys to rest. After Thanksgiving, the Christmas transformation would begin and those were long days and short nights.

"They all went to their cabins to shower and costume up," Wes said, returning with a paper towel to clean up the foam splatter. "Should be back within the hour."

"You sure went all out," Jared said. Wes' undead make-up was quite impressive.

Wes dropped the paper towel in the waste basket. "I figured if we have to work till midnight, may as well make the most of it."

Jared liked Wes a lot. Over the past eleven months, he had gotten to know Wes really well. The guy was the poster child for perseverance. Born in the backseat of a patrol car to a heroin addicted mother, his life had begun destined for trouble. After four arrests as a teenager and almost dying from an overdose at twenty, he had cleaned up and gotten his life in order. His parole officer helped him secure a job at a construction company known for helping the wayward. He had worked there for three years before responding to a newspaper ad about Riptide Island.

Despite everything Wes had gone through, the guy maintained a positive attitude. Wes told Jared one day that it was not how one started that people remembered, but how one finished. Jared thought that a superb lesson to live by.

The door opened and Ricky led Fernando, Desmond, Amp, Patrick, Brandon, Shane, Derrick, and Terry out of the chaotic corridor and into the shop. They all wore the denim overalls but no one decided to go with makeup.

"Bunch of boring asses," Wes said, laughing. "You guys look like a line dancing team from Moose Knuckle, Montana."

"Fuck off, dipshit," Patrick said, laughing as he looked around at his co-workers, recognizing Wes was right.

"I can't believe Larry is making us wear this stupid shit," Brandon whined. "And these overalls are rough. Must be made out of Naugahyde or something."

Jared listened to the banter while wondering who was missing. Then it hit him: the new guy.

"Where's Lawrence?" Jared interjected.

Everyone went quiet, looked around, suddenly realizing Lawrence was not with them.

"Not sure," Ricky said. "He was with us when we went back the cabins to ready for tonight."

Brandon nodded. "He was. I spoke to him. Running behind. Must've had to drop the kids off at the pool."

Terry barked a laugh. "Happens a lot, too. Kid's got the intestines of a squirrel. Thirty minutes after he eats, got to find the nearest toilet. Like clockwork."

"All right," Jared waved the nasty explanations off. "We'll give him a few more—"

The metal door opened and Lawrence stumbled inside. The first thing Jared noticed was the pasty color of his face. His hair was soaked like he had taken himself to the pool instead of "the kids." He walked funny, too. Like his equilibrium was off. Kind of leaning.

"You okay, Lawrence?" Jared asked. A silly question. The kid was obviously sick.

"Um, I guess," Lawrence mumbled. "I just don't feel so hot."

"You look like shit," Desmond said, stepping back to put distance between himself and the sickly kid.

"Feel like it, too," Lawrence said, his eyes rolling in the sockets like marbles.

"Tell you what," Jared said, pushing up out of his chair. "Why don't you let Brandon make sure you get back to your cabin, and you sit tonight out? We'll be fine."

Lawrence swayed like a stiff wind suddenly whipped through the building. "Yeah, that might be a good idea."

Jared nodded at Brandon, who opened his mouth to protest but noticed the stony "I'm not in the mood" look on Jared's face. His jaws clapped shut as he took Lawrence by the elbow.

Lawrence turned back toward the door, reacting to Brandon steering him. "It came on me all of a sudden," he said to Brandon as they stepped into the chaotic corridor. "I even blacked out while I was talking to Scuba outside my cabin. I woke up feeling like the sky was falling. Weirdest flu I've ever had."

"That's all we need," Amp proclaimed in his deep baritone, hands flapping at his sides. Always animated when talking. Always over-dramatizing the situation. "That kid walked his bony-ass up in here and brought his germs to spread to all of us. Now we all gonna be sick."

"Ease down on the apocalypse banter, Amp," Jared cautioned. "No need to sound the alarm. He was only in here for a second."

"One second's all we need," Amp added. He crossed his muscled arms and leaned against a worktable. At six-four, Amp was an imposing figure. A gym rat. With a goatee cut thin and tight and his bald head, he could've been a football player for the Steelers, a pro wrestler, or a porn star. For some reason, he chose Riptide Island. Rumor had it he was trying to escape some trouble back in St. Louis.

"I'm sure everyone will be fine. If the bug is catching, we'll have no choice but to deal with it."

The radio on Jared's desk sparkled awake. "Sixty-five, this is twenty. You read?"

Cindy. Out of breath and panicked.

"Read. What's wrong?"

"Got an emergency over at Cascade Canyon. Hurry."

Jared rushed out the door. Hoping the emergency wasn't something wrong with Cindy. He pushed past the throngs of costumed workers headed to their stations. Only an hour remained before the park re-opened, and everyone was in a hurry to be on time and ready. Larry could be an asshole at times, but Jared had to admit he ran a tight ship. Employees who arrived here to work knew the expectation up front. Do your job, be punctual, be safe, care about the visitors, care about your co-workers. It was practically Larry's mantra.

Jared turned down a small hallway that took him to one of the sixteen staff elevators. He stabbed the button and waited with impatience. Before the doors opened, the rest of his maintenance crew hustled toward him.

"Wes, you and Amp come with me," Jared said. "The rest of you go back to the shop and wait. I may need you to bring me something and it'll be quicker if you're on standby. If I call, you need to double-time it."

They nodded and left Wes and Amp with Jared.

"Double-time it?" Wes said sarcastically. "You're sounding like Quinten now."

"Fuck off," Jared smirked.

Amp cackled as they stepped inside the elevator.

Night had descended on Haunted Island. Normally brightly lit after dusk, the park was now shrouded in darkness. Ambient lighting enhanced the feeling of the macabre. Fake fog drifted a few feet above the concrete walkways, though the occasional island breeze ran its flirty fingers through the mist, breaking it up. Flowerbeds were now makeshift graveyards, old and crooked headstones standing among the shrubbery. Larger flowerbeds held ancient coffins smeared with wet earth, spit out of the ground like a cancerous tumor. Hidden speakers gave life to howling monsters and whistling winds, creaking doors and rattling chains, chittering rabid bats and scurrying creatures. Spiderwebs wrapped tree limbs and light poles like swamp moss. Workers continued to fine tune the decorations as opening hour crept closer.

"Are we really letting little kids in to see this?" Wes asked, gawking. This was his first Halloween on the island. "Gonna scare the pants off them."

Wes knew the answer to that question, so Jared didn't bother with an answer. Instead, he picked up the pace and leaned into a hard walk. Jared knew the park like the back of his hand, yet he still found himself double checking the direction due to the dramatic transformation. He had seen the concept drawings back in March, and had known what to expect, but seeing the ghoulish images brought to life, in the dark, was striking.

Cascade Canyon came into view and Jared caught movement. He squinted through the gloom. It was Cindy frantically waving. Jared broke into a jog and closed the distance. Cindy dashed around the side of the ride through the normally locked employee entrance. He followed her to the small shack that housed the machinery for the ride.

"Hope you haven't eaten yet," she said in a cryptic whisper, nodding toward the inside of the shed.

A female employee dressed in a skeleton costume—mask off—kneeled next to another employee, male. Her pretty face was bone-white and her eyes showed signs of shock. The male was slumped over a turbine engine, unconscious or dead. Jared wasn't sure which. He leaned over the body and involuntarily jerked.

"Holy shit," Jared hissed. He'd heard the horror stories of amusement park employees having accidents—usually through their own negligence—and losing a finger or a hand, but he'd never seen it in real life. This guy's arm was caught between the industrial strength chain that turned the pulleys and the spiked pulley itself which was attached to the turbine his body now draped. What was left of his arm anyway. "Has anyone called Dr. Lyla?"

Cindy nodded. "Yes, but she didn't answer. I sent Billy to find her."

"Is he—?" Jared was afraid to say the word.

"He's breathing," the girl in the skeleton costume answered, voice flat. "Was breathing, anyway."

"You need to get him out," Cindy said, stating the obvious.

Jared clinched his fists as he thought about the best way to proceed. If he took the turbine apart to remove the pulley, that would loosen the chain and allow them to get his arm loose. But that would take time. It would also take time to reassemble, putting the ride out of commission for tonight. One of the most popular rides in the park. Which would have Larry spitting napalm. The other option, and the best for tonight, was to cut a link of the chain, remove the chain from the pulley, get the guy out, and reattach the chain with a new link. It was a temporary fix that would need to be addressed before the park re-opened tomorrow, but would work for tonight.

Jared snatched the walkie talkie from his side. "Patrick, you copy?"

"Yessir, gotcha," Patrick answered immediately.

"I need a chain link brought down to Cascade. The spares should be on Rack M, Slot B, Drawer W. Bring it, a grinder with a new cutting blade, and some tools. Be lightning quick with this. We got a serious situation."

"Roger."

Jared was thankful Patrick kept further comments to himself. He was generally loquacious to the point of annoyance.

"What's the plan?" Cindy asked.

"Cut the chain, move him out of here, replace the link, get the ride operational."

Cindy pointed at Jared's belt. "I think we need to wrap a tourniquet around his arm. He's lost a lot of blood and it's still dripping." The blood continued to spread and fill cracks and crevices in the rough concrete.

"Good idea." Jared pointed to the electrical panel in the corner by the door. "Amp, throw the breakers for these motors."

Once the power was off, Jared unbuckled his belt, lifted an awkward leg over the machinery, and lassoed the leather around the mutilated arm. He tried not to focus on the torn muscle and ripped flesh, or the jagged pale tip of broken bone jutting out. He failed. Bile seared his esophagus, but he gulped it down before he added his cheeseburger dinner to the bloody floor. Jared cinched the belt tight against the scrawny bicep and pushed the prong through the nearest loop.

Footsteps announced Patrick's arrival. His thick hair was a sweaty mop and he was huffing like an eighty-year-old climbing Mount Everest, but he had what Jared needed.

Jared took the tools. "Patrick, I got one more assignment for you then you can take it easy for a while."

"No problem," Patrick said around deep inhalations.

"Go up to Doc's office and bring her back."

Patrick nodded and disappeared.

Wes climbed around the machinery to hold the chain while Jared cut the link. If the chain dropped on its own it might tear more meat from the kid's arm.

"Amp, when I cut this link, Wes and I will untangle his arm from the chain and pulley so you can lift him out of the way."

"Got it," Amp said and moved into position behind the boy, arms dangling at the ready.

Jared took a deep breath and pushed the spinning blade against the steel link. Sparks flew against the shed wall until the link plopped to the bloody concrete. Wes slowly tugged the chain, causing the arm to wrench sideways.

“Stop!” Jared yelled a little too aggressively. Then, softer: “We have to be careful not to rip off what’s left.” He swallowed. “Try *lifting* the chain off the pulley rather than pulling on it.”

Wes nodded, twin trails of sweat sliding down his zombie cheeks, ruining his makeup. Using his thumb and first finger, he pinched the chain near the pulley, grimacing at the mess caked inside the greasy joints, and lifted. Wes’ fingers were wet from perspiration, but he managed to remove the blood-slick chain without dropping it. Amp grabbed the kid and lifted him off the turbine while Jared supported the mangled arm.

“Where to, boss?” Amp asked.

“Take him to the clinic.” Jared met Cindy’s teary eyes. “Go with Amp, support the arm. Take Miss Skeleton with you. Wes and I have to get this ride up and running. Okay?”

Cindy held his gaze a moment too long. She was obviously shaken by what happened tonight, but he also saw something else. Maybe he was misinterpreting. The moment was strained, panicked. Emotions running high. Adrenaline pumping, fear permeating the air, nerve-endings rapid-firing, heart thumping. It was understandable if he was reading it wrong. But what he thought he saw was longing. Weird timing, but everyone reacted to trauma in different ways. Some wanted to be alone. Others wanted comfort.

Finally, she nodded, wiping the tears from her cheeks. “Okay.”

After they were gone, Jared and Wes went to work repairing the ride.

“I certainly hope this isn’t a premonition of how these next two nights are gonna go,” Wes quipped while wiping the blood off the chain.

"Me too," Jared agreed.

Ten

Dave sat on the couch in the small living room of their cabin. *Family Matters* was playing on the console TV but he wasn't watching. He was tuned to a different show: the lifeguard pumping that poor woman's dead chest, blood bubbles foaming around her shattered nose. Set on replay. Over and over. Picture presented in technicolor. Down to her pink and blue bathing suit. Even the bracelet on her freckled wrist. Gold with a heart dangling from a tiny loop welded to the main ring. Inscribed with writing too tiny to read. Fingernails painted devil red. As were her toes. Skinned shins from the fall, the thin flesh rolled back and dangling loose.

Dave pushed the palms of his hands against his eyeballs, trying to force the images away. Which he knew was impossible. He still had nightmares about Molly. That woman would now join his daughter to wreck his sleep. The afterbirth of trauma.

Dave jumped from the couch, marched to the freezer. He cracked one of the four plastic ice trays to loosen the cubes, dumped three in a whiskey glass, and poured a finger of Old Forester. The burn failed to blur the picture playing in his head, so he dumped more in the glass and kicked it back. Heat bloomed in his gut like an atomic bomb, climbing his throat. The video skipped, went blank. He was back to the present. In the kitchen of a vacation cabin, with his family. He poured another finger, sipped on the flames.

"Probably not a good idea to get drunk before we spend the next three hours chasing our kids around the park," Penny said softly from behind him.

Dave turned to her. "Sorry." He always had to make a concerted effort to be more open. It wasn't an easy thing for him. To shed any layer of protection, exposing the fragility of what lay beneath. Allowing himself to be vulnerable. After Molly, he'd retreated deep inside himself. Worse than usual. Until Penny threatened divorce. That harsh light cut through the darkness in a way nothing else could. The idea of losing his wife, his family. He'd gone to therapy. Alone at first, then with Penny. Gradually, climbing out of his shell. He learned that she needed him to let her in. That it promoted a bond that proved virtually unbreakable. He sighed, dumped the rest of the bourbon and ice into the sink, rinsed the glass. "I keep seeing that poor woman lying beside the pool, the lifeguard trying to save her. Arrived here on a boat to have a great time and now she's leaving in a box. Life is unfair."

Penny wrapped her arms around his waist, nudged her head against his chest. Her blonde hair smelled of coconut. Her favorite shampoo. "I know. It's so unfair. But wallowing in guilt won't help her. Unfortunately, nothing will. Life goes on. It's cruel to do so, but nothing will change that." She raised her head, kissed him gently. "I'm sorry you saw that. I'm sorry you're dealing with it. And I don't mean to sound callous, but we are still on vacation. A much needed and well-deserved respite, I might add. Having dealt with our own shit over the past two years. You and I need this. Our kids definitely need this. Our family unit needs this. Can you try to put this to bed?"

She was right, of course. Allowing what happened to ruin this for the family was nothing short of selfish. It sounded heartless, but what else was there to do? As Penny said, life goes on. "I hear you. And you're right. I guess when I saw that, it took me back to Molly. That's a wound that refuses to heal. Just bleeds from the slightest reminder."

Penny wiped away a stray tear. "We'll never fully recover from that. We can only push forward for Van and Jessica."

Dave straightened. Stood a little taller. He wanted his kids to have a memorable night of fun. Not of watching their father sulk. "I'm going to get ready. By then, it should be time to head down to the park."

Penny kissed him again. "Sounds good."

Dave showered in cool water. Refreshing after the heat of the day. Which was relentless down here near the equator. He'd never experienced this type of humidity. The very air seemed to drip with moisture. Thick to breathe. Almost like being underwater.

Back home in Nebraska, the summers were hot but not especially humid. Winters tended to be a little brutal. Digging out of the driveway for work six months out of the year was always a test of patience. After experiencing this type of heat, he longed for some snow.

He dressed in shorts and a Haunted Island t-shirt he bought from a memorabilia shop, brushed his hair, and clapped his hands as he entered the living room. "Who's ready for some scares?"

Van started hopping. "Me!" His costume—surprise, surprise—was *Ghostbusters.* Complete with a proton pack strapped to his back.

Jessica was Ariel from *The Little Mermaid.* Dave wasn't sure how much she was going to enjoy wearing a fake red wig around the park once she started sweating, but to each their own. "Dad, this is *not* going to be scary. Fun, but not scary."

Dave was amused by her bravado. Jessica didn't like horror movies. Or even tense movies. He rented *E.T.* on VHS from Blockbuster after they missed it in theaters, and Jessica ran out of the room wailing. Said it was too scary. "Oh no? Why do you say that?"

"Because this is a family park," Jessica stated matter-of-factly, tossing her fake red hair over shoulders. "It'll be like the carnival they have at church every year. And that's not even scary to the little kids, much less to us older young adults."

Dave laughed. "Young adults, huh? You're not even a teenager yet."

"Soon, Daddy. Soon."

Don't rush it baby girl. "Okay, young adult. Let's go check it out. Even if it is lame."

The ten lines at the Gate 4 entrance were already twenty head deep. At least. Most of the adult visitors wore costumes and all of the children were dressed. Excitement rippled through the crowd.

The purple ambient lights went out, casting the crowd in almost total darkness; the half-moon provided only a meager glow. Organs started playing an epicedium, anguish and heartbreak riding every mournful note. The sound came from everywhere.

Smoke billowed from atop the twelve-foot-tall brick wall that surrounded the park and through the thick wrought iron of the massive ornate gates. A growling gargoyle burst out of the dense fog, hobbling the length of the wall. Some kids gasped, others buried their innocent faces against mom or dad's leg. Another beast burst from the opposite side of the gate. Two witches followed each of the monsters out, stepping to the edge of the wall, casting sinister glares upon the waiting crowd.

"You think you've come to enjoy a night of innocent fun," the first witch squealed, her voice gritty and shrill, *"but you're entering a nightmare you can't outrun."*

The second witch dramatically threw up her arms and formed claws with her fingers before shouting in a voice almost identical to the first, *"The darkness that lurks all around, hides the many faces of evil unbound."*

The first witch floated in the air, her tattered black shroud billowing in the ocean wind, clapping like the sails of the ill-fated *Demeter*. She flew out over the startled crowd, and eyed those below like a vulture hunting carrion. *"Enter these gates if you don't fear, but, heed my warning, there be monsters here."*

The second witch flew out over the crowd like a bat, piercing cackle like nails to the scalp. Jessica wrapped her arms around Dave's midsection and squeezed so hard he thought she was trying to climb inside his pocket.

"At the ringing of the funeral bell," the second one quipped, floating back to her wall.

"You may join our haunted hell," the first witch finished.

They turned and vanished in an explosion of green smoke that pulled screams from the crowd.

A moment of stunned silence followed. Then a bell gonged three times. Each ring thick with benevolent foreboding. On the third ring, the purple lights snapped back on and the gates began a plodding, screeching opening. As the gates parted, ground fog poured out, seeping around the ankles of the visitors. Dave couldn't see much due to night and the crowd before him, but he knew one thing for sure: this was no church carnival.

And he would probably hear more screaming here than any haunted house attraction he'd ever visited.

Eleven

Pete and Nola stopped at the checkpoint to show credentials to the grim reapers at the gate entrance. One agent of death waved Pete through with a fake sickle. Pete moved to the side to wait on Nola, who seemed to have caught the eye of another reaper checking her badge. He said something Pete couldn't hear, she laughed, then moved on. The staffer watched her walk away a little too long before returning to duty.

"He stared at my ass, didn't he," Nola said with a grin. As if it happened all the time. If she had a habit of wearing tight-fitting cat woman outfits, it probably did.

Pete frowned. He barely knew Nola, yet jealousy tightened his chest."Yep. His black eyeballs almost fell out of the skull mask."

"Creepo," Nola said.

"What did he say to you?"

"It's not important." She laced her arm through his. "I ignore assholes. Or punch them in the nose. Depends on how I'm feeling. Tonight, I ignore."

"I'll try not to be an asshole then. I don't want you ignoring me." Pete added: "Or punching me in the nose, for that matter."

She stared at him with an intent that made it hard not to look away. Like she was diving inside, swimming around his head, learning the most intimate details of his thoughts and feelings. Invasive but welcoming all the same. No one had ever looked at him that way.

"Don't be too cute, Petey," she said softly. "I might have to kiss you."

"Tell me what I gotta say to make that happen and I'll never shut up."

Nola laughed, and it was the most beautiful thing Pete had ever heard. Like birds singing on a sunny spring morning. Her smile made everything brighter, better. "Okay, loverboy. Let's get going before we start ripping each other's clothes off."

"I repeat my last remark."

She doubled over this time, laughing until she had tears squirting out of her eyes. When she was down to giggles, she took his hand and pulled him along.

It took a while for Pete's attention span to move past Nola, but once it did, he was in awe of the park. The place was downright scary. The haunting music, the screech of unseen bats, the characters and creatures roaming the park: ghosts, goblins, more witches, ten-foot-tall circus freaks stalking the walkways, tormenting kids, vampires, mummies, werewolves. All bases were covered and the atmosphere was wrought with underlying dread.

"This is so cool," Nola said, yanking him to walk faster.

"Where you wanna go first?"

"The Haunted Asylum."

The brochure in his room gave scant details on The Haunted Asylum. Just enough to wet the appetite. An indoor maze. Terrifying surprises around every turn. A must-see nerve-shredding attraction. Sixteen-years-of-age and older only.

A chainsaw screamed to life and Leatherface burst from the darkness, attacking a group of teenagers who scattered like bugs. Except one girl who shrank to her knees in the puddle of fog. Leatherface hovered over her, chainsaw coughing black smoke, torturing the now crying girl. Her friends stopped a safe distance away, but refused to rescue her. Nola dragged Pete on past, and Pete was glad of it. He wanted to avoid being chased by a maniac with a chainsaw.

They passed a stand where a vampire was calling all passers-by to "Step right up and bob-for-eyeballs. Catch three eyes to when a prize." Nola darted straight to the bloodsucking creature.

"My boyfriend will try," Nola said, handing the vampire two one-dollar bills.

"All right boyfriend," the vampire quipped, "time to take a bite out of the skin."

Pete was too stunned by the boyfriend comment to do anything but gawk at Nola. She acted as though nothing happened. Adjusted a stray hair that dangled next to her porcelain temple.

"You got this," Nola said after a beat.

Pete blinked, and moved to the cauldron. A little dazed, and a lot confused. The water was green and smelled like the punch his mom made every year during the Christmas holidays. His dad also made a punch every year, but his smelled heavily of alcohol. Pete had slipped himself a cup once or twice.

The "eyeballs" were nothing but apples painted to look like giant eyeballs. Pete shrugged. "Okay."

Pete put his arms behind his back, and dipped his head in the cauldron. The apples pushed away from his face. The trick was trapping the fruit. He managed that by using the side walls. The first "eyeball" was the hardest, but once he got the hang of it, he pulled the next two out in under a minute. Nola hopped up and down, clapping. She leaped in his arms and hugged him tight. Even in the heat of the night, he wasn't bothered by the warmth radiating from her body.

"Which prize do you want?" the vampire asked.

Nola browsed the selection of lame horror-themed teddy bears, finally settling on a black—of course—t-shirt that announced "I WAS THERE!" Haunted Island 1989 with an aerial view of the island and park.

"Thank you," she said with a smile as they walked away from the eyeball pit.

"No problem," Pete said. But he was thinking about the boyfriend comment and the hug. More like daydreaming about it. His negative brain wanted to approach the idea that he would probably never see her again after this vacation was over, but he refused to go there.

"You okay?"

"Absolutely," he said. Trying to sound nonchalant.

Nola stopped, faced him. Stepped close, almost nose to nose. Her breath smelled like cinnamon. Her eyes glowed in the dark like the posters in his room when he used his neon light. "Did the boyfriend comment bother you?"

"On the contrary," he said.

"Contrary to what?"

"I liked it. A lot."

Nola smiled again. "You're cute when you're nervous."

"I don't think anyone has ever called me cute. My hair is long and thick, I'm bony, I have a tendency to hunch, I like metal, play in a band, and I'm not the most sociable person ever born."

Nola cocked her head to the side. "You haven't told me you play in a band. You just went from cute to a stud."

Pete blushed, suddenly tongue-tied.

"What instrument?" Nola asked, helping him out of the brain-jam.

"Drums," Pete managed to blurt. His kit was a piece of shit; a mixed-brand set bought at a yard sale. Cymbals were cracked, drumheads dimpled from the sticks, bass drum packed with two pillows to thicken the sound. Maybe one day he'd be able to buy a nice *TAMA* or *DW* set. But for now, his inbred set would suffice.

Nola bit her lower lip. "I'm gonna have to jump your bones now."

Pete laughed to mask the Lars Ulrich double-pedal hammering against his ribcage. "Most girls like guitar players."

Nola shook her head. "Not me, honey. I love drummers. Who's your favorite?"

This was a subject Pete was comfortable discussing. "Definitely Tommy Lee. Great drummer and even better showman. I saw Motley two years ago. Tommy's drum kit went over the crowd and flipped around. Coolest thing I've ever seen."

Nola kissed him. It happened so fast Pete didn't even kiss her back. He stood there stunned, staring at her. For the first time since he had met her, she seemed nervous. Gave him butterflies that a girl as beautiful as Nola was nervous around him.

Pete had only kissed a girl once. Jimmy Thorn had asked Pete and his band to play a skateboarding party Jimmy was throwing for a bunch of friends. They had agreed, excited about their first "concert." While Pete had been breaking down his cymbal stands, a little goth girl had come over and chatted him up. Wanted to take a walk. He had walked with her until she finally said she'd always wanted to kiss a drummer. Pete had told her now was her chance, and she had taken him up on it. He'd never seen her again after that night. He had always assumed it must have been really bad.

But when Nola pulled away from Pete, she stood there a few tense beats, eyes closed, not moving. He was afraid she was going to wipe her lips with her sleeve and stomp away. Instead, she leaned closer and kissed him again. Her tongue slipped through and found his own, and it was like being plugged into a *Marshall* amplifier with a *Les Paul* decked out with uncontrollable pickups. His body sizzled.

"Ugly as two pigs fucking," someone said. "You two are quite the pair."

It was the bully by the pool. Pete hoped the asshole would simply continue on by.

No such luck.

"I will say," bully said, eyes climbing Nola from toe to head, "you must love the bottom feeders, darling. This guy is a loser with a capital L."

"The only loser here is you," Nola clapped back. "Now run along before I hurt your feelings."

The bully nudged his friend beside him and laughed, like they were sharing some private joke. "You? Hurt my feelings? The only thing you can do to hurt my feelings is suck on my face like you did his."

Nola fake laughed, held her stomach, and doubled over. Slapped her knee. "You're almost as funny as chlamydia. Which I think your mother must've given you by the look of those boils peppering your dough-boy face."

The shit-eating I'm-too-smart-for-my-own-good grin fell from the bully's face like an avalanche. His neck went red and chased the color to his cheeks. "You fucking whore."

The bully took a step forward and Pete braced himself to defend Nola. He wasn't a fighter but this asshole was not going to lay a hand on her. A park employee, who overheard the name-calling, grabbed the bully by his arm. "I think it's time for you to move along, young man. Don't make me call security. They'll ship you back to Florida before you can blink."

The bully glared at the employee, but only for a moment. He was outmatched and knew it. He smirked at Nola and Pete. “See you around.”

“You better not,” the employee warned. After the bully and his friend was no longer in sight, the employee asked, “You okay?”

“Yeah, all good,” Nola said. “I’ve heard worse.”

“And that is truly a shame,” the guy said with a frown.

“Thanks for your help,” Pete said. He and Nola went in the opposite direction of their new nemesis.

After a few minutes of silence, Nola stopped. “Okay, I refuse to let that piece of shit ruin our night. Got it?”

“Absolutely.”

She rose on her tip-toes and kissed Pete. “Then let’s find a ride.”

He floated behind her like a balloon, tethered to her soft hand. The crowd of people were ghosts. There but not really. More of impressions than physical objects. Pete’s tunnel vision was acute and focused solely on Nola.

When they stopped, he looked up and found himself in front of Riptide Island’s Jungle Journey. Or, for tonight, Riptide Island’s Journey Through Hell.

“Thought you wanted to go to The Haunted Asylum,” Pete said.

“I do,” Nola answered, pulling him to the line, “but since we’re passing this on the way to the asylum, why not?”

Pete was game for whatever. He never thought he’d *ever* want to ride any of these, but Nola had a special way about her, a magnetism. Wherever she wanted to go, he was willing to tag along.

"You like horror?" Nola asked once they were in line.

"Love it. It's all I read and just about all I watch. You?"

"Same. What's your favorite slasher? *Halloween, Friday the 13th, or Nightmare on Elm Street*?"

"Definitely *Halloween*," Pete answered. He liked the other two but they were a little too campy to love. There was a seriousness to Michael that fit the genre better.

"You and I are on the same wave length. Halloween all the way." She added quickly: "Except for the third one. That was so bad I couldn't finish watching it."

"What even was that?" Pete asked. Pet had watched the whole thing out of spite, but he'd hated the movie. He was glad when the fourth one came out to erase the memory of the third.

"I don't know. Maybe they'll trash it and forget it was made."

The small kiosk gate before them swished open and a funeral parlor usher waved them aboard. Pete and Nola boarded the first car. A shrill whistle howled at the moon and the train jerked to a start. At the front of the car Pete and Nola occupied, an odd-looking man stepped into the middle aisle with a microphone in hand. He was pale and gaunt, short, with an odd-shaped bald head. He looked like he might've been dropped as a child. His dark brown eyes bulged from the sockets. He placed one hand on the back of a cushioned seat to steady himself from the side-to-side sway of the train, and recited a well-rehearsed dramatic campfire tale of the island.

"Good evening ghouls and goblins, my name is Sir Igor and I'll be your guide on this cursed voyage down the haunted rails of perdition. You are travelers in a story old as time. This train, these tracks, all lie on a land bedeviled by ancient malaise. Forever damned by forces beyond our comprehension. The unintentional founders of this hellish sanctuary were its first victims. Doomed from the start, Arthur and John Bangor, brothers, swam to shore when their boat sank off this island's coast after crashing into a wicked bed of corral. Stranded, they foraged berries and fruit. In need of more protein-rich sustenance, the two set off to explore the island. The savage jungle was most inhospitable.

They became lost and disoriented, incidentally venturing deeper into the mouth of the beast, never to be seen again.

"Until now!"

Bloody hands slapped the window beside Nola's head. She cried out and bounced onto Pete's lap. It was too dark to see faces but a pair of leaky handprints remained on the glass.

Nola appeared slightly embarrassed she had fallen for the jump scare, but Pete was not bothered.

"Sorry," she said.

"Don't be," Pete said.

The dim yellow lighting inside the train car winked a few times before blanking out, casting them in total darkness.

The gravelly voice of Igor cut its way through the oily depths. "O hollow night, bound to evil but lost to sight. Succumb to the stars, rise oh rise until the flesh chars. Ashes fall like rain, souls locked inside purgatories of pain. Seek out all those who spite, choked by the devil and loves to bite."

Thunder boomed inside the car, and the lights flickered. The whistle shrieked again as the train slowed, then stopped. A shadow flashed by the window. Feet thudded against the roof. The rear door of the car rattled in its frame. Maniacal, inhuman cries leeched between the cracks, seeping inside the car, drowning Pete with trepidation. He knew this was just pretend. Fake. Make believe. Still, his skin prickled. Nola squeezed against him, her body hot and trembling.

"Oh shit," she whispered, her breath hot in his ear, and pointed out the window.

The untamed jungle around the train was lit by a purple haze. Fog sifted through the underbrush. Figures danced and chanted, naked except for clothes covering their intimates, bodies painted red and black like a newfound cannibal tribe. Lying on the ground at their feet was the damsel in distress. Staked and tied to the ground with course rope. Her hair appeared black, and her pale body shook in fear. The tribal members halted and dropped to hands and knees, crawling around her, sniffing her hair, her legs, her flesh. One of the figures stopped at her head, a knife mysteriously appearing in his fist. He raised the blade and, with a native cry, drove it to the hilt into the damsel's chest.

The tribe member was immediately attacked. A batch of segmented arms wrapped around his body which leaned over the girl balancing on the knife handle. He tried to rise but was snatched closer to the captive. The other members panicked and scrambled backwards.

The lights flickered on inside the car and the train jerked to a start. Igor stood at the front of the car. His eyes flickered to the window, appeared confused for a moment. He recovered quickly, resumed his narration.

"Anarchy rules this island. Eons of morbid decadence. Twisted and foul, the ancestors only know turmoil. It's the fruit that nourishes their soulless remains. Riptide Island now resides inside a landscape of bedlam. Everyone who visits this land is doomed. Even the creatures of the night."

The train screeched to a concussive stop, lights flickering off again, strobing in seizure-inducing patterns, then dying out, plunging Pete and Nola in` darkness once again.

Outside, more dull purple lights illuminated the jungle. A small pond sat at the edge of the trees. The water rippled and two eyes glowed just above the surface. Seeming to float. A wolf jogged out of the wilderness to the pond. Its head flicked back and forth, as it searched for warning signs of trouble. It eyed the train warily before dipping its snout into the water for a drink. Reflective eyes floated on the surface. Inching closer to the wolf. So slow the water failed to ripple a warning to the doomed animal. Pond water burst into the air as the alligator seized the wolf by its head, dragging it into the water. But, like the damsel, the wolf became the attacker as its body transformed into a writhing ball of arms, unleashing its wrath upon the alligator. The train jolted and began moving again, lights blinking rapidly before staying on.

Igor was gone. Pete searched the car but the madman was no longer in it. A voice spoke over the speakers thanking them for partaking in the adventure and wishing them safe travels. The train arrived at the depot and Pete and Nola hurried off.

"That was actually pretty frightening," Nola said once they were walking off the boarding platform. "The effects were crazy intense."

"I've never seen anything like it," Pete admitted. He'd been to a few haunted houses and hayrides and that was the most convincing ride he'd ever been on.

"It looked like those people were really being attacked," Nola said.

Twelve

Jared barged into the doctor's office, ignoring the busted wooden door frame. The lobby was empty, so he searched the patient rooms. Cindy and Miss Skeleton were quaking in each other's arms, sobbing. Amp stood in the corner, chocolate skin drained of color. The kid with the messed-up arm lay on the gurney. His lips were purple, skin splotchy, his body still. The white sheet covering him to the neck lay flat, no breath to animate its rise and fall. Jared didn't need to ask what happened.

The reality was like mercury in his veins.

What a mess! He ran his hands over his face, took a deep breath to calm his grated nerves.

"Anyone seen doc?" Jared asked after he recouped a tenuous grasp of calm.

Amp's head dropped like a guillotine. "Haven't seen her, Billy, or Patrick."

"I'll go look," Wes volunteered from the doorway.

"No, you stay here," Jared said. "It shouldn't take this long or require this many people to find her. I'll go."

Jared knocked around plausible explanations that would account for doc's no-show status. Why people were searching and had apparently neither succeeded nor been seen since. She was supposed to be in her office tonight, prepared for possible injuries or illnesses or whatever she dealt with during these festivals. Over four thousand people were expected to attend. Her presence was mandatory.

An image of that kid's purple lips sprang across his vision like some morbid autopsy slideshow. Jared shook his head, hoping to erase the memory from whatever mental folder it was stored. The last thing he needed was to have those hellish snapshots haunting his dreams.

He mounted the steps to Lyla's cabin. The lights were out, but Jared was undeterred. He had to have positive confirmation she was not here before going Indiana Jones on the rest of the park. Which would be like searching for the Ark Of The Covenant.

The front door was ajar. Alarm sirens squalled in his head as he pushed it open far enough to squeeze inside. With the dense tree cover, the moon was no help, leaving the cabin cast in a thick murkiness. He kicked something with his foot, and was rewarded with glass shattering.

"Shit," he whispered. Not sure why he was whispering; the cabin appeared empty. It *felt* empty. And that was weird because it also felt like someone was watching him. He ran his fingers along the wall in the area where a light switch should occupy. It took a minute but his fingers flipped the switch and the living room brightened. Trailing arbutus lay in a small puddle of water and broken glass. The mayflower was native to the island and grew plentiful. Many of the workers had some in their rooms to add color to the otherwise bland, rustic space.

A board creaked, stopping Jared in his tracks. The noise came from the back of the house. All of the employee cabins were built to the same specs and floor plans allowing Jared to know where the sound originated. The bedroom.

He tip-toed toward the narrow, short corridor. Picture frames lined the walls on either side of him. Photographs of wild animals. Lyla was an amateur wildlife photographer. Her favorite animals to shoot were lions, tigers, bears—*oh my*—elephants, zebras, and giraffes. When she wasn't being a doctor, Lyla went on exotic expeditions, constantly snapping photos to document her travels. Jared asked her once if she ever considered hunting moose or deer and having it stuffed for display and she looked at him like he was insane.

"I cry if I see a dead deer on the side of the road," she'd answered. "I don't hunt." Disgust seeped through her words, and it was clear she'd held a grudge ever since. They were polite enough as co-workers, but were certainly not friends.

The bedroom door was closed. He turned the knob, pushed it open, wincing when the hinges squeaked. He slid his hand along the wall, flipping the light switch. Two bedside lamps snapped on, illuminating an empty room. The comforter was the definition of magazine cover perfection. Tight and wrinkle-free, the ends tucked, corner creases razor-thin. The pillows were fluffed and the excess fabric on the open end of the pillowcases folded neatly away. Jared knew nothing of Lyla's past, but her tidiness suggested former military. The rest of the bedroom was neat to the point of obsessive. Nothing on the closest nightstand but a lamp, alarm clock with bright red numbers, slim tan telephone with extra-long coiled cord, and a well-worn paperback copy of Whitley Strieber's *Communion*. The nightstand on the opposite side of the bed held nothing but a lamp and a photo of a smiling older couple Jared could only guess to be Lyla's parents.

Jared checked the closet, found it empty save a neat line of nursing scrubs, separated by tops and bottoms. He found it odd that not a single article of personal clothing hung next to her work uniforms. No jeans, no t-shirts. But now that he thought about it, he'd never seen her in civilian clothing. She wasn't one to fraternize with co-workers.

He was tempted to check the dresser, but he didn't want to leaf through her panty drawer. He was already being invasive, searching her private quarters. Going much further entered creeper territory.

Instead, he checked the bathroom—spotless—and the kitchen. Not only was she not in the cabin, it appeared as though she hadn't been there all day.

Then why do I feel like I'm being watched?

He couldn't shake the unsettling sensation. With Lyla clearly not in the house, that left the surrounding forest. The curtains were all pushed to the side; probably an attempt on her part to brighten up the shaded place. Someone could be watching from outside. Made no sense, but what else could it be?

"Fuck this," Jared blurted. He slammed the door on the way out and marched down the path to the main employee walkway, glancing back once to assure himself no one had appeared out of thin air. The unease lifted once he was beneath the fluorescent lamps lining the walkway for safe evening travel.

He tugged the walkie-talkie clipped to his belt. "Patrick, you copy?"

Patrick didn't answer.

Jared tried again. "Patrick, you copy?"

When he didn't answer again, Jared tried a new angle. "Maintenance? Anyone seen Patrick since he brought me the chain link?"

Desmond answered. "No, sir. And Brandon hasn't returned yet either. They're probably holed up somewhere hiding out."

Unacceptable if they were. But Jared wasn't convinced. Brandon, maybe. But Patrick and Billy had seen what the chain did to that poor kid. They would not be hiding. They would be searching for doc.

Jared decided to start by checking with each of the shack and street vendors. They were in the thick of things, so to speak. Perhaps one of them caught doc or Patrick passing by.

Jared entered the park through an employee gate, waited for it to close and latch, then headed for the nearest street vendor. A vampire with a cauldron of eyeballs.

Thirteen

Julie sat on the front porch, puffing on a cigarette, knee bouncing up and down. She was late, really late, and would probably get in trouble, but she didn't care. She hadn't seen Leon since he returned from the fishing trip. Scuba either. She'd dismissed their weirdness then, but now Julie was worried it had been a bigger deal than she thought.

She'd asked herself what happened out on that boat a dozen times in the past hour. Obviously, one of the guys had gotten hurt, but he'd walked away on his own accord. Julie had witnessed it. Other than his shirt being torn and a little blood, he had looked fine. It made no sense for Leon and Scuba to act so weird, then disappear.

And disappear where? The island was a self-contained land mass. Nowhere to go.

"Except by Leon's boat," Julie said to herself. Shocked she hadn't considered this before. She'd already called Glenda at the Boarding/Departure Center and was told neither Leon nor Scuba had left on the last ferry. The only boat remaining was the fishing boat.

She smashed the smoldering cigarette into the stained decking boards of the cabin steps, and walked as briskly as her short legs would take her. One of the physical attributes she used to loathe but now accepted. As a teenager she'd always been the shortest one in her friend group. It had been a huge advantage in gymnastics, but not so much when the need arose to travel somewhere quickly.

What reason would Leon and Scuba have to leave the island? Leon had only returned to the mainland once in the past year, and that had been to attend his father's funeral. Scuba hadn't left since he arrived before the park opened. Neither Leon nor Scuba had family; not anyone they cared to visit or share communications with anyway. Leon had an ex-wife who lived in Memphis, but he loathed her with a fiery passion. He'd never step foot on U.S. soil to visit that cheating bitch.

Except maybe to kill her, Julie thought sarcastically. Leon had the temper of a viper if pushed hard enough, but he'd never harm a soul.

Julie pushed the exit bar outfitted on the gate to enter the marina. She could see the dock almost immediately, and sighed with relief. Leon's boat wobbled aimlessly in the rising tide, bouncing safely off the rubber dock bumpers, tether ropes alternating between loose and taunt.

She was happy he had not left, but that only presented more questions: where was he and why was he hiding?

"Excuse me? Do you work here?" A female voice preceded the clopping of flip-flops on deck boards.

Julie turned to find a pretty brunette marching toward her. Her poof danced against the night breeze and her ponytail swung back and forth like the pendulum on a souped-up grandfather clock. Behind her, five other women followed like soldiers. Anger wafted off all of them through clenched jaws, furrowed brows, and stiff strides.

"Yes, I'm Julie. The secretary. What can I do for you?"

"My name is Monica Garrett," the brunette announced, tone blunt as an axe blade. "My husband, Ralph, and my friend's husband's" —Monica threw a thumb over her shoulder at the women behind her— "went on a fishing trip today, and have yet to return. I see a boat at the end of the dock. Does that mean they *did* return?"

Julie got the feeling this happened often. The boys planned to play eighteen holes but played nineteen instead. Or met down at the local watering hole after work to soak the day away with a few brewskis, and a few became a few dozen. These women were sensitive to their husbands' antics. Julie nodded. "They got back earlier. Around four-thirty or so."

Monica hissed, and spun to her not-so-shocked friends. "Those bastards. On vacation and they pull this shit again."

"Screw 'em," one of them said. Which seemed to surprise the rest. She was demure, almost proper. Out-of-date glasses, hair a little too perfect. The odd duck in the pond. Eager to please and always happy to follow the leader. She seemed to enjoy the looks. Feeling like an outlaw. "I say we find a bar, tell the DJ to turn up the volume, and do the same thing to them they always do to us."

Monica smirked. "You know what, Teresa? You're right. Screw 'em. Whatever they can do, we can do better. And I know just the place we can go."

The six women stormed back the way they came, Monica in front.

Poor fellas. No wonder they snuck away.

Failed to explain Leon and Scuba, though.

"Unless, they're at a bar with the husbands." Fishermen loved to drink as much as they loved to fish, and that adage held true for Leon and Scuba. Leon preferred the bar at Riptide Resort over the others, and Scuba followed Leon like a shadow. The bartender, Cynthia, always poured generous amounts of RotGut for Leon. Or so he claimed. Cynthia's ample bosom and flirtatious personality allegedly had nothing to do with it.

Leon would get in trouble with Larry for not working tonight, but Leon was the best fisherman below the Mason/Dixon. Especially when factoring his meager salary. Larry would chastise Leon a bit, then pat him on the back with forgiveness and happily send Leon back out with the next charter crew.

The knot of tension loosened in Julie's chest, knowing where he was now. She debated checking in on him, but that would be a bad look. He'd always said one of the ten thousand reasons he hadn't reconciled with Lorraine was because she had no respect for his personal space. Julie had sworn under oath not to be a dark cloud raining on his parade all the time. Maybe the accident on the boat shook him up and he needed to regain his equilibrium.

Whatever the case, she was going to give him time and latitude. She'd go to work helping in the park and try to cover for him if the need arose. Hopefully tomorrow Leon would feel better and be back to his normal self.

Fourteen

The Haunted Asylum was a dungeon. Flaming torches lined the damp stone walls. The concrete floors were rough and dingy. The sound of a squeaking rat scurrying away drew Dave's attention to the dark edges of the room, but there was no sign of a rodent. Shouts of outrage and insanity capered among the shadows. Whimpering, whispering, chanting, gibberish. Moaning, groaning, grunts of pain. Exactly what he would expect in a sanitarium. It was so realistic, Dave had to tell himself this was fake. An attraction at a theme park. A waterpark, no less. Nothing to be afraid of.

Penny glanced at him, her lips a thin bloodless line of nervousness. He nodded and stepped in front. She hooked her finger through his belt loop, pulling the kids closer. Someone screamed ahead, and Jessica jerked beside his leg. Dave hesitated a moment, then moved out of the current area he assumed was the holding room; where everyone waited their turn when it got busy.

Dave cautiously pushed through a set of black curtains, revealing an almost pitch-black corridor that went left. Moving slowly down the corridor, sickly yellow lights suddenly winked on. Twin little girls in matching red dresses and white slippers stood shoulder to shoulder beneath the amber glow.

"Oh hell," Penny breathed on Dave's gooseflesh-riddled neck.

His scalp felt like tiny cockroaches were scurrying across his skull, nervous legs skittering as tiny feet tapped the freshly shaven skin. Dave swiped his head, and continued moving toward the creepy twins. He wanted to turn back. For the kids.

"Daddy," Jessica whined, "I wanna leave. Can we turn around?"

Dave glanced back the way they came. A door now stood where the curtains were hanging moments ago.

"Sorry, pumpkin. This is a one-way only attraction." Dave leaned closer to his daughter, locked eyes. "This is all fake. Okay? Nothing will happen to you. Just stay close. If it gets scary, close your eyes."

The lights went out, dropping them in a tenebrous pool of nothing. Dave could hear Penny's shallow, panicked breathing and his own hurried heart thumping in his ears.

Dave reached out and touched the rough stone wall. Realized it was not real stone, but Styrofoam made to look like the work of medieval masons. He followed the wall until it ended and turned right. This was where the little girls had stood moments ago. Now it was empty of threat. Fingers on the wall, he continued down the next corridor. Twenty feet further, a spotlight clicked on in front of them. This spotlight was attached to a streetlamp standing next to the wall. The earlier rough concrete floor was now a paved road. Trash fluttered against prison bars on either side of the alley. Another streetlight clicked on some thirty yards ahead. The blackened silhouette of a man in a salesman hat stepped beneath the murky glow. Dave stopped, arms protectively outstretched, waiting. This looked familiar. A sense of de-ja-vu swept across him. When the strangers arms stretched out to either side like tentacles, and his fingers sparked off the steel bars like a grinder on a steel beam, Dave knew. This was *Nightmare On Elm Street.* Dave wasn't much of a horror movie guy, but he had seen the movies.

"It's Freddy," Dave said.

"Well, Freddy's coming for us," Penny whispered, her fingers clutching Dave's t-shirt like life support. "Maybe you can ask for an autograph before he beheads us."

Deep, smoky laughter resonated down the corridor. Freddy suddenly darted toward them. He disappeared in the dark void between streetlights, and never emerged. Dave wasn't sure if he trusted the illusion. Maybe the madman was hiding, waiting for them to explore further. After what felt like one hundred Mississippi's, Dave took a test step forward. Nothing happened. He took two steps, and again nothing happened.

Until the streetlights went out, plunging them in complete darkness again. Dead ahead, two red eyes blinked into existence. Low to the ground. About the height of a really big dog. A rumbling growl throttled toward them.

"Daddy, is that a real dog?" Van croaked. He was no longer pressed against Dave's leg. Had, in fact, backed away. "I don't like big dogs."

Van had been chased by a dog wandering the neighborhood last year. Dave had intervened and run the dog off, but not before the damage was done. Van had been traumatized by the incident and now quaked in his shoes when he saw a canine, big or small.

The red eyes blinked, then disappeared.

Dave exhaled slowly, hands on his knees. He reached back and took his kid's hands, picked up the pace to the next right turn.

This corridor resembled the "holding room." Same flaming torches, same rough floor, same "stone" walls. More steel bars lined each side in what could only be holding cells for the insane. Louder caterwauls echoed from unseen sources, madness driving the cacophony to the point of chaos.

This will be interesting.

He checked on Penny. Fire danced on her retinas, and her skin glowed orange. She bit the fingernails of her one free hand while her feet fidgeted against the floor like some new dance move that would soon be all the rave on *American Bandstand*. She was quite beautiful when she was nervous. And when she was not.

"You ready?" Dave asked, voice low.

Penny nodded. "Not really."

The first cell on the right held a body hanging on a meat hook against the wall. Dave slowly scanned the body in an effort to figure out the illusion, thus alleviating the fright. It was done so well, he couldn't find an answer. Obviously, it was fake, and that was good enough he guessed.

In the cell on Dave's left was a man on his knees in the middle of the floor wrapped in a straightjacket. His hair was wild as river bush, and his hazy glasses thick as telescope lenses. He whispered gibberish while staring at a dead waterbug lying legs up before him. The man raised his head and stared at Dave and Penny.

"It's coming," the man hissed. He spoke in what Dave assigned as a British accent, but since he had never heard such outside of a movie, he couldn't be positive. Could be Scandinavian for all he knew. "Coming home. I must keep meat on my bones. For it. It'll be famished after the long journey. I'll be its first meal upon arrival. And you'll be its last."

The deranged man dipped forward and pinched his yellow teeth on one of the tiny hind legs, and tossed his head back to launch the insect into his mouth. He bit down with a crunchy pop and yellow innards squirted from between his pale lips.

"Sick," Penny gagged. "Let's go."

"That was awesome," Van said. His scrunched face said gross but he was smiling all the same.

The next cell was occupied by a body bag lying on a gurney. The black sack was inhabited by the shape of a body. No doubt a mannequin or dummy. Far and away the most boring scene of the attraction thus far. Until the bag trembled. Dave stepped closer to the bars. The bag twitched at the feet, then went still. The zipper at the head moved. Sluggish and awkward. As the bag separated, sprigs of hair poked out. A cadaver-white face rose to the spotlight shining upon the gurney. The bag continued to spread like flesh beneath a scalpel. Once the upper torso was clear, the thing sat up. Its head rotated with bony clicks until its bloodshot eyes settled upon them. Thin, fragmented arms flared from the corpse's ears like a nest of living tree limbs.

"That's it, I'm done," Penny yelled and hurried down the corridor without even glancing at the cells, Jessica on her heels.

Dave and Van chased after them, but didn't catch up until they exited the building.

The heat was like a mallet to the face after the cool confines of the asylum, but Dave ignored it. Penny and Jessica stood near a raised flowerbed that had been converted into a miniature graveyard.

"I've been to haunted houses and haunted hayrides before," Penny explained, "no big deal. They are never scary. In fact, I'm usually laughing. The way those masked galoots run up to you and growl and try to invade your personal space, it's always comical to me." She pointed at the building housing The Haunted Asylum. "But that's fucked up. I almost wet my pants when that body sat up."

Dave laughed and hugged her. It felt good to be the protector. The comforter. "It's fine, honey. All is good."

"Yeah, yeah. If you say so. But I've got to find a restroom before we get on another scary ride."

It occurred to Dave that tonight was the first period of waking time since Molly passed that he had not thought of her. This caused an envelope of fear to open within him. As painful as it was to think, remember, and miss her, he also relished that pain. It meant she was with him. That she was not forgotten. That she was still loved and missed. He wasn't ready to not think of her, though he'd always known that with time, such would happen. Nothing was more cruel than life. The persistence to continue without flinching or pausing. Aloof and without care. Blind to atrocities, deaf to the cries of millions in anguish.

Penny stepped in front of him, hand on his chest, drawing him from his thoughts.

"You okay?" Her eyes searched his.

"Yeah, I'm good." No need to preach to her; she'd heard it already. Many times.

She dropped her voice to barely audible. "The kids sense when you climb back into the basement to wallow."

She was right. As usual. Van and Jessica stared at him, body language quiet and worried. They were affected by what he wasn't saying as much as by what he was. The wounds were healing, but slowly, and the slightest breach drew blood.

Dave nodded. "Yeah," he whispered. He clapped his hands, smiled to show all was right in the world. "What's next? I think I want to ride The Jungle Journey. Anyone game?"

Kids were resilient. They wanted to be happy and have fun. Van and Jessica were no different. Each one smiled, unease dissipating in the heat of the night, and, in unison, said, "Oh yeah."

"Let's go get in line," Dave said, ushering them along.

Passing the Tilt-A-Whirl, Dave caught a case of the creeps. Three costumed guys and a woman in hospital scrubs stood in one of the makeshift graveyards, staring up at the stars, arms straight down their sides, hands shaking like they were having a seizure. Dave noticed a few people staring at the proceedings as well. He wasn't sure what horror-related sequence they were acting out, but it was very effective.

Made his skin crawl.

Fifteen

Jared slipped into the back door of one of the Riptide Refreshments huts. The cashier was a fairy with fangs. She twiddled a few green fingers at him and went back to ringing up a customer whose four kids were being loud, obnoxious little shits. Jared felt sorry for the fairy.

One perk for working at the park was free drinks. And he needed one now. After running around the park the past hour and a half in ninety-degree heat and one hundred percent humidity, he was drenched in sweat. Even his feet were soggy. His calves were tight, legs sore. He must've walked five miles. Three employees had seen Lyla since the park re-opened this evening, but he had yet to find her. She wasn't answering the walkie. On any channel, much less 9-1-1, the channel designated solely for her. It was mind-boggling that she was AWOL, but still moving around the park.

Jared downed a large cup of Riptide Cola in four gulps, refilled, snapped a lid on, and stabbed a straw through the hole. Fairy was pulling a pretzel out of the hot box, rolling her eyes, and cursing under her breath.

"Have fun," Jared said, and rushed out the door before she threw anything.

He took another sip while he mentally ran through the park map. There was nowhere he had not been. Which meant he was simply not at the right place at the right time. Maybe he'd try another sweep but he needed to change it up. Reverse the order.

Jared wiped the sweat trickling down his face, and turned to head back the way he had come. A couple of lovey-dovey kids walked past, teenagers with budding hormones, dressed like they were backup singers in a rock and roll band.

And that was when he spotted Lyla. Standing in one of the park's fifty "graveyards" with Patrick, Billy, and Lawrence by the Tilt-a-Whirl.

"What the—?" Lawrence was so sick he could barely stand two hours ago. Patrick and Billy were supposed to bring Lyla to the shed to help save a kid's life. Here they were hanging out in the park like visitors.

Jared ran to them. "Hey, what the hell are you guys doing? Lyla, we have been calling you for hours."

Lyla rotated to Jared, which stopped him in his tracks. Her eyes were bloodshot and her skin was white as milk. Then Jared remembered everyone was ordered to dress up in some form of fashion. Lyla had settled on creepy undead person.

Lyla stared at him a beat, head tilted to one side. Finally she said, "My walkie is broken."

"O-kay," Jared said, caught off guard by her slack demeanor. "Did Patrick and Billy not explain the emergency? We had a kid caught in one of the turbines at Cascade Canyon. His arm was torn up by the chain and spokes."

Her head slowly tilted upright. "Goodness. Is he okay now?"

Anger flushed Jared's face. "Fuck no he's not okay! He died. Do you get it? He died because of you."

Jared realized he had said way too much way too loud. He quickly checked to see if anyone within close proximity overheard the outburst. But there was too much noise, too much activity. No one heard a thing.

Lyla placed her hand on his shoulder. "I am sorry for your loss. Maybe you should take me to him. As a physician, I am the only one qualified to truly determine if a human is dead."

An image of the kid's purple lips flashed across Jared's eyes. *If he's not dead, I'm Ronald Reagan.*

"Fine. Let's go." He pointed a finger at Lawrence. "I thought you were sick."

Lawrence stared at him with maddening indifference.

Jared bit his tongue. This was not the place for him to explode on these assholes. It was not his job anyway. He had a boss and his boss had a boss. He'd take this shit show to them. Hopefully, people were going to be fired.

Jared thought of taking one of the underground routes; it was shorter and cooler. But he wanted these three imbeciles to sweat. A small, petty punishment, all things considered, but punishment nonetheless. He even walked as fast as he could, calves screaming and threatening to cramp the whole way.

Twenty minutes later, Jared climbed the stairs to the doctor's office. He led Lyla to the room where the body lay. Amp was the only person in the room, seated on a stool in the corner, distance-staring at the floor. Cindy and Miss Skeleton had left. Jared couldn't blame them.

"You happy?" Jared asked Lyla. "He's fucking dead."

Lyla stood over the kid. Face complacent. She laid her head on his chest for a moment, and went back upright. "All of you step out so I can do an examination."

Amp stood up quickly. "Lyla, any fool can see—" He stopped mid-sentence. Lyla's eyes had snapped to Amp, and for the first time, Jared saw something dangerous, wild. Amp threw his hands up. "Whatever. I'm going back to maintenance."

Amp pushed past Jared, footfalls abating as he left the building.

Jared followed Lawrence, Billy, and Patrick out to the waiting room. The three of them exited the front door and disappeared in the darkness without a word. Jared was too mystified by their actions—specifically Lawrence and Patrick—to say anything. He wouldn't admit it to anyone, but he was creeped out by Doctor Lyla's demeanor. She was a little ... odd ... under normal circumstances, but her reaction to this whole ordeal was unlike her. Eccentric though she may be, she was a great doctor and cared immensely for the patients. Jared had witnessed the tenderness and focus on multiple occasions. He had never seen the detachment she was showing in regards to that kid on the gurney, or this accident as a whole.

Lawrence and Patrick's actions were equally mystifying. Lawrence was the new kid on the block, but he had shown nothing but a willingness to learn and a great work ethic. Eager was the word Jared used to describe Lawrence to Quinten. He even possessed a modicum of common sense. Not an abundance, but enough to problem solve fairly efficiently. He had never laid out of work. To see him sick earlier and mostly fine now threw Jared a little. Add in the disconnected, robotic elements—like Lyla—and the result was unsettling.

Patrick had been here since day one. Not the brightest lightbulb in the chandelier but serviceable and overall a good worker. He was a goofball, practical joker who was usually not serious about anything, but one who understood when it was time to get things done. Jared tolerated the funny guy because he knew he could depend on the serious guy when it counted. His behavior since leaving the shed to hunt for Lyla was out of character. The same mechanical, detached mannerisms as the others. And, most noticeable, the total lack of jokes. Not the slightest quip. Not even an ill-timed wisecrack that made the room wince rather than smile.

Jared had never spoken to Billy so he had no past experience to go on, but he noticed Billy acted exactly the same.

"What is going on here?" Jared whispered to himself.

He picked up a *Popular Mechanics* magazine off the coffee table sitting by the two couches in the waiting room. Two red Ford Mustangs on the cover. Comparing a '64 to an '89. That's as far as he got. He dropped the magazine back on the table as Lyla stepped into the room.

"He'll be fine," she announced flatly.

"Bullshit. His skin is white and lips purple. That boy is dead."

Lyla blinked and studied him for a long minute. "Are you a doctor?"

Jared propped his hands on his hips, exasperated. Knowing where this was going. "No."

"So your claim is based on what?"

"Common sense."

"Common sense has no place in the medical field. There is only fact or fiction. And it is a fact that Keith is still alive. He will require surgery to repair his arm, but he will live and be fine."

Jared moved to see for himself but the doctor stepped in front of him. "He is resting now. I have him sedated and hooked to an IV. I will stay here tonight and watch over him. You may go now."

Jared wanted to push her out of the way. See for himself the kid was breathing; he sure as hell wasn't earlier. But that would only make matters worse. Besides, if he was alive, Jared would see him soon enough.

Patience is a virtue. Or so someone said.

"I'll be back tomorrow." Jared applied a keen edge to the words. Showing Lyla he would not be put off with her speeches. "First thing."

"Goodnight."

Jared stomped down the stairs. More to show Lyla his anger than anything. As he marched down the employee path, he had an idea. He looked around to ensure he was alone, and darted into the trees. Dry leaves and limbs cracked and rustled underfoot. He tried rising to his tip-toes for stealth but the leaves crackled like tinfoil regardless. He hoped the earthquaking rumble of rollercoasters, the shouts of visitors, and the echoes of sinister music, distant as they were, would mask his movements.

The woods were almost pitch black, which helped him find his way to the doctor's office; the soft glow of lamps like a lighthouse to a weary sailor. He pressed his back against the cedar siding and waited a moment, listening for an indication Lyla had spotted his reconnaissance. Satisfied she had not discovered him, Jared crouched low, navigated around the HVAC unit, and moved to the window of the room the kid was in. He paused a beat, listening to the rollercoaster as it roared down the tracks, moving toward him as it looped and flipped. As the thunder grew, Jared raised his head to look inside. The shade was drawn. Only the thinnest of cracks on either side, not even wide enough to make out a single item in the room. Suddenly a spider lowered in front of his face, legs kicking as though it wanted to latch onto his face.

Damn! He jerked back, almost tripping over a fallen limb.

He stayed low and fled the scene. Back on the employee walkway, Jared had no idea where he was going. His brain was in overdrive, his body on autopilot. He was surprised when he found himself staring at Cindy's front door.

He turned to leave, but the door opened. "I was hoping you'd stop by."

She was in her nightgown; a silky number that pressed against her body, accentuated valleys and peaks. Her damp hair told him she was freshly showered. Jared could smell the sweetness of her body wash. He swallowed the lump in his throat. It took a great amount of self-control to drop his eyes to his scuffed work boots. "Sorry to bother you. I ... um ..."

She held out her hand. "Come in. Please."

Jared took her hand and stepped inside. Cindy's cabin was by far the coziest one he had been inside. She had taken the time to add all the comforts of home. Throw blankets and pillows on the couches and chairs. A large rug in the living room. Plants in pots and vases. Picture frames on the walls and end tables. Books on the coffee table. A few candles burning. Kenny G played softly in the background, just loud enough for a relaxing ambience.

She eased onto one of the couches, sinking in the cushions, and crossed her legs. Jared tried to avert his attention to something across the room so she wouldn't know he caught a flash of panties.

Damn, dude, he thought. *You're acting like you've never seen a girl before. Chill.*

Cindy patted the couch beside her, and Jared sat. He straightened his sweat-stained shirt and, for the first time, noticed the blood splatter. "Oh shit." He popped up off her plush, cream-colored couch.

"Here, let me have that," she said, standing. "It'll stain if I don't put something on it."

Jared unbuttoned and removed the blue work shirt.

"Why don't you go take a shower and I'll wash your clothes. I have a white robe that you can wear while your clothes dry."

"I don't want to impose. I can wash these at home."

"You're not imposing. Besides, after what I just saw, I probably won't sleep tonight, and I don't want to be alone." She held his gaze. "Do you?"

Jared shook his head. It was the last thing he wanted. "No."

"Go take a shower and I'll make us a drink. I was pulling out the glass when I heard you on the porch. Now I'll make two. Just toss your pants in the hall."

Jared tossed his pants in the hall and let cold shower refresh his skin, but the water failed to rinse away any of the painful residue of the accident. When he stepped out to dry off, a white robe was draped across the sink and his underwear were gone. His cheeks flushed. Only two other females had ever washed his underwear; his mother and his long-time ex-girlfriend.

He returned to the living room and found Cindy lying on the couch, a drink in hand resting on her stomach. Another glass sat on a coaster on the coffee table. She pulled her legs close and shifted to sit up.

Jared sat next to her feet, took a sip, relishing the heat that coated his stomach. For minutes they sat in silence. Any other time, Jared may have found this uncomfortable. But not tonight. As the whiskey softened his anxiety over the kid, he relaxed. Found comfort in Cindy's toes rubbing his leg.

"Every time I close my eyes, I see Keith draped over that turbine. Then I see him lying on the gurney. Lifeless." Cindy thumbed a tear from the corner of her eye. "I will have nightmares about this the rest of my life."

"What's his last name?"

"Brooks."

"I found Lyla," Jared said.

Cindy jerked upright. "Where was she?"

Jared took another sip to buy time. He wasn't sure what he wanted to tell Cindy. Maybe the actions of the doctor and others were all in his head. His heightened state of edginess and helplessness causing him to imagine things. If he told her these things, she may think he was crazy, kick him out with nothing but a bath robe covering his birthday suit. He decided to proceed with caution. "In the park. With Patrick, Billy, and Lawrence."

Cindy's brow furrowed. "What were they doing in the park? Why didn't they return to the doctor's office?"

Jared shrugged. "I never got an answer to that question. But here's the fucked-up part: Keith is alive."

Cindy cleared the couch in one bounce to her feet. "What? No way. He was dead. Like, call the coroner dead."

"I know that. You know that. But doc went in to examine him, then came out and assured me he was alive and would be okay. He needs surgery but otherwise he'll live."

Cindy plopped down on the couch. She swallowed the rest of her drink in one gulp, went back to kitchen to make another. "Did you see him? After she said that?"

"No. She wouldn't let me. Said she sedated him, and he was resting. Come back tomorrow."

Cindy sat back down beside him, sipped more whiskey. Finally, "Do you believe her?"

"I don't know. It's hard to believe; I saw the same thing as you. But she was adamant. We'll find out soon enough, I guess." Jared took a sip. To himself, he said, "And it looks like I'm Ronald Reagan."

"What?"

"Nothing, not important."

Cindy rested her head on his shoulder. The scent of her shampoo was sweet and oddly comforting. "I really hope she's right," Cindy said quietly. "Maybe knowing that he's alive will help me sleep."

"I know what you mean."

Cindy dropped her left hand on his exposed leg, trailed a glossy fingernail over a three-inch scar on his kneecap. "What happened there?"

"Funny story," he said with a clipped laugh. "The short of it is some friends and I were jumping our bikes on makeshift ramps in the street in front of my childhood home. You know, a plank of old wood and two cinderblocks. Some older kids came by and dared us to follow them down to The Pit. It was a place on the edge of our neighborhood where the city had dug out an area the size of a large swimming pool to use the dirt for road work. The older kids had built ramps on the edge of the drop and would jump bikes into the pit like Evel Kneivel. My friends and I were not allowed to jump into the pit, but that day, on a double-dog-dare-or-your-dad-likes-goats, I took the jump. My bike literally split in half when I landed. I'm not sure what sliced my knee; the bike or the rocks. Regardless, after a trip to the ER for stitches, I got my ass whipped and was grounded for a month."

"Doesn't sound like a funny story," she said. Her voice husky and tantalizing. The result of the whiskey.

"It wasn't at the time," Jared said. "My knee hurt like a bitch and my dad used a belt to spank me. For some reason, the best stories always involve a little pain."

She laughed and it was music to Jared. Without thinking he laced his fingers in the hand on his knee, squeezed. She raised her head and never hesitated to ease her lips to his. Like she was waiting for the moment and Jared complied.

Her warm, moist tongue tasted of alcohol. He was drunk on her immediately. Wanted more. But he held steadfast to the desperation that made him tremble. Stayed calm though he was enraptured. Slow and easy, gently, and Cindy responded by shoving him down on the couch and climbing on top. Her damp hair draped each side of Jared's face, tickling his cheeks. Blocking out the world so only the two of them existed. Cindy bit her lip, oh so wicked, then lowered to kiss him again. Slow and measured. Painstakingly. Jared throbbed all over, but continued his discipline. Cindy's lips moved from his mouth to his chest to his neck, and up to his ear.

She whispered, steamy breath pulling goosebumps on his scalp. "Let's go to the bedroom."

"Uh huh," Jared croaked. He wasn't sure if he could talk if he wanted. Every muscle in him quivered.

Cindy glanced back at him on the way to the bedroom and grinned. "Someone seems happy to see me."

Jared had nothing cool or smooth to say so he kept quiet. Laid on the bed. Enjoyed the show. Her pulling off the nightgown. Dropping the silk panties. Crawling on all fours across the bed to him like a ravenous animal on the prowl.

Jared was happy to be the prey.

Sixteen

Pete and Nola held hands as they reluctantly walked back to their hotel. A make-out session had been short-lived; a lemonade stand vendor caught them and ran them off. Despite the unfortunate incident with the bully, the night had been perfect. The most incredible time of Pete's young life. Whoever designed the haunted park had hit a home run. Every aspect was first class. the most fun ever. Experiencing it all with Nola only elevated it greatness. He wished the night would never end.

And to think. "I didn't want to come when my parents first told me about it," Pete confessed. "I refused."

Nola laughed. "I imagine that went over like a lead zeppelin, didn't it?"

Pete loved the play with words. "My dad's exact words were 'I brought you into this world, boy, and I can take you out of it.' " His dad had lots of those sayings. "But now, I'm glad that I came."

"I'm glad you came too. Otherwise, I would've been bored tonight walking this place with my lame, straight and narrow parents."

"Ouch, that hurts. I'm just here for your entertainment."

Nola laughed and dropped her arm around his neck. "I'm just kidding and you know it. Today has been the best day of my life. And it's all because of you." She kissed him on the cheek.

"Let's make that day better, shall we," someone said from behind them.

Pete turned, recognizing the voice of the bully, but he reacted too slowly. He never expected more than a verbal exchange. The fist hurtling at him barely registered until the pain washed his vision of all color. He shook his head and tried blinking his focus back. He heard Nola shout "NO!" a split second before another freight train battered the side of his head. The world went blank and silent. Nothing hurt in that void. There he roamed, in the cold black, for a time indistinguishable from the second hands of a clock. Weeks may have passed. Or years. Until a sound reverberated through the dark chamber, relocating constantly, filling his head with synthesized warbles. He hobbled toward the root of the sound, faintly recognizing it. Wanted to move closer, and as he did, the volume and density increased. As did the pain. Maybe it was best to retreat. Hide and wait for the hurt to abate.

But the song of a siren pulled Pete like a weary sailor on troubled waters. Fighting seemed a waste of energy. Fatigue crippled him, everything felt heavy. He relinquished and floated to the surface. When he opened his throbbing eyes, his vision was blurred. He blinked in time to catch Nola being helped to her feet by a female while a man with a military buzzcut dropped to his knees and leaned over Pete.

"Can you hear me?" The man asked. He sounded far away, yelling from a mountaintop.

Pete winced. The man didn't speak loud but the words were like ice picks in Pete's skull. After a moment, the stabbing eased and Pete nodded.

The man looked up at someone outside Pete's field of vision. "Call the doctor. This kid has a concussion at least, and maybe some broken ribs."

At the mention of his ribs, Pete realized his whole body felt like he had been pushed off a cliff. He wiggled his toes and electric-fire bursts impaled his legs.

More like pushed out of a plane with no parachute.

He licked his lips. "Where's Nola?"

The man jerked around to look behind him. "He wants you."

Nola fell beside him, weeping black mascara. "Are you okay?"

"I don't think I'm gonna make it. Tell the kids I love them."

Nola's face flashed surprise, confusion, then settled on the realization that it was a joke. She cried out, "Oh my god, do not mess with me right now!"

Pete barked a harsh laugh and his shattered insides made him pay for the revolt. He bit his bottom lip to hide the tears.

"Ma'am, who did this?" Buzzcut asked. Must be park security.

"I'm not sure who he is," Nola said, wiping her face, smearing the makeup like war paint. "He's a teenager. White. Heavyset. Wearing a white Panama Jack t-shirt and solid blue swim trunks. Brown hair. He messed with us earlier today. I embarrassed him, so I guess this was payback."

"Did you see which way he went?"

"No. I shoved him away, then fell on Pete so he couldn't hit him anymore. When I looked up, he was gone."

"Thank you," the man said. Pete heard retreating footsteps then the man started talking again. "Barbara, this is Moe. Call the front desk of every resort and ask about a teenage male, white, brown hair, white Panama Jack t-shirt and blue shorts. Find him and call me back. Over."

Conversations overlapped one another as Pete laid on the asphalt walkway, trying to ignore the last few gawkers leaving the park in the final minutes before closing. The security guard was quick to run anyone off who dared to stop and stare.

"This is not a freak show ladies and gentlemen. Move or be moved. The choice is yours."

One female said she wasn't having any luck hailing the doctor. A male said he thought he remembered seeing the kid not thirty minutes ago. Said the kid bought a drink from his shop, which was just around the corner. Remembered him because he was one of the few people in the park not dressed for Halloween. The male also said he noticed the kid's wristband—a requirement to get in the door of the accommodations where the guests were staying.

"What color?" The security guard asked.

"It was red."

Pete didn't know which colors associated with which resort, but red was not the color of his own wristband. The kid was staying somewhere else.

"That's the economy resort. Tsunami Suites. I'm going to get that little shit." The security guard bent down over Pete. Tall and slightly heavyset himself. Face oily with sweat. A goatee. Name-tag on his blue officer uniform read Moe. An intimidating figure. Pete wished he could be a fly on the wall to watch this guy drag the bully down the hall by his ear. "You take it easy 'til doc gets here. Do you want me to call your parents?"

"No sir, not yet." Pete's mom would be a mess and his dad would grab a pitchfork and go hunting the village ogre. No need to add to the drama.

"Okay, I'll be back." The guard disappeared.

Once Pete was sure Moe was gone, he pushed himself up on his elbows. A dozen slivers of glass punctured his lungs, or so it felt, leaving Pete gasping, but he wasn't deterred by the discomfort.

"Pete, what are you doing?" Nola asked quickly, the words running into each other.

"I can't just lay here in the middle of the walkway." He took a deep breath and steeled himself for the next flash of pain, and rolled over to his knees. He was surprised the move only caused a mild twinge. "I need to see how bad it is. I don't think anything is broken."

"Please go easy," Nola pleaded. She hooked her arm under his and helped him rise to his feet.

The ground tilted to the side, leaned backward, then rose toward his face. Only with Nola's help as a crutch was he able to avoid a face-plant. Sour bile squirted into his mouth and Pete was sure he was about to hurl right there in front of Nola, but he swallowed it back with a grimace and took slow, deep breaths. The guy who worked a beverage hut was still standing to the side, watching.

"I know you're closed and I hate to ask, but could I get a Riptide Cola? I've got money in my pocket if I can dig it out. Feeling nauseous."

"Not a problem. I'll be right back."

"You want to sit down?" Nola asked. Every time she looked at his face her eyes got moist. He didn't need a mirror to know that bastard messed him up pretty good.

"No, I need to stand. I want to try walking around. Get my legs back."

Pete took a few tentative steps, testing his stability. His knees were weak but held him upright and the pavement was no longer trying to toss him on his ass. Small miracles.

The guy returned with what the park called The Monsoon. Their souvenir thirty-two-ounce cup, full of Riptide Cola. Everything on the island was a sales pitch or an advertising campaign. Brilliant marketing strategy.

"Thank you," Pete said with a nod. He dug out his wallet. "How much?"

"Nothing. You paid enough already." The guy gently slapped Pete's arm and moved back out of the way. Maybe he was waiting for Moe to return.

It was a short wait. Pete was about halfway through The Monsoon and feeling better—at least from a woozy and nausea standpoint—when the bully came trudging down the walkway with Moe's massive hand clamped around a bicep. Two adults were trailing close behind. The parents.

The bully was not happy that he had been caught. It was written all over his face. Pete guessed his family was leaving on the ferry in the morning. The bully must have figured that by the time anyone linked him to this beating, he would be back on United States soil.

Bully's mom saw Pete and started crying. In that instant, she knew her son was in trouble.

"This him?" Moe asked as he pushed him closer to Pete.

"Yes," Pete said. His mouth was feeling funny, like it was swelling. Sounded more like *Yeth.*

"Liar!" Bully blurted. "I don't know you."

Pete smiled, though it hurt his split lip. "Show us your hands." *Thow uth your hands.*

"What?" Bully immediately shoved his hands into his now red shorts. He was also wearing a different shirt. "I'm not showing you shit, nerd."

Bully's head was suddenly knocked forward from a slap by his mother. "You better tell the truth Johnathon or so help me god I will snatch the life out of you." She looked at Moe. "When he got back to the hotel room his white shirt had blood on it. He said he tripped and skinned his knuckles. I was stupid enough to believe him. The shirt is soaking in the kitchen sink so it doesn't stain." She moved around Moe and came to Pete, placed her hand gently on his swollen cheek, tears streaming down her face. "I am so so sorry. He's done this before. I thought he was getting better from counseling. Obviously not."

"It's not your fault."

"I didn't do it, but it is my fault. I'm his mother. The buck stops with me. I have to do better, and when we get home, I will."

"Do you want to press charges?" Moe asked Pete.

"Yes," Pete said glaring at Johnathon. To Johnathon's mother, "I'm sorry. He's been messing with me all day. And rather than fight straight up, he jumped me from behind."

"Liar!" Johnathon hissed.

Nola raised her hand like she was in class. "Did you forget I was there, asshole? I saw the whole thing. You did this, then your buddy got a kick in before you two ran off like the pussies you are."

"Wait, what buddy?" Moe asked.

Johnathon's mom answered with an exasperated sigh. "That would be Fulton. He's here with his mom who is my best friend. They are in 204, the room next to mine." She wagged a finger at her son. "I can't believe you involved him in this. Sarah is going to lose her mind. And probably never want to come around us again."

"He's lying. I told you."

"Let me see your hands."

Johnathon stared at the ground in defiance. Moe snatched on one arm, yanking a hand from the pocket. Johnathon tried to shove it back down, but his mom grabbed it and raised it to the light. The flesh on all the knuckles were ripped and bleeding.

"I told you I fell."

"No one falls and catches themselves with their knuckles," Moe chastised. "If that had happened, the palms of your hands would be skinned, not the knuckles. I've seen enough fist fights in my day to know what's what."

Johnathon saw the excuses were futile and went silent.

"Ma'am, how old is he?" Moe asked Johnathon's mom.

"Just turned eighteen," she sighed. "This trip was his birthday present."

"I'm afraid I have a rude present to give to you. I'm calling port to have them send the ferry back to pick you guys up. You have to leave the island immediately. The other family as well. Port will call police and they will be waiting to arrest him and his friend for assault and battery when you arrive back to Florida. From there, I'm not sure what happens, but they are both in serious trouble.

"Furthermore, he and his friend are now banned for life from the island. You and your friend, Sarah, are welcome to return, but neither Johnathon nor Fulton can ever step foot on Riptide soil. We do not tolerate violence here. Our customers' happiness and safety are our top priorities. I am truly sorry for all of this, and I hope you understand."

Johnathon's mother wiped more tears from her face, and nodded. "I do. We're already packed; we were leaving in the morning anyway. What are you doing with him?"

"There is a security HQ on-site with two jail cells. They have never been used, but tonight they will be. Fulton will be joining him. Just until the ferry arrives. I have to personally escort both of them on the boat and across the water to the port where they will be detained by authorities."

"Jesus," she whispered to herself. Out loud, she said, "Okay. What time should we expect the ferry?"

"In about two hours. I have to call and request a special return trip."

"Well Johnathon, you've been trying to go to jail ever since your father died. Looks like you're finally getting your wish." With that she left, the man who Pete now knew to not be Johnathon's father, sheepishly in tow. Pete knew what whipped looked like and that man fit the description.

Hearing verbal confirmation of what was to come sunk Johnathon like a ship. His face drained of color and his defiant shoulders lost all resistance. He went where Moe steered him without another word, now a broken dog without a home.

"We've had no luck getting doc on the phone or radio," a female employee said. Her name tag read Keri. "You want me to walk you to her office? Maybe we can catch her before she leaves for the night."

Pete hurt all over, but what he really wanted was a shower and his bed. "No thanks. Think I'll head back to my room and lick my wounds."

"Okay. I'm very sorry for what happened."

"Thanks." Nola nuzzled underneath Pete's arm and helped him out the park's double gates, which closed once they were clear.

The trip was short but still took forty minutes. It was after two in the morning when he finally reached his room door. The lock was an electronic reader tied to his wristband. The light turned green and the mechanisms inside clicked indicating the door was now unlocked.

She helped him through the door of the dark room, then stopped. She kissed him, her soft lips like a soothing balm on his cut. In his ear, she whispered, "I don't want your parents to wake and find a girl in here. You good?"

Pete nodded, whispered: "Thank you. See you in the morning."

Nola smiled, backed out of the room, and quietly closed the door.

Showering was a painful, yet soothing experience. The water burned the cuts to his face but massaged his bruised muscles. He managed to get dressed in his sleeping shorts but pulling on a t-shirt was impossible. He snuck into his bed without waking his parents whose room was separate with a closed door. As he lay in the dark, the aches and pains causing him to constantly readjust, all he could think about was Nola. The taste of her lips, the feel of her body pressed against his. Her jokes. All the nuisances of her personality that made her so perfect. To him anyway.

He dozed off to her smile.

Seventeen

Though it had been a late night, Dave still rose at six for his morning jog. He quietly closed the bathroom door to change into shorts and running shoes, skipping a shirt. Another scorcher was in the forecast.

On the beach, he stretched, loosening the tight calf muscles. Another engrained routine from his college days. Enjoyed the slightly cool, brisk wind coming in from the west. Across the Atlantic Ocean, the sky brightened from eggplant purple to a bruised blue. The sun was still lying in bed, hiding beneath the covers, but it would be up soon enough. With it would come the heat. One hundred four degrees on Halloween Day. Back home, it was snowing.

Dave shortened the morning stretch. A break in the rules, but a forgivable one. He'd probably shorten the run as well. Another violation. And so what? He was tired from yesterday. A long day and a longer night. At least ten miles of walking. He pulled the kids out of the gates at exactly midnight. Van and Jessica had milked the park for everything it offered until it stopped offering. They were asleep before their heads touched the pillow.

He set off at a casual pace, taking it easy on his fatigued body. Getting old was for the birds. Twenty years ago he could've run around the entire island without breathing heavy. Now he slow-jogged to allow the blood to circulate so he wouldn't pull a hamstring or throw a hip out of socket.

At least my feet are in the sand of a beautiful beach and not in the snow.

There was that.

Enjoying a much-needed break from work was therapeutic. After Molly, he had buried himself in work. Aside from Sundays, he hadn't taken many days off since the funeral, even working most Saturdays. Hiding, not coping. Anything to avoid thinking about her being taken from this world, and the haunting, excruciating knowledge of her last moments. After years of grinding that axe without real downtime, he had begun to feel burned out. Going to work was no longer a passion; it was a job. The salty air, ocean waves, sunrises and sunsets, uninterrupted time with his family, was helping serenity reestablish itself within him. It was a fitful peace, prone to partial relapses when taking unexpected trips down Memory Lane, but they were steps in the right direction of rediscovering a little more of his old self.

The squawk of a pelican forced Dave from his thoughts. He had almost reached the end of the beach extension. Twenty yards ahead, a thirty-foot tall jetty dropped into the water, guarding the rest of the island from the beach. The rocks glistened in the sunlight. Knobs of corral clung to the lower stones like malignant growths. Spiny limbs of seaweed drifted with the waves. Dave jogged in a lazy circle to head back the way he came when his eyes swept across an anomaly. With all the natural vegetation—palm trees, salt meadow cordgrass, large-frond shrubs, sea oats, and a bunch of other types Dave had never seen or heard of—anything not indigenous to the island stood out like a sore thumb. Dave stopped moving and raised his hand to block the sun's harsh glare like the bill of a baseball cap. He squinted, sure it was a play of shadows. As he got closer, he realized the shadow was a body. A kid, about sixteen, greasy black hair, black eye liner, black fingernails, lying on his back, legs crossed like an Indian. Head bent back, whites of his eyeballs showing. Dave quickly felt for a pulse, telling himself to stay calm. Relief flooded through him when he felt a faint thud on his fingertips.

"Hey, kid," he said, rubbing the kids shoulder. Dave shook him gently, and something fell from the kids hand. A crack pipe. "Jesus."

Dave was not a doctor. Wasn't sure if he should leave and go get help, or carry him back. The idea of leaving a teenager who was unconscious from smoking crack to get help seemed dangerous. If he returned and the boy had died, Dave would never forgive himself.

"Hang on, buddy," Dave said, hoisting the boy into his arms.

He walked as fast as he dared and by the time he reached the lobby to Corral Cove where the main office was located, Dave's arms were limp as noodles. The receptionist behind the check-in/check-out desk watched him enter the storefront doors with a perplexed look on her face. Not sure what to think. She met Dave in the middle of the lobby before he reached the counter.

"May I help you?" She asked curtly, eyebrows raised.

Dave situated the boy in his arms before he dropped him on the tile floor, caught his breath. "My name is David Evans, I'm staying in villa number twelve. I went on a jog this morning, and I found this kid unconscious in the bushes down by the rock wall at the end of the beach. I think he smoked crack. I need help."

"Oh dear," the woman said, looking around like she was more concerned with eavesdroppers than the kid. She pulled a walkie off of her side and called for a manager to come to the lobby immediately. She then pointed to a couch located in a sitting area. Dave laid the boy on the couch and checked his pulse again.

"Is he alive?" She asked. Dave thought it more a perfunctory question than one of actual concern.

Dave nodded. "Yes, but his heartbeat is weak. I can barely feel it."

A short, balding man with a handlebar mustache and dark green eyes approached. "What's going on?"

"This is Mr. Evans," the woman said, nodding at Dave, "and he is staying in twelve. He went on a jog and found this unconscious kid down by the rock wall. Appears to be drugs."

The manager unhooked his walkie like a trained gunslinger in a street fight. He turned a small knob several clicks, then pressed a button to speak. "Lyla, this is Stuart at Coral, you read?"

Dave scrutinized the rise and fall of the kid's chest while he waited. Looked for any sign of further complications. A dreaded sense of deja-vu took his breath as the scene at the dolphin pool flashed across his eyes. Dave had to grab the back of the couch to hold himself upright. No way was he going to have to watch another human receive CPR in less than twenty-four hours. No way.

"Lyla? You copy?"

Stuart was holstering his walkie when the speaker crackled. "Yes?"

Stuart yanked the black plastic box back to his face. "I need you down here in my lobby. Got a drugged kid passed out on the couch."

"On the way."

Stuart shook Dave's hand. "Thanks for your help. We'll take it from here."

"If you don't mind, I'd like to stay with him until the nurse gets here. Just to be sure he's okay."

"Lyla's a doctor," Stuart corrected. "He'll be in good hands with her. But, yeah, sure, you're welcome to stay. Glad to see there are still some good people in the world." Stuart whispered something to the receptionist, and left the lobby.

"I'm Gabbie," she said. "Can I get you a water?"

"No thanks. I'm fine." Dave kneeled next to the couch and wondered about the boy. Where was he from? Where were his parents? How did a teenager get crack and know how to smoke it? The boy was a skateboarder. The black t-shirt with a figure performing a hand plant on Mars, the Airwalk hi-tops, the cargo shorts. The go-to clothing for the half-pipe crowd. Dave knew about it because he had been a skateboarder when he was a teenager. College soccer took over and he sold his board, but he had kept up with the booming sport. Even bought Van a board last Christmas and enjoyed watching his son show an interest. Van had already chosen the board he wanted next: a Tony Hawk with the hooked beak logo.

"Is this your son?" someone asked.

Dave looked up. The doctor was pretty but haggard. Her brown eyes were rimmed in red circles, face pale and slick. Her blondish-brown hair was pulled into a disheveled, scrunched pony-tail. She looked sicker than the kid on the couch.

"No, I found him. I don't know who he is."

The doctor nodded at a boy standing behind her. Maybe a candy-striper for the busy Halloween celebration. He was average height and weight, with black curly hair. He was wearing ill-fitting white scrubs; a little too tight around the torso and waist, and a little short for his height. He, like the doctor, appeared to have the flu or some sort of summer cold. He lifted the skateboarder like he was a feather and walked out a side door without a single word.

"Thank you for your help," the doctor said. "We will take good care of him." She disappeared, leaving Dave with more questions than he had before.

Gabbie returned to her post behind the desk. She smiled at Dave like all was right with the world and went back to work answering the phone.

When Dave returned to his villa, Penny was on the phone. Her reaction to him walking in the door was anything but normal. Shocked. Put off. She ended the conversation quickly with a quiet "Gotta go, bye" and hung up.

"How was the run?" Penny asked, stepping flirtatiously to him, kissing his sweaty chin and neck.

Dave wasn't sure how to answer. He was still puzzled over the exchange with the doctor. She had not asked a single question other than, "Is this your son?" She hadn't asked about the drug. Hadn't evaluated the kid on the couch. No questions about the parents. Nothing. Her demeanor had been cold and stiff. She had looked awful. Her helper had looked sick as well.

Then he found his wife on the phone and acting weird.

"Who were you talking to?" Dave asked while she hugged him, her head lying against his sweaty chest.

"Um, that was Renee. I called to check on Martin. He was sick when we left."

Martin Pierson was a good friend of Dave's, a golfing buddy. Penny and Renee, Martin's wife of twelve years, had started hanging out more after Molly. With Dave and Penny both grief-stricken and damn near inconsolable, Renee and Martin had stepped in big-time, providing a support system rivaled by no one in such a situation. The couple had been there for Dave and Penny at their lowest. The friendship carried on after Dave and Penny finally got their act together and now they ate dinner together on the regular. Dave and Martin played golf once a week. Penny and Renee had a girls' night out at least once a month.

There was nothing odd about her calling Renee to check on Martin. It was what friends did.

Then why does something feel off?

Her reaction when he walked in? Sauntering to him like a runway model and kissing him all over, slow-grinding her hips against him? That was not like her. She was flirty, sure, but not outwardly sexual. It usually took three or four cocktails to unleash her inner inhibitions.

Surely I'm being paranoid, he thought. After the unnerving discovery of the kid, and witnessing the lady die at the dolphin pools, everything now carried a negative undertone. His perception was clouded. Hopefully, a little park fun would wipe the confusion away and provide clarity. He'd see that it was all in his head.

Just let it go.

He wrapped his arms around her, pulled her tight, enjoying the feel of her body against his own. The comfort she always provided. "How's Martin? Feeling better?"

"A little. Renee says he's hoping to go back to work Monday." She looked up at him. "How was your run? You didn't answer."

"You'll never believe this," Dave said, and told her everything.

"That is crazy." Penny cinched the belt on her robe to close the front before sitting on the couch in the living room. "Where did the doctor take him?"

"I have no clue. I assume the urgent care they have here on the island."

"Do you want to swing by while we're out today? Check on him."

Dave had already thought of that. "Yes. I do."

"Okay, we will." Penny stood. "I'm going to check on the kids. You taking a shower?"

"Yep."

"If they are still asleep, I'll join. I think you deserve it after all of this."

Dave forced his lips into a smile, more uneasiness nudging him in the gut. He'd read somewhere that one sign a spouse was cheating was they would cover it up by being especially intimate with their partner.

Shut up!

He ignored the mental banter and started the shower.

He lathered a wash rag with soap as Penny stepped in. Despite his misgivings, he forgot about the kid and the lady by the pool. And the doctor.

For a while anyway.

Eighteen

A thin blade of sunlight cut through Jared's eyelids, dragging him from a dream about his mother. He fought to stay in that imaginary world where she was still alive and happy. Her hair was golden. She was in a field of sunflowers, laughing, and spinning in circles. Her sundress billowed in the breeze like sheets on a clothesline. She had never been that way in real life, not that he was aware.

That was how he knew it was a dream.

He failed to stay inside that blissful world, and the room came into a blurry view, leaving him feeling lost. The sheer curtains over the windows were not his curtains. The softness of the mattress beneath him was not his mattress—his being more firm. He turned his head and it all came rushing back. Cindy was still asleep. She lay on her stomach, facing Jared, her freckled bare back exposed. Her lips were slightly parted, features relaxed, peaceful. He stared at her, wondering how this was going to go when she woke. She had never shown an outward interest in him, though he had shown subtle signs of his attraction to her without saying it out loud. She had always seemed oblivious to any of his advancements.

Fast forward to last night. Had that been a case of right place, right time? Had he simply caught her in a vulnerable moment where she needed comfort? Had the alcohol played a part?

She hadn't started drinking yet when you knocked on her door, he told himself.

True, but he still caught her with her guard down. She'd been weakened by what had happened. Nothing to strengthen her emotions, keep her from making rash decisions.

Her eyes fluttered, then opened as she licked her lips. She looked at him and, for a moment, his heart sank. She was having a mental crisis, thinking, W*hat the fuck have I done?* But then she smiled and raised her hand to his face, her tender fingers caressing his cheek.

"Good morning," she said, sandy and adorable.

"Morning," Jared said, hoping he was hiding the mixed burst of relief and joy that detonated inside him. "How'd you sleep?"

"Hmmm ... like a baby. I haven't slept that good since I got here." She inched closer, kissed him gently. He was not put off by the morning breath, and she apparently wasn't either.

"I don't think I've ever slept that good," Jared said, brushing a few stray twigs off her forehead. "I never dream, but I dreamed of my mother. Dancing in a field of sunflowers. That's how deep down I was."

"Tell me about her."

Jared was surprised. Not one girlfriend had ever asked him that question. Even Evelyn, whom he'd dated for three years. No one had ever wanted to know him on a deeper level.

"I don't remember much. She left when I was young."

"She died?"

"Yeah, suicide. She said she was going to the grocery store. When she didn't come back, my dad had my grandpa drive us home. Our trailer was packed and there was a goodbye note. I don't remember what it said.

"Then one day, she shows back up. Wants to reconcile. She made a mistake. She was sorry. She had met a man and got caught up in a workplace romance. The guy was funny and wild. Rode a motorcycle and lived in a camper. He excited her and she thought that's what she wanted. Turned out he was also an abusive alcoholic, which she didn't want."

"Your dad take her back?"

"He wanted to. He told me years later that telling her no was the hardest thing he'd ever done. He still loved her. But he said that he wasn't going to be with someone he had to worry would leave at the drop of a hat for any 'swinging dick.'"

"I imagine that was hard on you," Cindy said, fingers caressing his forehead.

"I cried when he told her no. I wanted my mom back. I wanted everything to be normal again." Jared cleared his throat. He hadn't told her the worst yet. "The thing that haunts me about that day is I was in my bedroom, ear to the thin, brown paneled door listening to the conversation. Hoping they could work it out.

"My dad said 'No, sorry, but I can't live like that.' My mom cried softly for about thirty seconds. She said she was sorry for everything, said for him to tell me she loves me dearly, then I heard my dad yell 'NO!" just before a gun went off."

Cindy stared at him in horror. Her lips moved but she said nothing.

Jared wiped a stray tear from the corner of his eye. For the millionth time, watched the memory of his hand turning the doorknob, running down the hall, and finding his mother on the shag carpet, blood leaking from a hole in her temple. His dad kneeled next to her, screaming. The room smelled of smoking gun powder and hot piss. His eye latched onto the paneled wall behind the couch. A gob of brain matter clung to the wood. Chunks of bone and blood draped the couch cushion like a throw blanket.

"I've never been able to get that image out of my head," Jared said after a quiet moment. "My dad lived a few more years, but the guilt weighed on him heavily, and he eventually drank himself to death."

"Oh my god," Cindy gasped.

"I used to have nightmares about it almost every night," Jared said. "At some point, the nightmares went away and now I never dream. Not that I can remember anyway. I have a few pictures of her holding me, one of her and my dad just before I was born, a few others, but all I see when I think of mom is her body sprawled on the floor."

"The dream you had last night must've been pretty awesome then," Cindy said.

"Probably the best dream I've ever had. She looked so happy."

Cindy said, "It's horrible you have to carry that."

"Funny thing is, I don't remember most of my childhood. Like hardly anything. Snippets. Snapshots so faded I wonder if they're memories or fragments of dreams. But I remember that day. Vividly. I can still smell the gunpowder."

"That's your trauma response."

"You a shrink?"

"No, silly, but I went to college. Even paid attention. And I learned that people who barely remember their childhood most often experienced trauma. Forgetting all of it is a way for the brain to create a safe environment. Mentally, anyway."

Jared was always anxious. Always worried he would fuck up, do something wrong. More psychological damage. He kept that to himself. He said, "It's probably best that I don't remember a lot of it. It was pretty bad until I was old enough to move out on my own."

Cindy leaned to him, the sheet falling from her breasts. She raised his head with her finger, kissed him gently. "You should be proud of yourself."

Another first. "Yeah? Why's that?"

"You had a choice after that. Stay down and become a tragic story yourself, or climb back to your feet, dust off, and walk tall. You chose to keep pushing forward and by doing so, you became a responsible adult and a good man. Your mom would be proud of the path you chose. And your dad."

Jared changed the subject. He was not one to wallow. Last night had been so perfect he wasn't going to spoil it by living in the past for too long. "What does *"Dum spiro, spero"* mean?"

He wasn't aware of Cindy's tattoo until last night. On her stomach, just below her right breast. In italics, riding the ridge of a rib. Sexy as hell.

"'*While I breathe, I hope,*'" she recited. "It's a personal mantra I adopted from my grandmother. She was a nurse in World War Two. She said the things she saw made her question humanity and our place here. But she always hoped for a better future for mankind. She had the exact same tattoo. I got it the day after her funeral to honor her."

"Do you have any idea how long I've had a crush on you?" Jared blurted. Shitty timing, but he wanted her to know.

"Same as the amount of time I've had a crush on you. Since day one."

This admission caught Jared off guard. "What? You serious?"

"Yes."

"Why have you never said anything?"

"Did you say anything? Besides your cute but corny little come-ons?"

Damn. She got me. "You noticed."

"Oh, yeah, I noticed. I thought it best we stay professional. Try, at least."

"What do we do with this?"

Cindy's head cocked sideways and she looked at him like he was a fool. "Well, we are going to make out for a few minutes. Then get ready and go check on Keith. After that, we will go to work. Tonight, I'm staying at your place."

Jared rolled the dice. Choosing honesty. "I can't do casual. I want that out in the open. Just in case."

"Good. I can't either. Now shut up and kiss me."

Jared kissed her, and the make-out session morphed into round two.

Nineteen

Pete stared at his reflection in disbelief. One eye was almost swollen closed, the view a thin, blurry rectangle. His jaw was tender, causing him to wince every time he opened his mouth. By far the worst was his torso. His ribs felt like someone ran over him with a car, then put it in reverse for good measure. Purple patches dotted his sides and back.

The mirror fogged from the heat of the shower. The hot water had loosened him up last night, and he hoped for the same this morning. A knock at the room door stopped him before he climbed in. He waited for one of his parents to answer, wondering who would be calling on them this early. Had to be housekeeping.

"Good morning," his mother said. "Can I help you?"

"Hello," a female voice answered. "I am Doctor Lyla. I heard your son Pete was in an altercation and injured last night. May I check on him?"

Pete's heart dropped in his chest. He had yet to tell his parents what happened. He had snuck into the bathroom this morning without either of them seeing him.

"You must have the wrong room," his mom said, confused. "Pete's fine. He's taking a shower."

"Have you seen him this morning?"

A moment of silence. "Well, no. But if he was hurt I'd be the first person he would come to."

Usually. Sorry, Mom. Pete opened the bathroom door. His mom gasped when she saw his condition.

"What the hell, Pete?" She started fussing over him, inspecting his swollen eye, raising his arm—he almost shouted as a current of pain shot up his chest—to look at his bruised ribs. "Who did this?"

"I'm fine, Mom," Pete grunted. "Some guy jumped me is all." He was not in the mood to narrate the whole incident, though he knew his mother would not stop the interrogation until he gave her a full debriefing.

"Is all? Is all? Peter Toy Ray Palmer, you better start explaining."

"Pete," the doctor interjected, "I would like for you to come with me so I can properly examine you. It is park policy in these circumstances. For obvious reasons."

His mother gave the doctor a you-better-butt-out-of-this look. "Why does he need to come with you? Why not just check him here?"

"The office has all of my gear. I cannot be thorough here."

The last thing Pete wanted was to go to a doctor's office, but he was almost giddy with the idea of escaping the wrath of his mother. Even if only temporarily. "I'll go. Just let me change."

Pete ignored his mother's stormy glare. He shut off the shower, slipped on the shirt he slept in last night, biting back the groan that tried to escape, and eased by his mom to follow the doctor. "I'll be back in a bit," he said. "I'll tell you everything then." Before stepping into the elevator, he shot back to the imposing figure standing in the hall with both hands on her hips. "You and dad can head on to the pool. I'll find you."

The shiny steel doors slid shut and the elevator started a smooth decent to the hotel lobby. A faint smell of grease and gears reminded

Pete of his grandpa's garage. It was machines, motors, bearings, wiring, and oil. Cologne to mechanics.

Pete side-eyed the doctor. She was standing ramrod straight, staring blankly at the door, not even blinking. She was a curious woman. Eccentric delivery. Strange mannerisms. Zero personality. Reminded Pete of *The Terminator*.

A bell dinged to announce their arrival to the first floor and the doors lid open.

"Pete!" Nola exclaimed, standing by the door, waiting her turn. Looking at him, then the doctor. "I was coming to see you."

"Doc wants me to go to her office, look me over."

"Oh, okay." Nola nodded at the doctor who remained blank. "Can I see you when you get back?"

"Who are you?" the doctor asked.

"His girlfriend," Nola said quickly.

Butterflies fluttered inside Pete's stomach, numbing the pain.

"You may join us. If it is okay with him."

Pete's brain was still stuck on Nola being his girlfriend. It took a moment for the question to form. "Yeah, absolutely."

The walk to the doctor's office was uneventful. Lyla led Pete and Nola on the employee path, and it was busy as staff hurried to get where they needed to be before the park opened in two hours. Pete found the unofficial behind-the-scenes tour to be interesting. It reminded him of a show he had seen once. A news anchor was live on-air sitting behind a massive desk. His jacket was impeccably tailored, his power-colored tie a perfect knot, but when the anchor finished taping, and stood up, his pants were pajama bottoms. That was a superb example of Riptide Rapids. In the park, everything was pristine. All the embellished buildings perfectly painted. All the walkways pressure washed and clean of debris. Flowerbeds without a single weed. Presented in such a tailored fashion, it was awe-inspiring.

Behind the walls, it felt like a Hollywood movie set: clean and tidy, but plain. There was some shrubbery, though not much. The backs of the buildings were flat and bare, lacking the charming details found on the park-facing sides. No craftsman-style windows, no Victorian eaves, no ornate entryways. The word that came to Pete's mind was utilitarian.

In other words, pajama bottoms.

The doctor climbed the steps to a cabin with a large placard reading Riptide Urgent Care above the entrance. Pete noticed the door frame was splintered around the strike plate, as if someone had kicked it in. Inside, the lobby was simple but tidy. Two couches, a pair of cushioned armchairs, and a coffee table with a few scattered magazines filled the space. A desk with a silver-plated receptionist sign summoned those in need of a doctor to check-in. The walls were painted a winter green. A color chosen for its calming effect.

"Follow me," the doctor said as she walked through an open door.

Through the doorway lay a hallway with exam rooms to either side. She stepped inside the first door to the right, numbered ONE on a small sign stuck to the wall beside the door casing. The space was small, square, and resembled every other exam room Pete had ever been inside. Various posters informed patients about common applicable medical conditions: dehydration, heat stroke, urine color, hydration tips, potentially concerning melanoma signs, and a skinless body showing organs and their functions. A small counter with a stainless-steel sink waited in the corner by the door. Above the counter hung two double-door cabinets with glass fronts. Inside were new packages of gauze, antiseptic spray, a box of latex gloves, and other boxes with words too long to pronounce.

"Take off your shirt, then have a seat on the exam table. I will be back in a minute."

Once the doctor left, Nola assisted Pete in removing his shirt. As he lifted his arms, his skin seemed to crack. Nola gasped at the sight of the bruising. "Jeez."

"My sentiments exactly," Pete agreed. He wondered what happened when Johnathon reached the mainland. He wished he could've been there to see the handcuffs slapped around his wrists, and the look on his pimpled face when he was shoved in the police car. Pete hoped Johnathon had to spend the night fighting off a gang of thugs. But he probably spent the night in a comfortable cell, alone, with a TV and a Nintendo, playing Mario and eating ice cream. It seemed typical for guys like him.

Nola lightly traced the bruises on his ribs with her fingers, sending a shiver through his skin. Goosebumps rose, and in that moment, the pain from the bruises seemed to fade away.

The door creaked open and Nola jumped back, a deviant smile tugging at her lips. The doctor entered with a boy of about nineteen in tow. The boy moved to stand by Nola, which Pete found odd, but he said nothing. The doctor stepped in front of him, and removed a stethoscope draped around her neck like a pet snake. She positioned the two prongs with rubber tips in her ears then placed the business end on Pete's chest. It was an ice cube being rubbed on his bare skin. She moved the stethoscope around his chest, then placed it on his back, listening to his lungs. She pulled the prongs from her ears, draped the instrument around her neck, then pulled a penlight out of her pocket. "Follow the light," she said.

Pete followed all of her instructions as she examined his eyes, ears, and throat. Then raised his arms so she could get a closer look at the bruising. She spoke little, her voice flat and monotone.

"You appear fine. Let me check your eyes again."

Pete stared into the light, its brightness swallowing everything around him. Yet, he felt an odd sensation. Doctor Lyla was close, her dark outline appearing at the edge of his vision. He caught the scent of her breath, hot and earthy, just as a strange, tingling sound slipped from her lips. Nola spoke, her voice sounding distant, like an echo stretched across time and space. Something wet slipped inside his ear canal, probing like a wet worm. Pete tried to jerk away but the doctor held his head steady, her grip like steel clamps.

The light jolted away, the thing in his ear disappeared, and suddenly the doctor was standing by the door, staring into the hallway. Her arms were at her side and her hands shook like she was having a seizure. Pete looked to Nola and found her white as a ghost. The boy next to her was at military attention and his hands mimicked the mannerisms of the doctor.

"What the fuck?" Nola mouthed.

Lyla stopped shaking so quickly Pete wondered if he had hallucinated. She nodded at the kid without saying a word. He quickly left the room. "Stay here," she said, and closed the door.

Nola tiptoed to the door, and pressed her ear against the wood. She turned the knob, and found it locked. "Pete, we have to get out of here."

"What happened a minute ago, when I was looking at the light?"

Nola handed him his shirt. "We'll talk about that when we are out of here. Let's go."

Dull voices worked through the walls. A male voice. Not the boy who stood by Nola. Though he never spoke a word, Pete was sure this voice belonged to someone else. Someone older.

Nola grabbed his hand. "What are you waiting for? Let's go."

"There's someone out in the waiting room. We should just beat on the door, get their attention."

"We don't know who it is. They may be like the doctor." Nola went to the window, opened the shades.

"What do you mean? 'Like the doctor.'"

Nola stared at him, irritation pushing her features to show Pete what she looked like when angry. "We. Don't. Have. Time. For. This." She waved him over. "Let's go. Now."

Pete was confused, and wanted answers, but underneath everything, he saw Nola was frightened. Terrified even. He pushed off the table, moaned as he slipped into his shirt, went to Nola.

"Turn the latches," Nola instructed. "I can't."

The latches were covered with some sort of slimy material. Like a silicone caulk. After two tense minutes, he got both of them loose, and Nola slid the window up.

"Oh shit," she breathed.

The window opening was completely covered by a thick spiderweb. So thick, in fact, it was like a blanket. Pete looked around the room but found nothing to clear the web. He saw no alternative. He jabbed his hand through the middle of the weaving and cinched his fingers around the mass as though it were a comforter. He twisted his arm and ripped the web with his fist.

"Stop!" Nola whispered and went still. Pete heard retreating footsteps, and another pair getting closer. The doctor was returning. Nola ran to the chair she sat in earlier and jammed it under the doorknob, barricading them in the room.

A second later, as Nola backed away, the knob twisted, followed by a thud as the doctor pushed the door. The chair held. The next thud was more powerful; the doctor laid her shoulder into it.

"Open the door please," the doctor called. "I can make you better. Both of you."

A trickle of sweat slithered down Pete's spine, and now he, too, was terrified. He understood Nola's desire to get out of here. He clawed at the spiderweb, pulling the matted silk through the window and tossing a wad on the floor. Some web still clung to the edges of the sill, wispy ends trailing in the breeze, but Nola stuck a leg through and folded her body to escape. She dropped awkwardly to the ground, landing in the leaves.

"Hurry, Pete," she said, standing and holding her arms out.

Pete was halfway out when Nola warned him again. "Pete, you have to hurry. Spiders. Lots of them."

Pete wasn't sure what she meant, but had no interest in finding out. He flung himself out the window, landing on his bruised side. Bursts of stabbing agony held his breath captive in his lungs. He tried to exhale but nothing worked, the pain short-circuiting his organ functions. Nola was not sympathetic. She jerked him by the arm until he was on his feet, pointed at the cabin. Thousands of spiders blanketed the cedar siding. Almost every inch of the exterior wall was covered with the scurrying arachnids. But something was wrong, and the mystery drew Pete toward the cabin.

"Pete? What are you doing? Let's go."

Pete raised his hands, palms out, as he stepped closer. The insects crawling down the side of the cabin were unlike anything he had ever seen. They looked like spiders— mostly—but he noticed tiny tentacles jutting out of their hairy bodies. Little worms twisting and squirming. One leaped from the windowsill and Pete jumped back to dodge the attacker.

A hand clamped around his arm. "Let's go!" Nola hissed.

They made it to the employee path where they barreled into a couple of park employees, one a female in office attire and a male with an outfit like a maintenance man would wear.

"Woah, you two okay?" The man asked. His badge said his name was Jared.

Pete exchanged glances with Nola, both realizing the same thing at the same time: this was the man they overheard talking to the doctor a few minutes ago.

"Were you just at the doctor's office?" Nola asked, words spilling out quickly.

Jared's eyes flicked back and forth between Nola and Pete, sorting through a response. He glanced back at the cabin fifty yards away. The doctor was standing on the front porch, watching them. Nola and Pete backed away.

Jared, noticing their reactions, grabbed Pete by the elbow. "Come with us."

Twenty

Julie unlocked the office door, switched on the lights. She dropped her purse on the counter by the ringing phone, and answered the obnoxious thing.

"Thanks for calling Riptide Charters. This is Julie."

"Julie, it's Larry. I walked the park earlier and noticed Leon and Scuba were not on the dock getting the boat ready for today's charter. Is something wrong?"

Julie closed her eyes, sighed deeply. She was planning to call Larry this morning, but had been procrastinating since five-thirty a.m. when she awoke to an empty bed and still no sign of Leon. Her stomach clenched from stress. Not only was Leon not here to do his job, but she was worried sick about him. She loved him deeply and the thought of him being missing sent her damn near into a panic.

Now she would have to try to explain this to Larry, who was not the most understanding boss. "Larry, we have a problem."

"I don't want to hear problems," he said sharply. "We are booked solid through next summer and we don't have time for problems."

"We may not, but the problem still exists." She opened the bottom drawer to the right of her chair and snatched up a bottle of antacid pills.

Larry let silence hang in the air like the blade of a guillotine waiting for a neck to sever. Finally, he asked, "What's the problem?"

"Leon and Scuba are missing," she said, wincing as she braced herself for what was coming next.

"What do you mean," Larry growled, "they are missing?"

Julie gave Larry the cliff notes version of the events from the past twenty-four hours, hitting only the high points.

"Did they take the ferry back to the mainland yesterday? Maybe they needed a break. From what I don't know. Day drinking and floating around the Gulf?"

"No, I already checked. But Leon wouldn't do that. He'd tell me if he were leaving."

"Have you checked with yesterday's charter group?"

"Um, well, as of last night, the charter group are also missing," Julie said. "The wives came looking for the husbands yesterday evening."

"Did you bother checking the bars? Leon loves bourbon."

"I didn't. Figured he would come home once the bar closed, like normal."

"Well, why don't you call the bars and the guys from that group now that it's morning, and ask them?" Larry phrased this like an impatient father speaking to his child. "Seems pretty sensible to me."

Asshole. "Will do," Julie sound through gritted teeth.

"Call me back after you talk to them. As soon as. You hear?"

"Yes," she said, but a click on the other end told her Larry hadn't waited for answer.

One part of Julie's job was gathering information from those wishing to charter the boat for a day. Including the hotel in which they were staying, and room number. Julie would then leave a Thank You postcard—a photo of the Riptide Charters fishing boat on one side and a personal, handwritten note with reservation date and time on the other—lying in the middle of the bed on the morning of the patrons arrival. This served two purposes: to show the customer a genuine appreciation for the business, and a reminder of the booking.

Julie opened her customer logbook, found the information on the guy who had chartered the boat: Mike Ackerman, 58, pharmacist, from Hampton, Virginia. Staying at Driftwood Haven, room 226. Julie dialed the number to the front desk from memory. Asked for Mike's room. It was answered in the first ring.

"Hello?" A woman, anxious.

"Good morning. This is Julie over at Riptide Charters. I think we met last night."

"Yes, I remember. Have you found him?"

This threw Julie for a loop. The question insinuated Mike was still missing. Julie was careful. "Did he not come back to the room last night?"

"No, he did not. I drank a little too much at the bar last night. Came to the room and passed out. I woke up twenty minutes ago and he is not here. Hasn't been here."

"Have you talked to the other wives? Have any of the husbands returned?"

"That's the problem," the woman said, angry and scared. "None of us have seen or spoken to our husbands since they left to get on *your* boat yesterday morning. We are thinking about calling the police."

"I understand. Totally. Give me a little time before you do that. We don't want to make the situation worse."

"Not sure how it can be worse, but okay, we'll wait a little longer. If we haven't heard anything by noon, we're calling the mainland."

Julie dropped the phone in the cradle and leaned back in her chair. She was no longer concerned. She was petrified. Her stomach writhed as if she had swallowed a handful of earthworms.

Eight people were missing. Which was impossible. This was an island in the Gulf of Mexico. There was nowhere to go.

Except to the back side of the island, Julie thought.

Why go back there? A ten-foot-high green electrified chain-link fence was installed during construction several hundred yards behind the cabins as the final park perimeter. Larry even labeled the land beyond the fence as a no-trespassing zone, warning that violators would be prosecuted.

If one were to ignore all warnings and threats of penalty, one would have to scale an electric security fence. Leon was not going to voluntarily subject himself to shock and was not nearly spry enough at the creaky age of sixty-one to climb. Beyond the fence lay a dense wall of feral vegetation Julie wouldn't walk through if her life depended on it. Dangerous animal life roamed the land, part of the reason for the electric fence.

No way Leon and the husbands ventured beyond the park perimeter. They had to be somewhere inside the park. For lack of a better explanation, they were hiding.

She dialed Larry.

"Hello?"

"The husbands are also missing," Julie said. "All of them. We have eight people who were on that boat yesterday, returned from the trip, then disappeared and haven't been seen since." Julie had not told Larry about the bloody clothes and torn shirt. She continued to hold that information until it proved pertinent.

"That makes no logical sense," Larry said. "Where would they go? And why?"

"I don't know. We can ask when we find them."

"Okay. I'm calling security to start a sweep. I also want a radio message sent out to every employee on the grounds to be on the lookout and to call security immediately if they see anything suspicious."

"Just a heads up. The wives are threatening to call the police in Florida. We have until noon to find them."

"No, no, no, they can't do that. That could lead to a shutdown and we can NOT have that. We lost too much money when we closed for Hurricane Hugo last month. Not doing that again. I'll reach out to them and put the kabosh on that shit. What's the room numbers?"

"I only have Mike Ackerman's room," Julie said, and told him the resort and room number.

"I'm on it."

"What should I do?"

"Stay where you are in case Leon or Scuba show up. Now let me go, I have another emergency to deal with as well."

"What's going on?"

"The ferry broke down last night on an emergency trip back to the island. It had to be towed back to Florida. The engine suffered catastrophic failure. Now I have three hundred people stranded on the dock in Florida and two hundred stranded here on the island with no way to get them where they need to go. I also have two juveniles still in detention who were supposed to be transported to the mainland last night after they jumped and beat the shit out of a kid for no reason, and said kid is likely to sue the park for damages. Happy fucking Halloween." Larry slammed the phone down so hard, Julie jumped in her chair.

"I really don't like you," Julie said as she hung up. She popped two more antacid tablets, too busy thinking to taste the bitterness.

There were lots of places to hide in the park. Mechanical rooms, landscaping warehouses, storage facilities, etc. But all of those locations were only *temporary* hiding spots and all of them were locked and only accessible by maintenance or staff directly associated with said building or room. Mechanical rooms were opened daily since maintenance and staff inspected the equipment there before the park opened. Landscaping warehouses held lawn equipment, and mulch bins, and fertilizers, and all sorts of items she had no clue about, but the landscaping crews worked seven days a week year-round keeping the grounds pristine. There were multiple storage buildings, one housing all the props and pieces for this extensive Halloween makeover. Another held the Christmas decorations, and yet another held the remaining furnishings for the other, lesser celebrated holidays.

Christmas, she thought suddenly. No one would go in the Christmas building until it was time to start decorating the park for that joyous holiday. Which wasn't for another month.

Julie jumped out of the chair, slamming the door behind her on the way out, pressing the lock button before the door latched. It was a trek to the back of the grounds where they hid the buildings from site. She took the Riptide Charters golf cart.

A pebbled trail ran along the perimeter fence line from one side of the park to the other and was mostly used by the landscapers. Julie took that trail, staying on her side of the narrow lane to avoid the influx of groundskeepers heading to various areas of the park to give it a final polish before the gates opened.

Eleven minutes later, Julie parked beside the building holding the Christmas decorations. It was a sizable metal structure, green sheeting helping it blend into the forest. She looked around, the only sound that of birds chirping and weird clucking sounds coming from only God knew what sort of creature. Slim streams of sunlight poured through minor openings in the leafy canopy over her head, producing shimmering puddles on the grass and green metal skin. The temperature was a good fifteen degrees cooler here and Julie was grateful. She'd never lived in a place where the heat was as relentless in October as it was in June. Like living in an oven that never shut off.

She unclipped the key ring off the belt loop of her khaki work shorts, and flipped through the selection of about a dozen until she found the one labeled Christmas. All employees had a key to the "Holiday Buildings" due to Larry's insistence that everyone pitch in when time to decorate rather than hire specialty crews to come in and do it for them. Julie unlocked the door, and eased inside, stepping quietly for some odd reason. A few spiderwebs caught her hair and she waved the threads away. Pitch blackness lay before her, and in it, not a living thing crept.

Not even a mouse, she thought without humor. Besides a few spiders. Maybe.

Julie flipped the light switches beside the door and the florescent high bay lights blinked on, low at first but slowly brightening as the filaments heated. The warehouse was neat and tidy. Rows of metal shelving held hundreds of plastic containers, and those plastic containers housed the ornaments and trees and lighting and angels and Santa Clauses and elves and fake snow and a thousand other pieces that transformed Riptide Rapids into Riptide's Christmas Wonderland the whole month of December. All the containers were on pallets and a gas-powered forklift waited in the corner for someone to come along to put it to work.

Julie waited a moment longer for the lights to fully illuminate the warehouse, then set to checking each row. Looking for what, she had no idea. A group of eight men hunkered down in a tight dark space, playing hide-and-seek from their wives?

Julie shook her head, feeling stupid for coming here. But since she was here ...

The building lacked any rooms except for a small closet with a toilet, which was empty save a few push brooms, a dustpan, and a dirty toilet bowl. All four corners were empty and the place showed no signs of anyone having been there since last year. She stepped out the door, and locked the deadbolt once it was closed.

"Hi."

Julie screamed and spun in a jerky circle to face her attacker.

It was a short Hispanic man, his blue shirt labeled Manuel. He smiled at her with bright white teeth that filled his open face. "Sorry."

Julie thumped her fist against her chest in hopes to silence the knocking on her sternum. "Damn you scared me."

"Sorry," Manuel said again, English lilted and broken. "Okay?"

"Yes. Might need to see doc about some nitroglycerin but otherwise I'm fine."

Manuel nodded and smiled, no clue what she was talking about.

"Manuel," Julie said after she caught her breath, "have you seen eight men moving around back here—or anywhere—that maybe seemed out of place? Two would've been park employees but the other six would've been civilians. Sound familiar?"

Manuel's smile faltered and his eyebrows dipped as he dissected the question. Looking for familiar words or phrases. His head moved slightly side to side as he found nothing to latch onto.

"I saw them," another voice said. Julie peaked around Manuel and found another Hispanic man sitting on a muddy landscaping utility cart with shovels loaded in the small bed in the back. "Yesterday on the way back to our warehouse."

The man spoke in Spanish to Manuel, explaining, the sentences spilling from his lips so fast Julie couldn't make out a single word. Manuel smiled again and nodded at Julie. "Yes, yes."

"Where did you see them?" Julie asked the guy on the golf cart. She wasn't interested in a language lesson. She wanted information.

"In the woods. By the fence. Just standing there. I thought it was weird. Told my boss about it, but he said to keep my nose out of it."

"Why would he say that?"

The man looked around as if an audience awaited his answer. "I could get in trouble for telling you that."

Julie read between the lines. "I don't care if you're here illegally. That's not my problem. These missing men are my problem. Okay?"

The man nodded.

"Take me to the place you saw them."

Twenty-One

Owen couldn't believe it. The ferry broke down? How did that happen? And no back up? A place this nice, no expense spared, five-star accommodations, fantastic food, fun atmosphere, with no way off the island if the main transport happened to shit the bed? What about in case of emergencies? Some gentleman with a lame ticker had a heart attack on The Ripper? What then? The park's Urgent Care wasn't equipped to handle a medical crisis like that.

He opened his mouth to shout at the man who was addressing the crowd in the waiting area of the Departure Center, when the man added some unexpected good news to counter the bad.

"As a token of our appreciation for your patience, we will be allowing all of you to return to the rooms you had rented and you can resume your vacation—meals included—on Riptide Island free of charge until we can either repair our ferry or bring in a replacement to take you back to the mainland. We will also be offering each of you a voucher for two free days on your next visit to Riptide Rapids."

The bustling crowd went silent. Kids shouted in excitement while parents shrugged and agreed almost en masse that a few more days wouldn't hurt. Amazing the effect the word "free" had on people.

Owen was bursting with the desire to get back home. He had a story to write. His editor was waiting. To make the cut in the January

1990 New Year, New You edition, Owen needed to have the article written and turned in, clean as possible, by the end of November. Extending his "vacation" was not ideal from a deadline standpoint. He hadn't brought his trusty Smith-Corona electronic typewriter, but he had packed multiple legal pads for notes. He supposed he could start writing long-hand and transpose over to typeset once he was back in his office. He'd have to make do.

Owen grabbed his bag, and hurried back to the lobby of Bluewater Bay, the beachside resort where he had stayed for the past week. Renee, the receptionist, was happy to return the card to him, repeating most of what the gentleman at the Departure Center had already said, and adding new information.

"You'll receive an alert message via room phone with a date and time for departure once the ferry returns to operation." She held out the card, smile plastered to her shrewd face. She reminded Owen of his high school librarian, Ms. Shaw. An air of high brow sophistication permeated from her like cheap perfume. "Thank you for choosing Bluewater Bay."

Owen grunted and took the card. He hadn't the time for pleasantries. He ignored the small crack in her facade when he failed to share in the fake exchange. Enjoyed it, in fact.

The room was exactly as Owen had left it two hours ago. Housekeeping had yet to make the rounds. Two unused bath towels still hung from the bar in the bathroom. He dropped the DO NOT DISTURB hanger on the door handle to discourage disruption.

He unpacked—again!—then tore the plastic wrap off a fresh legal pad, laid a loaded plastic baggie on the desk next to the pad, and sat at the cramped desk in the uncomfortable office chair. The meager accommodations made him appreciate his home office: a massive red mahogany desk bought at a real estate auction, the plush leather chair that had come with the desk, the coffee mug full of pens next to his typewriter, the bookshelves laden with fiction and nonfiction books. Fiction books—King, Koontz, Barker, Laymon, McCammon, Douglas—to help guide him through a novel idea he wanted to write at some point in his life, and nonfiction books to help guide him through life as a freelance writer.

The notes Owen had taken on a legal pad were sporadic. Observations, feelings, findings, hearsay, facts. Most of the information had been garnered from the resort bars. Park employees loved to talk once they were sufficiently lubricated. A shot of whiskey here, a beer there, and the tongue wagged at both ends. Stories of a haunted island were the most prominent. People disappearing during the construction phase, weird sightings, strange noises at night, even a claim of a strange light beaming into the sky from the uninhabited side of the island. Owen was never able to find more than one worker living on the island to corroborate the light beam story, but still, he found it interesting. The park even included the haunted narrative into the Jungle Journey ride, sort of a tongue-in-cheek response to the outlandish tales. It made for thrilling theater. And Riptide Rapids seemed to embrace it.

He needed to form a narrative from these random accounts. To help him do so, he needed the contents of the plastic baggie. He spread the three back pocket pamphlets, the laminated island map, various trinkets and artifacts, across the desk. One of the pamphlets provided a brief but concise history of the island, dating its existence back over 130 million years. Formed by now-dormant volcanic activity, it was believed to have been shaped by a meteor crash some fifty million years ago. The island was claimed by Cuba but sat untouched until a United States investment group, Grandiose Capital Investment Corporation, decided to buy the island and convert it into a vacation destination. It took six years of development and five years of construction, but they managed to build Riptide Rapids on an island where everyone in the business said they would fail.

"Blah blah blah," Owen said. He could care less about the age of the island or any of that development crap. He cared about the angle. He cared about the spin. Facts weren't required, any good defense attorney would tell you that. He just needed a story so salacious it made everyone forget the truth and focus on the fantastic.

Owen first heard about the island from his niece, Angela. She and her family had come here on vacation last year and brought back some various novelties. Her youngest boy, Ian, had excitedly shown Owen some unusual rocks. Owen was not a rock expert by anyone's imagination, but he was a novice in geology. He carried a mild interest in the field. And the rocks Ian dropped into his palm that day had led Owen to where he now sat in the Bluewater Bay resort. The rocks had been unusual to say the least. Owen knew of only three types of rock: igneous, sedimentary, metamorphic. Ian's rocks were none of those, as far as Owen could tell. That was the first oddity that sent Owen down the Riptide Island rabbit hole. The second was the constant mild heat that radiated from the things. Owen placed them on top of ice in the ice cube trays in the freezer and closed the door, left them for ten minutes. He had assumed the rocks would freeze—or turn cold at the least—and continue to sit on top of the ice cubes. He had been wrong. The rocks had sat in a puddle of water. Not only had they been warm enough to melt the ice, they had been warm enough to maintain a temperature above freezing.

Ian hadn't wanted to part with any of his treasures, but Owen gave him ten bucks and a promise to return the rock if Ian would grant him permission to take one of them. Ian had relented, and Owen took the rock to a friend who was more versed in the field of study. The friend had made the same observations Owen had, and, ultimately, suggested

Owen take the rocks to someone with a degree. Namely the highest regarded geologist in America, Dr. Evelyn Pembroke.

But the wheels had already started turning in Owen's imagination. He found that he really wasn't interested in the rock's origins anymore. He was a freelance writer by trade, and his number one customer was *Daily Bizarre,* a supermarket tabloid that currently ran in third place to *The Star* and *The National Enquirer*. JoJo Timpone was the editor and he was obsessed with placing his newspaper in the number one slot. He pushed all of his writers, in-house and freelance, to up the ante. Give him the juiciest, most scandalous, most over-the-top stories they could wring from their fingertips. The bigger the star, the crazier the story, the heftier the payday. Nothing was off-limits or out of bounds. Lawsuits be damned.

The potential for this story had grown by the minute. There was also a nice monetary gain to be collected if he could spin the story just right, and the rocks provided an angle that rode the coattails of a popular current trend: extra-terrestrials. Green men from outer space. This amusement park and its origin story played perfectly into the hands of someone like Owen who was adept at tossing a tantalizing word salad.

Riptide Rapids had been an instant hit, successful from opening day. It had made national news. The advertisements were commonplace during the daytime soap operas of *The Young And The Restless* and evening television shows like *Wheel Of Fortune*. Ads ran regularly in all the big magazines, from *Good Housekeeping* to *Playboy*. Hell, even Johnny Carson gave it rave reviews on his show after a visit with his family. Sears and Roebuck sold a line of t-shirts for the attraction. Riptide Rapids carried universal appeal, drawing record visitors from abroad.

The brighter the spotlight, the bigger the story.

That was Owen's motto. And he saw huge potential in Riptide Rapids and the island it inhabited. Sensational, fantastic, headline grabbing. Didn't matter it was fiction—most of it anyway. It only mattered that the story spread like wildfire. That sort of attention could put them out of business.

Wouldn't that be something? Little old Owen Newman, Mr. Unpopular back in high school, now the destroyer of public perception and grim reaper to a fashionable family vacation hot-spot.

Owen smiled and put pen to pad. The first draft of Riptide's downfall awaited.

Twenty-Two

"Where are we going?" Van asked, putting on an exaggerated look of confusion. "Cannonball is the other way.'

Dave shook his head. *Kids only hear what they want to hear.* "I need to check on something first. Stop whining and follow."

Urgent Care was just around the corner. Hopefully the kid was okay. Or going to be okay. Dave had smoked pot back in his high school days, but that had been the heaviest he'd been willing to try. Kids now were trying shit without regard to personal safety. It was dangerous, and he hoped this was a wake-up call to this young man to stay away from drugs.

Urgent Care came into view. On the front porch stood the doctor and an animated, angry woman. The woman was shouting at the doctor who appeared unfazed. Dave caught the question "Where's my son?" and knew this was the mother of the kid he found.

Dave broke into a quick walk and mounted the stairs. "Ma'am, ma'am," he said gently, trying to de-escalate the situation.

The woman looked at him like he was crazy. "Don't ma'am me. This bitch won't tell me where my son is."

"I'm the one who found your son," Dave said. "That's why I'm here; to check on him."

The woman's frazzled demeanor changed instantly. She combed her fingers through her morning hair, and crossed her arms over her chest. "Sorry, I'm just upset. I woke up and found Paul gone. I go looking for him and find out he's here. And now this so-called doctor won't tell me anything." She wiped her nose, took a deep breath. "I want to see my son. That's all."

"What's your name?" Dave asked. Silly question under the circumstances but he wanted to know.

"Susan."

He whipped around on the doctor. "Where's her son?"

Her face remained blank, unemotional. "I am not at liberty discuss patient information with anyone not related," she said. Flat, monotone, cold.

"I'm his mother," Susan hissed, "and you won't tell me either."

"I do not know who you are," the doctor said. "You must present identification."

Dave could not believe his ears. This doctor was mentally unstable. *Something* was clearly wrong with her. He'd been to enough doctors in his life, but never had he spoken with a doctor who was disengaged from the job of providing care and comfort. This was no doctor.

Dave stabbed his finger at Lyla's face.

"Dave!" Penny chastised, pulling on his arm. "Chill out."

Dave ignored her. "I don't know what's going on here, but I am goddamned going to find out." To Susan, he said, "I think we need to go see security. If they don't do something, we're calling the mainland and reporting a crime."

Susan nodded emphatically. "Damn right."

They were at the bottom of the steps when the doctor spoke. "Fine. You can see him."

Susan ran back up the stairs, Dave following.

"Suddenly I can see him," Susan snarled, nose to nose with the doctor.

"I had to know you are family. We have strict policies about that. As does the medical profession."

"Well, aren't I lucky to have you looking out for my best interests?" Susan snapped and stepped back, waiting for the doctor to open the door.

To Dave, Lyla said, "You are not allowed. You are not family."

"He—" Susan began to protest, but Dave held up his hand.

"It's fine. You go see your son." He glared at Lyla. "Something's not right here. I'm gonna find out what that something is."

The walk to the Ripcord was like lost time. When he stepped in line, Dave couldn't remember the trip there. It was a blur of smoky snapshots without substance or color. His families conversations were lost as well. He heard nothing but the voices in his head. His conscience talking, tossing the two exchanges with the doctor back and forth like a backyard game of catch. Examining the words for hints or clues. Observing her strange demeanor with closer scrutiny. Like her walking for instance. He hadn't paid much attention the first time, but on recall, he remembered how unnatural it seemed. She reminded him of a video he had seen once of a newborn deer taking its first steps. Clumsily stumbling about, tripping and jerking back to standing, only to trip again.

Maybe she was in an accident recently and haven't fully recovered.

His sensible side, making a sensible argument. One Dave needed to consider. But common sense disproved that contretemps. If she had been in an accident and had not recovered yet, she wouldn't be the lead caregiver on this island. Unless the powers-that-be were extremely negligent and not afraid of criminal and civil liability. And Dave knew that not to be true. One didn't buy an island and build this type of universal attraction without planning and enacting shrewd business measures. The number one goal being to eliminate any chance of litigation by carefully scrutinizing every aspect of the property and daily activities on the island. From the rides, to the park, to the employees. No stone left unturned, no circumstance unvetted.

The doctor had a different kind of problem.

"Dave?" Penny cut through the contemplation.

"Yeah?"

"Have you not been listening to us?"

"Sorry." Dave pushed the internal investigation to the side. He was still on vacation and his family needed his attention. "What's up?"

"The kids are hungry," Penny said with feigned patience. "You were such a hurry to leave this morning, we didn't feed them breakfast."

"Okay, yeah, we'll hit the nearest restaurant after this ride. Sound like a plan?"

"Can we go to Amazonia?" Van asked, raised on his tiptoes to show how important an agreement was to him. It was a natural characteristic to him that Dave never got tired of seeing. It reminded him of Van at the age of two when the toddler first started doing it.

Amazonia was one of the top-tiered restaurants on the island. It was not part of the food plan Penny had paid for when she booked the vacation. It was a pricey meal and Dave had been avoiding the pleas from all of them—Penny included. With only two more days left before departure, Dave relented. "What the hell. Yes, let's do it. After the Cannonball."

Cannonball was a ride that strapped ten thrill seekers into chairs before dropping them from eighty feet in a sudden, stomach-churning plunge. A burst of water erupted around them near the bottom, mimicking the splash of a real cannonball into a pool. Dave stumbled out of the exit gate, trying to swallow his stomach back down where it belonged.

"Can we do that again?" Van asked, clapping.

"Never," Penny said before Dave could get it out.

If Dave hadn't been so focused on settling his stomach, he might have missed the woman standing off to the side, watching them from a distance. When he finally noticed her, a wave of chilling déjà vu washed over him. He realized that even in the lost time journey from the doctor's office to the Cannonball attraction, he had seen her. His brain must have dismissed the sightings, preoccupied with the doctor and knowing that her existence here and now was impossible. She was wearing a sundress now, but it was unmistakably her.

He'd last seen the woman's body being lifted onto a stretcher and removed from the dolphin swimming area. And she'd been dead.

Twenty-Three

"All employees," Barbara, the security office receptionist announced on the main radio channel, "please be on the lookout for Leon Thibideoux and Scuba Jebailey. They may be accompanied by six civilians. If you see them, please call the security office and provide information on their whereabouts."

Jared turned the volume down. He was too busy to do anything about Leon or Scuba.

The two teens sat side by side in office chairs, visibly shaking. The boy, Pete, kept brushing his long black hair out of his face, exposing quite the shiner and a swollen jaw. His knees bounced and he picked at his fingernails. The girl, Nola, hugged herself as though cold, and rocked almost imperceptibly. A nervous tick she was probably not even aware she was doing. If the door to the maintenance shop opened they jumped, and looked ready to bolt. Jared hated they were scared, but was pleased to see they reacted at all. Not robotic and detached.

They had been through it. Now it was time to know what happened.

Jared used his feet to pull the chair in which he was sitting closer to Pete and Nola. The wheels clicked over an expansion joint in the concrete. Cindy remained standing.

"Listen, I can see you two are upset, but I need some information."

"You're not in trouble," Cindy added, stepping closer.

"Right, you're not in trouble." Jared leaned forward, placed his elbows on his knees. "It's just, I've seen some strange stuff the past twenty-four hours, and I think you might've seen some strange stuff too. I'll tell you mine if you tell me yours."

Pete licked his puffy, blood-crusted lips. "Okay. Fair enough. But you never answered if that was you in the doctor's office. Before we bumped into you."

"Yes, that was me. That was us, actually." Jared motioned to Cindy.

Nola joined the conversation. "Pete was jumped last night by some boy in the park. As you can see, the asshole got Pete pretty good. Doc came up to Pete's room this morning and insisted he go with her back to the office to check him out."

"Why couldn't she check you in the room?" Jared asked, trying to get the full picture.

"I don't know," Pete said. "My mom asked her the same and doc said she could do a better job at the office. I said fine and went with her."

Nola took over. "On the way to the office, I noticed the doctor walked funny."

"Funny how?" Cindy asked.

"Like her legs didn't work right. Like—" Nola looked at Pete for help.

"I didn't pay much attention at the time, but yeah, now that you mention it. It was like her legs were broken or something," Pete said.

"I don't know. It was just weird when she stepped it was like her knees didn't sync up timing-wise with the ground. It was jerky. Newborn"

"Like those circus people who walk on really tall stilts," Jared threw in for good measure.

"Yeah, kind of like that," Pete nodded.

Nola continued. "Then we get to the exam room and that's when everything got super weird.

"She tells Pete to take off his shirt and sit on the bed, then she leaves the room. I help Pete out of his shirt then she shows back up with an assistant who looks like he might be eighteen or so, and the assistant stands beside me. Like *right* beside me. I'm uncomfortable at this point because there is a bizarre vibe in the room."

Cindy sits in an office chair, glides closer. "The doctor doesn't have an assistant. She works alone. She deals with vertigo, and sunburns, and heat strokes, and small kids bumping their head at the splash pad. Hardly a need for an assistant. What did he look like?"

"About six-foot, average build, brown curly hair, glasses. Wearing scrubs."

The air got trapped in Jared's lungs. *No way.* Jared asked, barely a voice to apply to the words, "Was he injured? Right arm wrapped and in a sling maybe? Anything like that?"

Nola shook her head. "No, he was standing to the left of me and placed his right hand on my shoulder while the doctor examined Pete. I remember looking down at it because I was suddenly terrified. His arm was normal."

Jared leaned back in his chair, the trapped out whooshing out of him.

"That's impossible, Jared," Cindy said. "He was dead, and his arm was almost completely severed."

It was Pete and Nola's turn to sit forward.

"What did you say?" Pete asked.

Cindy recounted the accident last night, finishing with the doctor assuring Jared Keith was alive and would be fine.

"There's no way we're talking about the same guy," Nola said. "This guy was fine."

"Did he have a scar on his cheek?" Cindy asked, pointing to her own face.

Nola nodded. "Yes, actually he did. He was pretty tan and the scar was lighter so it stood out. It was right below his cheekbone, straight across."

"That's Keith," Jared said, still not believing. "Holy shit."

"I did notice something else with him," Pete said. "He was wearing scrubs, but they didn't fit him right."

"Yeah, that's right," Nola agreed.

"They were too small, and the shape was wrong."

Nola snapped her fingers. "They were women's scrubs. My aunt is a nurse. His scrubs looked like her's. The shape and fit and all."

Jared was reeling. The world was advancing forward quickly, no denying it. He had a friend that just two years ago had gotten a telephone installed in his car. No need to use pay phones anymore. Computers were in schools now, and claims were rampant they would become household commodities in less than a decade. Rear-projection TVs the size of a wall were now moving into homes. He saw a kid here at the park playing a video game on a handheld device called a *Game Boy*. Compact discs were replacing cassette tapes. He wouldn't be surprised if electric and self-driving cars were on the horizon.

The advancements in society were like something out of *The Jetsons*. But to his knowledge, scientists hadn't discovered or patented limb regeneration technology.

Then how did Keith repair his arm?

"Fuck if I know," Jared said.

"What?" Cindy asked, puzzled.

"Nothing," Jared waved. To Nola: "What happened after they came into the room? When the vibe was weird."

"Doctor Lyla started examining Pete. I was really uncomfortable with the assistant resting his hand on me, so I concentrated on the doctor and Pete. Her exam was also strange. She was running her fingertips down his chest while listening to his heart, then down his back when she was listening to his lungs. Caressing."

"She was?" Pete asked, brow furrowed.

"Yes. You were acting like you were tired. Your eyes were watery. Out of it." She looked back to Cindy, then Jared. "This is where it gets batshit, and I still question whether or not I was hallucinating." Nola took a deep breath. "The doctor said she wanted to check his eyes again. She put the light to his eye, leaned in close, and turned her ear toward Pete like she was listening to him whisper. It was over in a second because you guys showed up, but I saw legs come out of her ear and wrap around her head. Tiny, segmented legs. Eight or ten of them. Then she jerked away and she said she'd be right back. She took Keith with her and locked the door. We heard your voice but we didn't know you then. We used that distraction to get out of there. Then we ran into you two. Literally."

"I faintly remember her checking my eyes again," Pete recounted. "The light blinded me then I felt like I was drowning without being in water. Then the light was gone and Nola was telling me to get my shirt on."

"What is going on?" Nola asked. "I mean, you guys said Keith was in an accident and died but he was there in the room with us. The doctor has weird shit crawling out her ears and trying to, I don't know, pass it to my boyfriend. I love a good horror story as much as the next guy, but I don't want to be part of one."

Horror story was right. Jared wasn't discounting what Nola thought she saw, but she had to be hallucinating. Segmented legs don't crawl out of people's ear. There had to be a logical explanation.

Keith is alive and his mangled arm miraculously healed overnight. Got logic for that one?

Jared hated reason. Sometimes.

"There were also spiders," Pete said, breaking the heavy silence.

This rang a bell of recognition with Jared. He waited for the eureka moment but nothing came. "Yeah, I've seen spiders here, many times. We're on an island that sat uninhabited for thirty million years."

"Have you ever seen them weave a web thick enough to be a throw blanket and cover an entire window?" Nola asked, edgy and obviously irritated by Jared's response. "Or have you seen so many of them the side of a house was completely smothered?"

"No, I have not. Is that what you saw?"

Pete answered, "That's what we both saw. I had to stick my hand through the web and tear it apart so we could climb out the window. It was full of eggs."

Pete held up his hand, eyes widening when he noticed some strands of web were still laced between his fingers. One tiny white bulb rested against a knuckle.

Nola gasped, slapped her hands over her mouth.

"What's wrong," Pete asked.

"I've been trying to place why the whole thing looked familiar. Legs crawling out of doc's ear and all. Now I know."

Pete was way ahead of her, the pieces clicking in place. "The Journey Through Hell."

Nola looked at Pete. "Those scenes were really real."

Twenty-Four

Julie stared at the hole, trying to make sense of it. Under the fence, a tunnel. Under the *electrified* fence. Finger marks in the thick soil, clawed and scratched. The AWOL group of men tried to hide their escape by scattering leaves over the excavation area. She found it only after noticing weedy clumps of dirt tossed haphazardly onto the forest floor.

Beyond the fence, stood another barrier. This one a wall of seemingly impenetrable wild jungle.

Has to be a way through if they made it, she thought, scanning the vegetation for evidence of passage: a broken limb, trampled underbrush, a gap big enough to allow a human to slip through, anything. From her vantage point, not a single tell-tale sign existed. The forest appeared untouched.

The Hispanic groundskeepers stood to the side, gibbering in Spanish amongst themselves.

"Is the power still on these fences?" Julie asked, interrupting their conversation.

"Sí." Alfredo pointed to a little green box with the red light glowing at the top of one of the posts. This was the power indicator. Designed for security to quickly check to ensure power was on and functioning while making their rounds.

"Can you turn it off?"

The two Hispanics exchanged glances. Finally, the Alfredo said, "I can, señora, but I would get fired. I need this job."

"You won't get fired. I just need to you to cut the power for five minutes so I can crawl under. Then throw the breaker back on and go about your day."

He looked to Manuel again, picking at his fingernails.

Julie approached him, patted his bicep to reassure him. "I promise you won't get fired. If anyone gets in trouble, it will be me. I'll say I cut the power. As far as anyone knows, you were never here. Okay?"

The man nodded. Still weary, but convinced. "Sí, señora. I'll cut the power for five minutes. But be quick. I don't want you getting electrocuted."

"That makes two of us." Julie pointed at the cart. "Can I have one of those shovels. I'll return it when I get back."

Manuel retrieved the tool, spoke to the translator, who passed the message along. "Manuel wants to know how you'll get back across when you return? If the fence is electrified?"

"I'll dig deeper," Julie said with a smile.

Handing Julie the shovel, Manuel said, "Por favor tenga cuidado."

"Please be careful," the translator interpreted.

Julie started digging quickly, careful not to touch the fence. She figured she had about eight to ten minutes for them to drive back to the block building that housed the electrical panels and energizers and cut the power. She had to be ready.

Sweat dripped from her face and her shirt was soaked by the time the hole was at a comfortable depth and width. Roots snaked across the opening but she would have to deal with them; the shovel blade was not sharp enough to cut them out of the way. She checked the red power indicator light to see if it was still on. It was.

Julie dropped to her hands and knees at the mouth of the dugout and waited for the light to switch off. Thirty seconds later, it went dark. She lowered her upper body into the trench. Roots dug into her boobs, grabbing at the wire of her bra. Julie ignored the discomfort, choosing to hope the hole was deep enough to let her ample bottom pass the fence. Getting stuck out here with no one around would suck like a pornstar.

Julie giggled, but it lacked real humor. It was relief, equivalent to the whistling of a coffee pot once the water started boiling. She was scared. For Leon and Scuba. For herself. She was leaving the protection of the park and venturing into the unknown. What lay beyond was fictional tales passed around among park employees while sitting on barstools and drinking whiskey. Julie was not a regular at the bars, wasn't aware of the variety of stories about the island, but she had heard a few campfire tales. Like Crystal Lake and Jason. Like Haddonfield and Michael. Like Derry and Pennywise.

She repeated the mantra "The stories are not real" over and over. Made up for the sake of entertainment. An ancient relish of the human condition. To scare others shitless. The reason Stephen King was so popular.

Julie's upper body finally cleared the fence, and she squeezed her elbows under her torso to push herself up. Loose, course soil had flowed inside her shirt collar and now scrubbed against her chest and stomach like sandpaper. She pushed her butt upwards against the fence to allow room to shake the dirt out of her shirt from the bottom. It worked, kind of, but one belt loop on her shorts was now hooked on the fence.

"Shit fire and save matches," Julie groaned, a well-worn proverb of her deceased father. She often used his favorite sayings as a way to keep his memory close. A former truck driver, Dick's adages were long—no pun intended—and almost always filthy.

Julie now regretted telling the two Hispanic's to go on their way when the power was back on. It would have been better to have had them swing by and be sure she hadn't been electrocuted before returning to work.

Julie used her elbows to push backward in an attempt to free the loop. She didn't care if it tore loose as long as her shorts stayed intact. Running around the woods in her granny panties would be most undesirable.

The fabric tore, but the loop slipped free from the chain-link. She twisted her neck as far as she could and saw only a small hole where the loop had been sewn onto her shorts. *Beggars can't be choosers.*

She wiggled side to side as she crawled up and out of the trench, lying in the weeds to catch her breath. It had been a hot minute since she had truly exerted herself and her body was letting it be known.

"Okay, okay," she said to her wheezing lungs. "I'll work on it."

An audible click from the green box informed her the power was back on. In the nick of time.

Julie shook the dirt out of her shirt and shorts, and brushed off her knees before setting off. She trudged through stubborn weeds that somehow found the will and strength to push through the thick blanket of leaves and forest waste to grow, carefully searching for an opening, a crevice, a sign of passage. A possible doorway came along and she stopped to examine. Something brushed her leg. Julie bit her tongue when she saw a spider climbing lazily up her shin. She knocked it loose and jogged away, choosing discretion over valor. Spiders and snakes were two chief weaknesses. Encountering one before making it fifty yards was not a good omen. A snake would end this search in half a blink.

The tree-line continued another three hundred yards before a rocky mound wrapped in briars ended her trek to the south. Julie had only seen one possible passageway that maybe/might be/could be a way in, but it was so tight she doubted it had been the entry point. She'd have to backtrack the way she came and proceed north.

It was when she turned to leave that the shadows shifted and the jungle offered a prize for vigilance. As she stepped closer, it became obvious this was where the men entered. A large frond hung from a broken branch, and the leaves underfoot appeared stamped. Julie ducked low and pushed through the foliage. A sharp limb scratched her arm, drawing a thin line of blood, and brambles snagged in her hair, but she was not deterred. More of the same lay ahead like some sort of elite military training obstacle course. She was not a soldier, and overwhelming doubt weakened her knees. How the men weaved their way through this was beyond her. She dropped on all fours to crawl under a mass of thorns, and climbed over a fallen log. Julie detected no further sign of the men's passage, and saw no end to this savage jungle, though she knew it ended at some point. It had to.

And what if you get stuck in here? The usual condescending nature of her mother. Always eager to sling an I-told-you-so in Julie's face like an angry baboon throwing shit. Happy to play the blame game as long as no one was blaming her.

Julie was even more pissed that on this particular occasion, at this particular time, her mother had a reasonable point.

Julie stopped, and dropped one bare knee into the mushy dead leaves. The jungle greeted her with uneasy silence. For the first time, she noticed the smell of woody mildew blended with a floral bouquet that eerily reminded her of a funeral home. All around, colorful flowers popped through the greens and browns, exotic blossoms that maybe had never been discovered, maybe weren't named. Around her ankles were tiny green leaves that *were* named: poison ivy. She was allergic to the stuff and would pay the price later. But for the moment, she needed to think.

Leon and the others had gone this way. She was sure of it. If they made it, she could make it. What lay on the other side of this savage hell, Julie was not completely certain. The unknown was what gave her pause. What was so powerful in its draw that the men would wrestle this miserable death trap? Was this some kind of exploratory hiking trip? Many a man and woman had braved brutal elements, paralyzing terrain, seemingly impossible obstacles, and boundless tests of perseverance in quests to conquer fear, to prove mankind's resilience, to push the boundaries of what was believed to be possible, or to simply shoot the middle finger at naysayers. Perhaps the appeal of danger had drawn them under that fence. The pamphlets in the rooms provided a certain mystique about this prohibited side of the island. Some would find the scant, yet fascinating details irresistible. Leon and Scuba knew better than to trespass here, but maybe the men made a satisfactory argument for disobeying the rules.

Sounds like bullshit to me, Julie thought. But bullshit was all she had to go on.

Julie saw no choice but to continue the search. Despite a nagging feeling she should turn around and come back with the proper clothing, a machete or a hatchet, and perhaps some backup, Julie pushed forward. She put her full attention on the task at hand. She broke the limb off a sapling and stripped the V-shaped end of leaves. The limb became a fork of sorts, helping clear limbs and foliage out of the way for easier travel. This was a trick her father showed her as a little girl, except he had used the limb with tines on the end as a rake to gather straw. He had used the straw to cover a hand-built structure made of random sticks foraged from the forest. He'd explained the structure provided crucial shelter from the elements, if one were in need of such. He'd called it bushcraft, and Julie had thought it a silly thing back then. Not so silly now.

"Thanks, Dad," Julie huffed. Though she was in deep shade, the humidity and the physical demand had her sweating profusely. A magnet for mosquitos and gnats. As if she was not uncomfortable enough already.

Julie was so caught up in grappling the jungle, she was not aware she was clear until nothing sat before her but jagged hills. She was about to drop the stick but thought better of it; a cane might come in handy when traipsing across the hazardous rocks that formed these mounds. The cover of the forest behind her, the sun sat in the clear blue sky like a cigarette burn. The temperature was easily twenty degrees hotter than it had been in the shade. Julie hadn't thought to spray herself with sunscreen. She hadn't thought about a lot of things.

Julie climbed the first rock, and instantly lost herself to the mission of not breaking a leg. She was so focused on each step, the cliff arrived before she knew it. She peered over the edge. Below was rocky beach, the turbulent waves of the Gulf slamming against the grey boulders with such force she could feel the mist way up here, some fifty feet above. The ocean met the sky thousands of miles away and nothing floated out there that she could see.

"What now?" she asked the wind. It howled in response.

To the right was more cliff that gradually petered out into the ocean and disappeared around the side of the island. To the left lay a slope descending down to the beach below. Beach was a kind word. It indicated a place to sit in a chair, toes in the sand, watching the waves lapping at the shore. Fruity adult beverage in hand, glass sweating, ice tinkling.

Below lay no such thing. This was a cruel, spiked area, as inviting as the grave. The visible sand was dark brown, riddled with broken seashells and the jagged backs of more stones.

Julie searched either side and saw no other option but down. Julie slowly scaled the rocks, reaching the bottom after what felt like hours. At least one of the why's was immediately answered. A black hole disappeared into the side of the cliff.

A cave.

Where it went Julie had no idea. It confirmed some of the rumors to be true. Other rumors about there being a warren of natural tunnels running beneath the island were unfounded, but Julie had a feeling she was about to discover a lot about this island.

Again, reservations about continuing alone and without proper tools—*or protection*, a tiny voice whispered—tried to force Julie to turn around. She was too invested now.

In for a penny, in for a pound. Another of her dad's sayings.

Julie carefully climbed the water-slick rocks, ignoring the screaming pleas of a colony of seagulls, and entered the yawning mouth of the cave.

Twenty-Five

"Jared."

Jared unhooked the walkie talkie from the charger on his desk. "Copy."

"Where are you?"

Jared and Cindy's wide-eyes met. It was Quinten, and Jared knew what that flat, monotone meant.

Cindy mouthed, "Oh, no."

Jared agreed.

Jared thought fast. No way was he giving away their location. "Um, morning Quinten, um I'm at The Reaper checking the, um, turbine to be sure it's still working after the accident last night."

As far as he knew, Quinten hadn't been told about the accident. He wasn't sure if Larry had been told yet either. A lot had happened since then.

Quinten was silent for a full, uncomfortable minute before speaking. "Be in my office in an hour. We need to talk soon, but I am walking into a meeting with Larry first." He paused before adding: "Bring Cindy also." The radio clicked and Quinten was gone.

No mention of the accident involving Keith. Which would have been priority one under normal circumstances.

"This is bad," Cindy said. "This is bad, bad, bad."

"Who was that?" Pete asked.

"Our boss," Jared answered. "Director of Maintenance."

"And the Larry guy?"

Cindy shook her head in disbelief. "That's the Park Director. The next stop up the ladder after him are the owners."

It was spreading. Whatever *it* was. Jared ran down a mental checklist of those he knew were probably infected: Quinten, Lyla, Keith, Lawrence, Billy, Patrick. And Larry was next. Possibly being infected right now as Jared hid in the maintenance shop.

Could there be more?

Probably. Anyone the doctor had come in contact with was suspect. That number may be as few as those Jared knew about or as many as a dozen more. Maybe dozens.

"What do we do?" Cindy asked. She was seated, and looked shell-shocked. "We're not going to meet with him."

"Obviously," Jared said.

"Then he'll know something's up. Surely Lyla suspects something's up. Nola and Pete escaped her grasp and she saw them pair up with us. Now Quinten wants to see us. Once they collectively figure out we know more than we should, they are coming after us."

"We don't actually *know* anything," Nola said. "We saw some strange shit, sure, but we don't, like, know anything."

"It won't matter," Jared said. He took slow, deep breaths to calm the rabbit's feet in his chest. "Maybe we don't know exactly what they're infected with or how they became infected in the first place, but they know we are not oblivious. We know enough to be a danger to whatever they are planning."

"Okay," Pete said. "What do we do?"

Jared only saw one option. "We get off this island." He checked his watch. "The last boat of the day leaves at three. That's six hours away. We lay low until then."

"I have to alert my parents," Pete said. "We were leaving tomorrow anyway."

"Me, too," Nola said.

"It's likely they will expect that," Jared warned. "Probably waiting for you to show up." He hated to say it, but they needed to consider all possibilities.

"All the more reason to go to them."

Splitting up was dangerous, but all four of them running around the park was bound to draw more attention than Nola and Pete moving alone. "Okay, but you need to be careful. Do not run. Do not walk fast. Casual. I suggest you split up as well."

Pete shook his head. "Absolutely not. I'm not letting her out of my sight until she is safely with her parents."

Jared figured as much. "Let her walk ahead of you. Fifteen, twenty feet. You keep your eyes open and pay attention. Got it?"

"Got it." Pete took Nola's hand and followed Jared to the elevator. Employees were moving about, some in work clothes, some in costumes. None of them gave Jared, Pete, or Nola a sideways glance.

"This will take you to a small building on the surface. Step out and go right to re-enter the park through the employee gate. Find your parents as quickly as possible. Be safe. Go."

Pete and Nola nodded as they entered the open elevator door. Jared returned to the maintenance shop for Cindy, and found her trembling in the office chair. Standing behind her, hands on her shoulders, was Lawrence.

"Hi, Jared," Lawrence said. Lawrence was smiling, a wide, morbid stretch of the lips, mouth full of bloody teeth. His voice was flat, bored. An unsettling combination.

"Lawrence," Jared said, enunciating his name slowly to buy time. Time to think. Hard to do under the circumstances. "Can you let go of Cindy, please? We were leaving."

"Oh, no, Jared." Lawrence continued to smile as he squeezed Cindy's shoulders. Tears streamed down her flushed, terrified cheeks. "I am afraid the time for leaving has passed."

Panic wormed its way into Jared's chest. Not just for Cindy, but for the implications behind Lawrence's presence.

Maybe it's random. He was in the neighborhood.

Perhaps. But that was a little too coincidental for Jared's liking. The walls were closing in. The infected were making connections, determining who was unaware and who was conscientious of … knowing. Cindy and Jared were now deemed a problem. Which meant Pete and Nola were in grave danger.

Stall.

Jared winked one eye at Cindy, then the other. Shot his eyes from her to Lawrence, back to her, held the gaze. He had no idea what he was going to do, but he wanted her ready. Her head bobbed forward ever so slightly. Jared sidestepped toward the work bench—and its multitude of tools—lined along the wall and held his hand up. "Lawrence? What's this all about? You're acting weird."

"I feel fine," Lawrence answered, hands massaging Cindy's neck. "Perfect, actually. When you meet with Quinten, you will be perfect as well."

Jared nonchalantly sidestepped again. "Why does Quinten want to meet us?"

"It is a matter of utmost importance. That is why I am here. To ensure you make the appointment. We are also retrieving the other two, Pete and Nola. They must attend this meeting as well."

The door to the maintenance shop opened and Wes slipped through. "Oh hey, I was wondering where you were. Are you ready to head over and switch that chain out? We gotta get the ride—"

Wes stopped speaking, finally sensing the tension in the room. His eyes flicked from Jared to Cindy to Lawrence to Lawrence's hands on Cindy's shoulders.

"What's going on?" Wes asked, taking a hesitant step forward.

"Wes, would you be so kind as to repair the chain yourself?" Lawrence asked, grip tightening around Cindy's neck.

Wes had lived a hard life. A life in the streets. He was a scrapper if need be and the sight of Lawrence holding Cindy must have set the back-alley cat off inside him. He stomped toward Lawrence. "I don't know what's going on here, but you need to take your hands off her right now."

It happened fast. Segmented arms shot out of Lawrence's ears and nose like lightning from dark, bloated clouds. Spearing Wes through his eye sockets and ears and nose. Wes was lifted off the floor, head thumping the ceiling grid, knocking tiles and a fluorescent light fixture loose. A thick, wormy tentacle shot into Wes' mouth. He choked and gagged as it pushed its way down his gullet. Lawrence's eyes rolled back in his head as bloated bulbs of something Jared couldn't identify slid down the tentacle from Lawrence to Wes.

Like rats in an IV line, Jared thought as he backed away.

Wes gulped each time one of the bulbs was dumped inside him.

This was how the infection was spreading. But it wasn't just an infection. It was a mutation. Each of the diseased were offloading a portion of the sickness into a new host. The host then became infected and mutated into ... whatever the hell these things were. And the cycle repeated.

It was a terrifying concept. One Jared never would've believed if he had not seen it himself.

Jared searched the work bench for something, anything that could be used as a weapon. Lawrence was distracted with Wes, his hands now removed from Cindy's throat. He needed to strike now if he and Cindy had any shot of escaping.

A nail gun lay on the counter, yellow air hose still attached.

Sure hope the compressor is on.

Cindy leaped from the chair and reached Jared just as he raised the tool. Nail guns were equipped with a safety feature that made it impossible to shoot a nail without pressing the tip against a hard surface. But Ferdinand dropped this nail gun a few weeks ago, breaking the tip, disabling the safety feature. Jared ordered a new nail gun from their tool supplier in Orlando but it had yet to arrive. With the amount of work needing to be completed for Halloween, the defective tool was still in use—*shhh,* don't tell OSHA—with only Ferdinand authorized to operate it.

Until now.

Jared pulled the trigger and a nail shot into Lawrence's chest. Lawrence stopped trembling instantly, his eyes rolling back to their rightful place, the tentacles dropping Wes' convulsing body to the floor. Lawrence gripped the nail with his fingers and wiggled the piece of galvanized steel free. It tinked off the concrete when he dropped it. A thin stream of orangish liquid poured from the wound, soaking his work shirt.

Lawrence advanced toward Jared and Cindy, opening his mouth again as tentacles burst from his lips.

"Fuck me," Jared gasped, and shot the gun again. Lawrence jerked and stumbled backward, but Jared barely noticed. He was already running, dragging Cindy along.

Twenty-Six

Larry slammed the phone down. He expected action, not justifications that lacked reason and common sense. Not one of these corporate fucks could explain what happened with the ferry. Not one could explain why there were no contingency plans in case the ferry broke down. Or, as in this case, suffered catastrophic engine failure.

What the hell does that even mean? Catastrophic engine failure.

His chest tightened and a sharp pain jabbed him in the ribs on his left side. He tossed two aspirin in his mouth and dry swallowed, grimacing at the bitter residue left on his tongue. This job would kill him one day. The responsibility of his duties. To the park. To the staff. To the thousands of people who visited the park daily, almost 365 days a year. The pressure was immense. Days like today, where everything that could go wrong, was going wrong, he wondered, why do it? Why put himself through this? As a life-long bachelor, he had no family. No self-serving wife to support, no spoiled children to blow his money. The house was paid off. Money was in the bank. His stock portfolio was thriving. His only personal obligation was to himself.

So why do it?

Larry knew the answer, as complicated as it was to explain. Even to himself.

The long and short was he loved it. He loved the power. He loved the pressure. He loved waking up each morning and arriving to the office and standing by this window that looked out over the park from his position of authority, knowing he had helped create Riptide Rapids. And now he managed the park and everything on the island. He was invested in its success—and invested in its stock. He hated the problems that came with running this type of vacation destination, but he loved that he always found a way to resolve the issue. He was the guy the staff came to when they couldn't find the solution. It was his gift. And his curse.

Knuckles tapped against his mahogany six-panel office door. He knew the knock. Heard it everyday.

"Come in, Cecilia," he called.

His receptionist, Cecilia, slipped her beautiful, exotic head in the half-opened door, and smiled at him. Her jet-black hair glossy in the office lights, mocha skin wrapping a perfect Brazilian body.

After a silent exchange, she said, "Quinten is here to see you."

Larry nodded. No words were necessary. She knew him well. In the office. And the bedroom.

The door opened all the way and Quinten entered. Larry was struck by how unwell his maintenance director looked. Hair messy. Clothing wrinkled. Complexion sickly. Eyes severely bloodshot. Then Quinten's body odor wafted across the room like a deadly breeze. Mildew and sour sweat. Nasty combo.

Larry swiped at his nose. "What can I do for you, Quinten? Please tell me you have word on that goddamn ferry. Those pricks at headquarters won't tell me shit."

"We have a problem."

Larry was again surprised. Quinten was former military. Drill Sergeant. He was tough but loquacious. A weird mix he pulled off well. His maintenance crew loved him, and Jared would go to war for his boss if necessary. To hear him sound disconnected, flat, monotoned was a little unsettling.

He's obviously unwell. Must have the flu or something. Larry moved to the plush leather couch on the opposite side of the office. Creating a little distance. Last thing he needed was to catch some damn cold.

"What's the problem now?"

"A park attendee and an employee died yesterday evening."

Larry sprung off the couch like it was in flames. "What?"

"Keith Parker. Works on," Quinten paused, eyes moving to the left, seemed to grasp for the information like fingers flipping through Dewey Decimal cards at the library, "Cascade Canyon. And Emma Jean Struthers, sixty, from Bangor, Maine."

"How the hell did Keith die?"

"Somehow got his arm caught in a gear in the mechanical shed. Lost too much blood."

"Jesus," Larry said, light-headed. "And the woman?"

"Tripped climbing out of the Dolphin Run pool. Bashed her face on the edge and died from a brain hemorrhage."

Larry's knees gave out and he dropped on the couch. He'd known bad things were coming. When one tilled evil soil, one reaped rotten crops. He was surprised an accident hadn't happened before now.

The news still cut him to the bone.

Larry raised his head to speak only to realize Quinten was sitting beside him. He stayed put, no longer caring about getting sick.

"We need to contact corporate. An investigation will be called." A seismic shift ripped through him as he realized the enormity of what was about to happen. The park would be closed. Millions of dollars would be at risk. He'd most certainly be fired.

He found that he cared. As much as he tried to convince himself otherwise.

Quinten smiled, his two front teeth dangling in bloody sockets. "I do not think that will be necessary. Both of them are actually okay now. They died, but we saved them."

Larry couldn't make sense of what he was saying. Crazy talk. "What do you mean?"

Quinten smiled, and Larry noticed one of his bloody teeth was dangling. Only the root holding it in place. "Let me show you something cool," Quinten said. Then his head exploded.

The pain was everything. The tips of his dyed hair hurt. His toenails felt like someone was ripping them off with pliers. His flesh seemed to unwrap from his body, loosen, stretch. Nerve-endings sizzled. Atoms mutated. And like a dream, Larry floated off the couch, through the clouds, into the cosmos, sucked across a vast ocean of time and space, stars at his fingertips, planets within his grasp.

Until all that remained was the void.

There, he experienced an awakening.

Twenty-Seven

The crowd was heavy. A sea of people everywhere, in a hurry to get in line, to ride a ride. Yesterday it had been a reasonable plight, even if Pete hadn't been interested himself. Today, as he tried to keep Nola in his sight while maintaining a low profile, it all seemed silly. A bunch of ants, running about with some chore or deed or mission in mind. None of them knew the fragility of reality. Not only was death always lurking at arm's length, but, as Pete learned just this morning, realities existed that most deemed fictional. Cool ideas for movies or books. Never in a hundred lifetimes would he have thought he'd be living such a scenario.

What climbed out of doc's ear? Pete wondered as he skipped sideways to allow a young couple pushing a stroller to pass.

He hadn't seen it, but Nola's description made him queasy. He'd literally been moments away from being infected. Or whatever it was called. And if he'd been taken over, Nola would have been next.

Pete almost tripped over his own feet when it hit him. The end game.

He quickened his pace and caught up to Nola, grabbing her elbow. She jumped, a small squeak escaping her until she realized it was Pete.

"You're supposed to keep your distance," Nola said, voice low.

"I think I know what this is about," Pete said, inspecting every passing face, overly paranoid. "They want to infect all of the employees. Then the visitors."

"Okay. Yeah, kinda makes sense."

"But it's more than that though. Think about it. If all these people are infected and return to the mainland and go home to their families, friends, and co-workers, they can spread it without anyone knowing. By the time a connection is made, if it's ever made, it'll be too late. They'll infect the entire North American population in months. Maybe less.

Nola's hands wrapped her stomach as if nauseated. Comprehending the magnitude of what they were up against, almost impossible to fathom. "What do we do?"

The fear was almost incapacitating. Pete could hardly think. But he knew what *not* to do. "We can't get on the boat and leave."

Nola pulled him aside, out of the middle of the walkway, near a webbed bush with a plastic skeleton climbing out of it. "Pete, we *have* to get out of here."

Pete shook his head. "Besides Jared and Cindy, we are the only ones who know about this. If we leave, everyone on this island gets infected and brings this to America. No matter where we go, how far we run, the infection would get us at some point.

"I'm scared to death, and I don't know if I have what it takes to fight these things, but leaving is for sure a death sentence. Not just for us, but maybe for humanity. If we stay, we have a chance."

"Then let's tell someone. How about that security guard from last night? He seemed level-headed."

"Tell him what? We went to see the doctor and a spider climbed out of her ear. And, oh yeah, by the way, they are trying to take over the world."

"That's just a theory at this point."

"I get that, but we know something bad is happening. We can *deduce* that more bad will happen if we don't do something about it. I can't leave knowing that."

Nola dropped her head in defeat, hair falling around her face. Pete wrapped his arms around her, as much for himself as for her. She laid her head on his shoulder and it was then that Pete saw Keith. He was fifty yards away, standing by the block building housing the restrooms. Conspicuous, but not enough.

"We're being followed," Pete whispered in her ear. Nola stiffened. "It's Keith."

Pete remained casual in his movements counting on the mass amount of people either streaming past or loitering while studying park maps, taking a bathroom break, or simply resting their legs to mask Pete's discovery of the reconnaissance.

"Where?" Nola asked, keeping her head down like a pro.

"Straight behind you. By the bathrooms."

"What do we do?"

There were only two options: try to lose Keith and find his parents, or try to lose Keith and find somewhere to hide. Pete wasn't sure if his parents stayed at the hotel or went on to the pool, but he hoped they were at the pool. The safest place for them right now was in public, out in the open.

Hiding was not without its problems. Namely, it required being secluded, and seclusion was the enemy with these people. They needed anonymity while they spread the infection. At least for now. If Keith caught them while hiding, the job of disseminating the virus was easier.

Hiding was defensive, allowing the doctor, Keith, and the rest to continue the contamination. Time was against Pete's small rebel contingent. The more people became infected, the more difficult the task of stopping this nightmare.

"Pete?" Nola called, snapping her fingers in front of his face. "Earth to Pete."

"Yeah, I'm here. Just thinking."

"Think fast honey. We gotta move to somewhere safe."

"There is nowhere safe," Pete said. "And that doesn't solve the problem anyway. We have to play offense the rest of the way."

"What does that mean?"

It meant taking the fight to the other team. Pete had no idea how to do that, but he was committed to figuring it out.

Maybe it was time to turn the tables on them. Stop running and hiding, start following and observing. Learn their habits. Find a weakness. Exploit it.

Easier said than done. When spiders crawled out of someone's face, bravado tended to melt to a puddle of piss.

"Come on," Pete said. He wasn't concerned about Keith anymore. Let the bastard follow.

"Where we going?"

"To check on our parents, then find Jared and Cindy."

Twenty-Eight

Corey's fingers were numb, eyes burned, head throbbed, and his ass hurt from sitting all night, but he was determined to finish coding this level of the game. He was close. The biggest bad guy was next. Then Corey could call it and get some much needed shut eye before jumping back into the next challenge. After a few hours of sleep, he planned to work until the trick-or-treaters started ringing the doorbell. He'd spend a few hours feeding those little crotch goblins enough sugar to keep them up until Christmas morning, then hunker down for another long night on Level Eight. It was back to work at Deep Sky the night after that.

A side hobby of his was building computer games. It started out as something he thought might be fun, but had since turned into an infatuation. He had created two previous games—both being junk—as models to learn what to do and what not to do. The fight game he was working on now, current working title *Fistful Of Vengeance,* was different than those two duds. Exciting, fast-paced, fresh moves, cool finishers, astonishingly creative weaponry. A winner, if he said so himself.

Computers were the future. What they were doing at Deep Sky with computers only reinforced his theory. Every home in America would have one of those machines in ten years. In twenty years, experts predicted, computers would run the world. Automation, computation, analytics, all streamlining daily functions, processing millions of gigabytes of information in nanoseconds. In the realm of entertainment, the growth would be even more dramatic. Video games experienced a growth spurt thanks to the Italian guy in the red hat, but that was only the beginning. Games would become more realistic.

Movie-goers would enjoy better graphics in big time movies—Corey wasn't sure anyone could top George Lucas' sci-fi trilogy, though, even with advanced technology. The writing was spray painted all over the wall in bright neon. And Corey wanted to be in the cockpit when that rocket left the terminal.

The phone next to his computer rang. Corey ignored it. It was probably his mom. She always called early. He'd asked her to wait until later multiple times.

"If I wait until later, you'll be in bed," she'd responded once before.

And she had a point.

He'd call her back.

Except the voice that spoke into the answering machine was not his mother's; it was his boss.

"Corey, give me—"

Corey snatched up the phone. "Hey, sir, sorry, was just trying to get to the phone."

"Corey, I was not here yesterday because of my meetings with NASA. But when I arrived this morning, I found a disturbing report on my desk about some sort of anomaly you and Max witnessed. What sort of anomaly? And why was I not called?"

Corey winced. Fucking Max. Always the do-good, ass-kisser. Obeying the rules down to the millimeter; mostly. Must've filled out a report before shift change without saying anything to Corey.

"Well, sir, it was no big deal. That's why I didn't call. A ghost in the machine, we believe. Max and I." Corey shut his mouth. He was always tongue tied around Simon. The man was stern with a capital S. Deep Sky was his baby and he was extremely protective of it. Five people had been axed in the past twelve months because of mistakes or lack of productivity. Corey felt the cold edge of a blade pressing against his neck right then.

"A ghost in the machine, huh? And how did you determine this?"

"Well, sir," Corey swallowed, "a mass showed up on the screen, a large mass. Like an asteroid. It showed up in Sector Seven, headed straight for Sector Eight, but it never arrived to eight. It disappeared. Completely. From all sectors. We searched and found nothing. Max and I agreed it must have been a glitch in the system."

"The system cannot show an asteroid unless there is one. Glitch or no. How long was this so-called ghost in the machine observed before it disappeared?"

"I would say one to two minutes."

"You observed a mass in Sector Seven for one or two minutes, and you didn't think I needed to be called?"

Corey thought of explaining the hour of the morning, but knew that would only accelerate his termination.

Not to mention I was high as a kite.

He stayed quiet, staring at the blinking cursor on his computer screen, stomach in knots, wondering if he was about to be unemployed.

Simon went on. "I need you to get in your car, and drive to work right now, while you still have a work to drive to. Start sifting through the data and figure out where this anomaly went. Is that understood?"

Simon's voice was level but miles from calm.

Corey understood. "Yes, sir. On the way."

"And call Max. Be sure to express the importance of haste. I expect you both here in fifteen minutes."

Corey squeezed his eyes closed to clear the sting. He hadn't slept in fourteen hours and now he was in for a long day of Simon standing over his shoulder like a mad parent. He'd have to suck it up and take it like a man. He needed this job, and loved working at Deep Sky. Most of the time. "Yes, sir. Calling Max now."

But Simon was already gone.

Twenty-Nine

Julie leaned against the rough, stony cave wall waiting for her eyes to adjust. The switch from blinding sunlight to total darkness was a hard transition on the pupils. Her ears and nose helped provide immediate feedback. The dominant odors were dank and musty, but an underlying redolence wormed its way through. Hot blood came to mind. Her stomach rolled, groaned. Again, she considered abandoning the mission, but was too far now. The men were close. She knew it. And they weren't simply hiding. Evil hung in the air like beef on a meat hook.

Joining the sickening stench was a faint echo. Julie leaned into it, head turned sideways, trying to decipher the nuances.

Slithering? In oil?

She wasn't sure, but that was how it sounded. Slick and slimy, slurping and writhing. She shook her head, the sounds too perplexing.

Her eyes finally adjusted and the cave became a dim corridor bending down toward Hell. No salvation available here. This was where man came to yield to the unholy while demons cited scripture written with blood. Hand in hand, what a congregation they presented.

Yield to what?

Despite the suffocating heat, Julie shivered, the cadaverous fingers of icy dread grazing the back of her neck.

The cave walls were jagged spears. Like a protective cloak to discourage those not confident in their christening from journeying further. Julie wondered who had carved this out of the bedrock. Machines could not be responsible. This had the look of hand and chisel. One insubstantial blow at a time for a thousand years. Tenacity and purpose driving the hammer, millions of strokes of steel upon steel. She could almost imagine a mangy, wrinkled man, all sinew, nothing but a loin cloth for modesty, hunkered in the darkness, tugging the entrails from the stomach of a screeching rat with his rotten teeth, drinking his own rancid piss to wash down the meal. Admiring his work. Proud, but hungry to finish. A few hundred more years and he would reach the destination. Somewhere further, an abyss home to unfathomable nightmares.

But not for long.

If I can hold my nerve, she thought, coming to a narrow alley at the back of the massive cave. The ceiling was lower, the walls tighter. Not yet claustrophobic but not far from it. These walls were a little smoother. The old man had taken his time to smooth the points. Julie's shoulders cleared either side by less than a foot. The rocky earth was squishy beneath her Reeboks as the grade gently descended, and plump water bugs scurried from her presence, tiny legs clicking. The smell was worse here, choking her. She tugged her shirt up over her nose to try to filter the stench. The smell of her sweaty body and the scented Avon lotion she lathered on that morning helped but wasn't powerful enough to smother it totally.

I'm close.

To what? What the fuck is going on here?

Not a single logical explanation came to mind. Hell, nothing came to mind. Julie was not an imaginative person. She had always struggled in English. Assignments like one-sentence prompts where she was to write a fictional story using the prompt as a guide. She loved to read other writers' fantasies and false realities, but she lacked the ability to create those herself.

What lay ahead, all the possibilities, were lost on her. She'd have to see it with her own eyes.

Something shifted in the darkness ahead. Wet and sticky. Julie stopped, held her breath. Though she now possessed night eyes, this deep inside the tunnel was like being buried alive. Pitch black and claustrophobic. Her movements were more based on feel than sight. She not only heard the shift, she sensed it. An imperceptible breeze, a pulse in the air as though a monster exhaled. Whatever it was moved away. Sliding. Slowly diminishing until it was gone.

Mostly. The writhing continued. Mixed with new sounds. Tapping. Or padding. And muffled, squelchy grunts.

Julie took a deliberate, deep breath, inhaling through her nose. Exhaled from her mouth. The blood-soaked air activated her gag reflex, but she drowned it in gritty spit and swallowed the repulsive mixture. Using the walls on either side for stability, Julie pushed forward. When her fingers dipped into a congealed wax coating the rock, she slapped the other hand over her mouth to mute the gagging cough threatening to give her away.

This was where the unknown thing was hiding before it slunk away. Probably caught her scent. Perspiration and body lotion.

Julie brought her gooey fingers up to her nose, took a tentative sniff, and instantly regretted it. Bile erupted from her mouth so violently it shot out of her nose. She wretched at her feet, morning coffee splashing on her shoes. After a moment her stomach settled, and she wiped her mouth. The tunnel was absurdly quiet. The slithering had stopped. All movement had halted.

They know I'm here, she thought with dread. Whoever—*what*ever—they were.

Julie was about to retreat when footsteps marched toward her, stomping in the slimy mud. "Julie?"

Goosebumps flashed up her neck. Julie couldn't see, but it was definitely him. "Leon?"

"What are you doing here?" Leon asked. The question suggested surprise, yet it lacked inflection, intonation, or emotion.

"I ... I came looking for you," she said, mind reeling. She had come looking for Leon but what had she planned to say or do once she found him? "And the others. Their wives are worried sick." Julie decided to add a little white lie. Hoping to put pressure to end whatever this was. "Security has called the mainland for assistance. Authorities are sending in a search party."

Leon smiled. She couldn't see it, but she heard a repugnant stretching of flesh. His words expanded with it. "Now, now, Julie. We both know that is not true. You came looking by yourself. Right?"

Julie stammered, "Well, um, yeah, I ... wanted to be sure you were okay. You acted weird yesterday, then disappeared. I was worried."

"I understand. We are glad you came."

He wasn't acting glad. Julie stayed quiet, trying to decide if she should run. This was wrong. All of it. Leon was the kindest man she'd ever met. He always greeted her with a hug and a kiss and pat on her butt. That was his love language. And she loved that about him. Understood him. This person before her was not the Leon she knew and loved.

Leon's emotionless vocal delivery was frightening, but Julie noticed he enunciated. Leon was a high school dropout who went to work on a shrimp boat at fifteen. He hadn't read a book since. When he spoke, the words sometimes jumbled together, sounding like a Frogmore Stew. He liked to tell people he spoke fluid Louisiana redneck.

Listening to his clear, diction-accurate delivery, Julie wondered what could clean up a lifelong speech pattern overnight.

"You are scared," Leon said. "I get it. Let me show you why we came here. You will appreciate our secrecy."

Cold fingers wrapped around Julie's arm at the elbow. She tried to pull away but the fingernails dug into her flesh as the grip clamped down like pieces of steel.

"Leon, you're hurting me," Julie whispered. An invisible hand squeezed her esophagus, cutting off air, allowing nothing but the faintest of speech.

"I do not want to hurt you," Leon said. "Come with me and everything will be fine."

Julie was too afraid to fight. She felt like Leon could snap the bones in her arm if he desired. Going with him would hopefully deescalate the situation. Then she could look for ways to escape.

"Okay," she whispered. "I'll go. Just ease up on my arm."

The pain subsided but Leon didn't relinquish his hold. "Walk forward."

Julie followed his instructions. The corridor was too narrow for them to walk side by side, so Leon squeezed around her, trailing close behind. She noticed his body felt odd, sickly and gaunt as though eaten by disease.

"Almost there," Leon said in her ear.

The air became thick with the smell of hot copper and shit.

"What's that smell?" Julie coughed.

"Afterbirth."

Darkness dissipated like smoke. A strange, faint glow showed Julie she was now in a chamber. In the ceiling above, a small incision allowed a beam of sunlight to cut through the blackness, exposing a horror Julie was not mentally equipped to handle.

"You are witness," Leon breathed in her ear.

Julie tried to discern what she was witness to, but the gruesome mass of squirming flesh and puddles of crimson fluid mixed with chunks of veined grey meat and pulsating "eggs" piled in the middle of the chamber were alien to her. The only materials that made sense were the neatly folded clothes next to the chamber entrance. Men's shorts and shirts which she recognized from the fishermen who passed by the office yesterday afternoon. And park uniforms. Uniforms worn by the housekeeping staff.

Against the far wall, tentacled bodies twisted together like slimy pretzels, creating the acoustic nightmare Julie had been hearing since entering the cave. She blinked to clear the burning tears from her vision. Hoping she was dreaming and the blink would clear the images. But, no, the scene remained. A visceral abomination of nature.

"What is this?" Julie croaked around the bitter bile crusting her tongue.

"You humans call it copulating," Leon panted with a passion Julie had never heard from him. Finally showing emotion. "We call it something that has no meaning. Not to you anyway."

"We?" Julie asked, but she wasn't really interested in an answer. Her bladder felt engorged and her knees were shaking so terribly she thought she might collapse then piss on herself for good measure.

Leon nodded, smiling, face rising to the hole in the ceiling as if gazing upon a God. "We. Children of the void. Here to reclaim something we lost long ago. Something vital to our continued existence." His eyes dropped to Julie. "You have never experienced anything like this, Julie. It is wonderful. No pain. No suffering. No mental anguish. No anxiety. No addictions. No hate. No bias. No death. Just peace. Sweet, sweet serenity."

Leon leaned down to her, and she thought he was going to kiss her, but his cheek brushed her own as he moved close to whisper something in her ear. Silently, he kissed her earlobe and despite the fear and repulsion that shuddered in her bones, Julie felt her skin rise. His warm and wet tongue slipped around her ear until the sensation became like a needle sliding inside her ear canal. She tried to jerk away, but Leon held her tight. A mass of segmented legs shot out around her face, wrapping her head. One landed over her eyes, the thin, hairy appendage blocking her view. She opened her mouth to scream but something wet with mucus slipped down her throat like a slug. The pressure built inside her ear until she felt a piercing pain, heard a pop like gunfire, then was blinded by an eternal future. Infinite as the stars and the swirling galaxies that lay beyond. And beyond those galaxies, in a place where nothing else could thrive much less survive, lay the children of the tomorrow.

Now her children.

Thirty

Dave couldn't shake the fear. No matter how many times he pretended the dead woman hadn't been following his family, no matter how many excuses he fashioned out of thin air, he knew in his heart of hearts, it was her.

And that was impossible.

He needed answers, to a multitude of questions, and he couldn't get them with the family under his feet.

Amazonia was an awesome restaurant with an immersive environment. A full-grown live tree grew up through the floor in the middle of the room and out of the roof. A waterfall cascaded down one wall. All sorts of dinosaur statues roamed the dining room floor. Pterodactyls hung from a ceiling designed to look like the tree canopy inside an actual jungle. The wait staff dressed like cavemen and women. Every dish was rustic and brought out on cast iron skillets and wooden plates. Forks and spoons were made of animal bones. Truly a spectacle and worth every penny.

The kids loved it. Van walked around posing with the different species of dinosaurs while Jessica took pictures using a disposable camera they bought at the front desk. The cost of having all of these pictures developed at K-Mart was climbing by the minute.

But Dave was so distracted he had trouble enjoying the atmosphere or the food. His knee jumped, his thoughts swirled, and he was ready to go. He waited until Van and Jessica had gone exploring the restaurant again. He made a show of holding his stomach with one hand and covering his mouth with the other. "Penny, I need to head back to the cabin. I don't feel so good."

Penny dropped her napkin and leaned closer to him. "What's wrong?"

"Feeling nauseated. Was feeling it a little when I woke up but it's gotten worse."

"Oh, okay. Well, um, I'll get the kids and—"

"No, no, you guys stay here, finish eating. Go on without me."

"We don't want to ride rides without you. We'll be an odd number. One of us would have to ride alone."

Dave had already thought of that. "The kids haven't been to the pool area yet. Why don't you go down there and hang out for a while? Make it easy for me to find you later. I'll take something to calm my stomach and lie down. I'll try to rejoin you in a bit."

Penny flaunted her fake pouty lips. Usually endearing, but not today. "Okay. But hurry back."

"Just tell the waitress to add the meal to our hotel." Dave escaped the restaurant without having to explain his ailment to the kids. Conspiracy theories were running rampant through his mind, and he couldn't sit still any longer.

Dave paid close attention to his surroundings on his walk across the park. If the dead woman was following him, she was doing a great job concealing herself. He'd considered approaching her if he saw her again. See what her reaction would be. Maybe he'd realize that it wasn't the woman who died at the dolphin pool. Just someone that resembled her.

You know better, he thought. But was not sure.

He'd deal with it if she appeared again. For now, he had a bigger concern.

His first stop was the reservation desk of his villa. Gabbie was still working.

"Hi, can I help you?" she asked with a smile.

"Yeah, I'm in bungalow 12. Dave Evans."

"Yes, of course. Our hero. Have you heard anything on the kid you brought in?"

"I think he's still with the doc. I saw his mother earlier. Very upset."

"I can imagine. Drugs will do that to a parent."

"Anyway, listen, could I get the phone records for my room? I dialed a number this morning that was written on a napkin, and then I lost the napkin, and I need to call that number again." Dave rolled his eyes and made a goofy face. "I'm such a klutz sometimes."

Gabbie beamed her patented I-deal-with-klutzy-people-all-day smile at Dave and clicked away on her computer. The printer behind her went to work and thirty seconds later she handed him a paper with the desired information. "Thank you so much Gabbie. And thank you again for your help this morning. You were a doll."

Dave shot her his own radiant grin, and hurried back to his bungalow. He sat in the chair by the phone and read the printout. Gabbie had given him a full listing of all calls made and received since check-in. Every morning, the same number had been called at around the same time. He didn't need to be Sherlock Holmes to see the pattern. The calls were made while he was jogging on the beach. And the number was not the Pierson residence; he knew it by heart. He dialed the mystery number on the paper.

"Good afternoon, this is Shaeffer, Pierson, and Locke. How can I help you?" a perky receptionist asked.

Dave was quick on his feet. "Is Martin in?"

"He is, but he's meeting a client. May I take a message and have him call you back?"

"No thanks, I'll try him later." Dave slammed the phone down, hand shaking. Penny had lied. She hadn't called Renee. She'd called Martin. At his firm. Where he allegedly wasn't working due to sickness.

Dave closed his eyes. "There's a reasonable explanation," he said to the empty bungalow. Sure there was.

A surprise party for Renee's birthday? It just passed in August.

A surprise party for Dave's birthday? Wasn't until April of '90.

The kids' birthdays? Already gone for the year.

Dave sat back and grappled with a dark reality. His wife, his wingman for seventeen years, mother of his children. Betraying him. With his best friend since college. Losing two staples in his life at once. And after Molly...

Why didn't I see it?

Small memories flashed behind his eyes. Little looks he'd observed but dismissed as nothing. Martin appraising Penny's ass when she walked away a few months ago while Dave and Martin sipped cold beers and grilled steaks in Dave's backyard. Dave noticed, but what guy wouldn't look—her ass *was* spectacular. During that same dinner night, Dave had walked into the kitchen to get another beer to find Penny and Martin talking quietly. They had acted normal and Dave hadn't given it a second thought. Three weeks before the trip to Riptide Island, Dave and Penny had joined Martin and Renee for a wedding. Renee's niece, Sasha, got hitched to a car salesman. During the reception, Martin asked Dave for permission to dance with Penny. Dave, of course, shooed them on the dance floor and took that time to dance with Renee. Innocent fun. Best friends enjoying an evening out. Nothing to be concerned about. Except Dave had noticed—again dismissing as harmless—Martin's hand creep a little low on Penny's spine. It hadn't been an aggressive cheek-grab, but the fingers had ventured beyond the friend zone. The party had gone past midnight and, later, both of them tipsy from champagne, Penny had wiped his memory clean of any potential concerns about stray hands when she unzipped her gown before they climbed into bed.

Many small shots of behavior that, singled out over time, had meant nothing. But when spliced together, a disturbing pattern emerged. Dave couldn't believe he'd missed the signs.

He swiped his hands across his face to dry the moisture dripping from his eyes. Nervous energy pushed him out the door and down the beach. Crashing waves and the steady urging of the wind soothed his anxiety. Allowed him to think. To wonder where it all went wrong. He and Penny had always been so happy together. Molly's death certainly strained the relationship, no denying that. Dave had been grappling with acceptance, the same as Penny. They hadn't been grappling together, not at first, and that had been the problem. Little by little each of them had maneuvered that emotional obstacle course in such a way that it had led them back to one another. Nothing had ever been the same as before, never would, but the two of them had found a rhythm. The *family* had found a rhythm.

So where did it stray?

Dave rewound the tape on the past two years. Slowed the play speed and tried to pick a tangible moment that would explain why.

Deep inside he knew the answer. Molly's death had broken the marriage. It started the day she had disappeared from the playground during a birthday party at the park. Dave and Penny had frantically searched everywhere before calling police. By the time the officers arrived, he and Penny had been in a full-blown panic. Penny had fainted. Dave had almost joined her. A dozen officers and the parents at the party scoured the area. The woods behind the park, knocking on neighbors doors, checking backyards. A roadblock had been set up around the perimeter of the park, and police searched any suspicious vehicle.

But Molly had disappeared without a trace.

The next three days had been like living inside a world made of the white noise you see on the television at night after the station signed off—usually with the American flag proudly waving to the sound of the national anthem. Dave hadn't been able to eat. His stomach had been twisted like a pretzel. All he had been able to do was sit by the phone now manned by Detective Adams and Detective Boatright. Search teams had been on the streets, looking under every rock. Other detectives had put pressure on CIs and snitches, questioning anyone out on parole, anyone who had a history of pedophilia, kidnapping, or had been deemed a person of interest for one reason or another.

No one had known anything.

Four days after Molly disappeared, Detective's Adam and Boatright had sat Dave and Penny down and broke the news. Molly had been found. By two boys fishing in the river. Police had pulled her body from the water.

Nothing prepared a parent to hear their child had died. It had been like drowning while someone repeatedly stabbed him in the chest with garden shears. Dave had never felt pain like that in his life and had hoped he never would again.

Three weeks later, police stormed the residence of William "Willie" Timothy. His fingerprints had been found on one of Molly's shoes. He had also been identified by one of the residents who lived beside the park as their landscaper. The resident told police Willie had been working that day, but vanished before he finished cutting the grass.

As police had kicked down Willie's door, a shotgun blast sent the team scrambling. Thirty minutes later, after a deputy spotted feet through a dirty window, officers had discovered Willie on the kitchen floor. His head had been blown clean off his shoulders, grey matter, bone shrapnel, and blood wallpapering the ceiling and cabinets. A double-barrel shotgun had lain beside the body. A search of the house had rendered a bedroom with chains and straps, bloodstains on the mattress. Tests had confirmed the blood to be Molly's.

Molly's last breath had been the end of her suffering, but it had been the beginning of Dave's. It had been the type of pain that etched constant thoughts of suicide into the skin of his psyche. And he'd almost done it. Sitting on his riding mower in his shop, gun in hand, safety thrown, chamber loaded. Easy to end it all and go see his baby girl. But a knock at the door had changed his mind. And his heart. He had wiped the tears away, hid the gun on a shelf behind some old paint cans, and opened the door to Jessica. His other baby girl. Who had still needed him. Despite the grief. Despite the pain. She had been dealing with her own sadness at losing a sister whom she adored.

How selfish am I? Dave had asked himself while Jessica waited for him to answer a question he hadn't heard. "Say again," he had said.

"Will you push me on the swing?"

He had closed the door and pushed her on the swing. For hours. A small and trivial act to most, but to Dave, it had changed everything. A new outlook. A reconciliation to his marriage. A slow emergence from the fog of loss to the clear skies of promise. Life changing.

"I like the beach."

Dave jerked at the voice which belonged to the mother of the overdose kid.

Susan? He thought that was correct.

"Yeah, me, too." Dave was put off by her presence. He wanted to swim in the dark waters of his thoughts. He realized he had tears streaming down his cheeks, and wiped them away.

Susan sat in the sand next to his feet. Oblivious to his mental strife. Dealing with her own problems.

Everybody's got 'em, Dave thought, and sat next to her.

"How's your son?" Dave asked, staring across the ocean.

"Fine. He will live," Susan answered. The weight of her despair pounding the words flat.

"Sorry."

Susan turned to Dave. Met his gaze, held it. "You are upset."

Dave had only met this woman briefly. Knew nothing of her beyond her first name and that she had a son who did drugs and almost died from that usage. Yet, something in her called to him. It happened earlier on the porch steps of the clinic. That was why he asked her name. It was the reason he threatened the doctor.

Before he could stop himself, Dave spilled his troubles on the beach. All of it. From Penny, to Molly, to the moment he sat next to Susan in the sand. He couldn't stop the purge. Even if he wanted. And the relief was enlightening. To say it, to let it out, leeching the poison from inside him. No longer alone on his king-sized bed of razor-wire.

Susan listened. Never interrupted. Perhaps glad to hear someone else had problems too. Not just her. "Sorry."

"Sorry to unload on you," Dave said. But he wasn't sorry. Not at all.

"I need a drink," she said after a moment of comfortable silence. "I have bourbon in my room. Care to join?"

Dave was confused. "There's no ... mister?"

"No." No other explanation. And maybe none was needed.

Dave stared at the waves washing closer to his feet, brushed sand off his lap. He was speechless. Not by her invitation, but by the excitement he felt. Like a schoolboy on his first date with his crush. He knew it was wrong. Knew the hurt had weakened him, turned him petty and immature. Knew this was not the answer. Knew it all and still wanted to go anyway.

Repercussions, rang in his ear like a funeral bell. He ignored it.

"I'd love to."

Dave should've felt guilt. He should've had reservations. He should've probed the reasons for the lack of sound judgement. But he refused. He had been betrayed by the one person he trusted most. His life was in shambles. He was headed for divorce, his children were about to be upended. He owed it to himself. This gift.

He followed her to Tsunami Suites like an obedient dog, tongue wagging as he took in her messy morning hair, pulled up in a bun, sexy as hell. Her neck, tanned and freckled. Her compact, athletic body. She walked funny, but it was probably because she was barefoot. Stepping on the smallest pebble would be painful.

Followed her inside her room, looking out over the pool.

She poured two glasses, handed him one. He clinked his glass against Susan's, anticipation as dark as the liquid sloshing back and forth. Dave took one sip before Susan grabbed the glass from his hand, sat it on the counter, and pulled him to her bedroom. She pushed him down on the bed, opened her robe. This was the first naked body other than Penny's Dave had seen in almost twenty years. A needle of guilt injected itself in his chest, but Susan was already on top of him, straddling his hips and the growth there.

"We are glad you came," Susan said.

For the first time since Susan arrived on the beach, Dave caught a detail he had missed in his grief and depression. Compelled by her, he'd overlooked the obvious.

She sounded like the doctor.

Susan's head detonated into a tangle of stick-like legs, writhing and lashing, bursting from her mouth, eyes, ears, nose. Dave screamed and tried to scramble from beneath her. Susan's legs clamped around his waist, holding him firm. Susan lowered herself to him, and Dave involuntarily pushed his head into the bed, trying to distance his face from the approaching mass of appendages wrapping his face. A lone, slender, slimy tentacle, different in color and design from the spider-like legs encapsulating his head, reached his lips, burrowing through even though Dave pinched them tight. The tentacle reached his teeth and slithered back and forth like a slimy tongue, searching for an opening. Denied access, it retreated only to slither up his lip to his nose, the tip probing inside the nostril.

Dave unleashed the pent-up fear, anger, and pain. It burst from him in a fit of rage and survival instinct. His athletic past proved valuable, the strength and conditioning he'd undergone since middle school. He was up off the bed and running across the bedroom with Susan in his arms before he even realized he'd done it. Momentum carried him through a pair of sliding patio doors, knocking them off the track where they shattered on the concrete. A few older couples lounged in the sun, napping, until the breaking glass startled them awake. Dave never saw them. He was racing blindly with Medusa strapped to his chest. Air replaced the concrete beneath his feet and he tilted forward to prepare for a landing. Water splashed around him and Dave sucked in a breath before he dropped below the surface of the pool.

Susan's reaction was as shocking as it was instantaneous. She detached herself from Dave and began twisting and thrashing, alien parts seizing as though being fried in boiling grease. An inhuman high-frequency shriek managed to erupt from the frothing water, sending panicked seagulls squawking away from the threat. Dave swam away quickly, climbed the ladder, and stood by the edge of the pool, watching in horror as Susan's skin blistered red, then black. Boils bubbled and burst. Even submersed in water, she smoked. The splashing slowly subsided, then stopped altogether. Susan's blackened body sank to the bottom and rested there. Severed, charred legs floated to the top of the water, a few flicking back and forth before stilling from death. Dave stared, disbelief like concrete around his feet. Shocked stupid, his brain unable to think. Pattering feet caught his attention and he looked up to find four senior citizens, two males and two6 females, disappearing around the corner of the building. Dave had the courtyard to himself.

Instinct and decorum said he should report the incident to the front desk. But Dave was on auto-pilot. Numb, removed from himself. Like an observer in someone else's nightmare. Walkways carried him across manicured lawns, past trimmed hedges and landscaping trees as though he were on a magic carpet ride. Floating, the world was bent and out of focus. Sunlight blinded him with its harsh, judging glare. Humidity wrapped around him, and squeezed. Further admonishments for his sins.

Cool air embraced him. Dave blinked, and reality reinstated itself. He was in his bungalow, standing by the air conditioner vent. The trip from Tsunami Suites was nothing but a forgettable blur.

Dave stumbled to the bathroom and his expensive lunch courtesy of Amazonia joined the blue water in the toilet. He undressed and practically fell into the cold shower. He refused to think, or remember. The water rinsed the worst of the disconnect away. Dave felt a little better by the time he dried off and put on fresh clothes.

Lying in bed, he replayed the afternoon in his mind, still struggling to believe what had just happened. Was this really real? Dave couldn't help but wonder if it was all just a dream. And he was about to wake up and laugh about it, relieved that his wife wasn't cheating on him, a dead woman had not come back to life to stalk his family, and monsters didn't exist.

He pinched himself and groaned. He was very much awake and this was very much real.

Frightening knowledge to carry. But worse, knowing the doctor was like Susan.

She, too, was a monster.

Thirty-One

Corey popped two Wide Eyed caffeine tablets and drowned them in half-a-cup of coffee. Max was on the way, and Simon was pacing. Simon had received a call thirty minutes ago from NASA about a report of strange images captured by the HPL0927 satellite. It was an obsolete relic that was not used much anymore and would become space junk once NASA launched their new modern marvel, The Hubble Space Telescope, next year, but still had imaging capabilities. Deep Sky used the satellite sparingly from time to time to help them in their endeavors.

While Corey waited on NASA to send the images, he began triangulating a theoretical path. Where it had potentially come from and where it had been heading. Academic guesswork at best.

Hayley, known as Comet to everyone at Deep Sky, was helping Corey with the project. She was a petite, dorky girl who wore her thin brown hair in ponytails every single day. She moved at the pace of a galloping horse and carried a business-like persona. She'd never called in sick and took her job seriously. She was smart as hell and her work ethic was out of this world. Needless to say, everyone loved her and hated her at the same time.

Comet yelled across the room. "Images coming up!"

Corey jumped to his feet as the photos loaded to the big screen. A blurry, pixelated shot slowly cleared to show a gorgeous view of Earth, a magnificence Corey never tired of seeing. At the edge of the frame, caught at the last second, was what appeared to be flames.

"Zoom in on the anomaly," Simon instructed as he stomped toward the front of the room.

Corey couldn't see anything other than the tips of flames, but he kept this to himself. He was on Simon's shit list. No need saying something that moved him to number one on the terminated list.

Comet painstakingly expanded the image while scrolling sideways right to left. Earth grew larger and fuzzier, as did the flames. She pounded the keyboard to use every ounce of image scaling capacity the system possessed to clear the fuzziness.

"That's the best it will do, sir," Comet said to Simon.

"What do you think, Corey?" Simon called from his position in front of the screen. "Still look like a ghost in the machine?"

Smart ass prick. Corey scratched some phantom itch on his scalp and pointed at the screen. "Well, sir, obviously not. But we still don't know what *it* is. All I see is a little fire. This has all the signs of a shooting star. And that could explain the reason we lost sight of it. It was moving so fast the satellites didn't have time to refresh and capture the next image."

Simon stared at Corey for a full minute without saying a word. As were the dozen other desk jockeys in the room. This was a cinematic masterpiece compared to the dull drudgery of normal day-to-day operations.

Finally, Simon said to Comet. "Give us the next one."

Comet clicked a few buttons and the first shot was replaced by another pixelated mess. Back in the server room, lights flashed and parts snapped and cooling fans whirred to life, scrubbing the large squares into a viewable portrayal of what had entered Earth's solar system.

Corey gasped. The entire room sprung to foot in unison as if a drill sergeant had marched in demanding attention. Mouths agape, they all stared in silence. Grappling with the impossibility. Logical, analytical minds witnessing a counter-balance to all they knew and believed. Scientific faiths—not to mention spiritual faiths—were being demolished at the very moment.

Corey knew how they felt. He couldn't believe what he was seeing. But for now, his internal debates were reactionary to the situation. How had that *thing* disappeared from their radar? *Why* had it disappeared? And what was it? Where did it come from?

Corey combed his fingers through his hair as the most important question came to mind.

Where was it going?

Simon was suddenly in Corey's face. He pointed at the big screen. "Does that look like a fucking ghost in the machine?" He chastised, spraying Corey's cheek with hot, angry spittle.

Corey only shook his head. "No sir. It looks like the spawn of Hell hurtling through space."

"And where do you *theorize* it was going?"

Corey felt deflated. This was his doom. "Earth."

Thirty-Two

Paranoia was like a cancer. Eating away at all the good. Rationale stood no chance in the wake of such a ferocious hunger. Everyone became suspect. Every eye was watching. Every ear was listening. Innocent bystanders were rogue agents following every movement, predicting future decisions based on past choices.

That's how Jared felt anyway. The park was packed, and each mom or dad, aunt or uncle, brother or sister he passed appeared to be on surveillance. Ready to report the location of the fleeing humans who were not willing participants in whatever fiendish scheme was at play on Riptide Island.

Even children were suspect.

Jared pushed through a cluster of people before Cindy yanked her hand away. He spun in panic, sure she was being snatched, to find her hunched over, hands on knees, gasping. He'd been running in a white haze, scared out of his mind by what he saw come out of Lawrence's face and what happened to Wes. He hadn't checked on Cindy.

"You okay?"

Cindy held up her hand, dropped four fingers, left one standing. *Just a second.*

Jared felt exposed out in the open like this. He scanned the crowd, checked each face for blank stares. Each body movement for weird mannerisms. Any sign that gave the perpetrators away. But everyone seemed normal. Eating sandwiches, drinking drinks, looking over the colored paper maps that showed the layout of the entire park, a mother soothing her daughter who scraped her knee when she tripped. Oblivious to the horrors happening behind the scenes.

Jared flinched at a flashback of Lawrence. "Okay, hey, we need to go."

Cindy nodded. "Fine, but where are we going?"

"To the marina. We'll hide there until the ferry comes."

Cindy fell in behind Jared as they carved a path across the park and arrived at the marina. Jared wiped the sweat from his forehead as he entered the Riptide Island Arrival/Departure Building. It had the feel of a government installation. Block walls, shiny linoleum floors, and drab colors. Hard plastic chairs with metal legs. Not a single luxury appointment anywhere. A stark contrast to the beauty of the park. The designers of Riptide Rapids wanted patrons in the park spending money, not wasting time in here.

Glenda Barnes, the receptionist, only added to the military persona.

Jared was surprised it was so empty, even if the ferry was hours from arrival.

"Hey Glenda," Jared said, aiming for nonchalant. Probably missing the mark.

"Jared." Glenda said flatly.

Jared would have been suspect but Glenda always sounded like that. Her features matched her voice; sour face, small, hooded eyes, blocky shoulders, thin lips. The woman was the definition of dreary.

"Listen, I have a family emergency and Larry gave me and Cindy permission to go mainland to handle it. We're gonna catch the next ferry and be back middle of next week."

Glenda wiped an imaginary crumb off the surface of the desk. "Afraid you're not going anywhere, sport. Ferry's broke down. Larry knows this. Why would he give you permission to leave if you can't leave?"

Cindy was quick on her feet. "Larry gave us permission yesterday actually, but we were waiting to be one hundred percent sure we really needed to go."

Glenda shrugged. "You missed the boat then, darling. The ferry broke down on the way back here late yesterday evening. Had to be towed back by a tug. Mechanics are on it but I hear there was extensive damage to the rotors and the engine. It looks like a few days at least. A week or so at most."

"Why was it coming back late yesterday evening?" Jared asked.

"An incident here on the island. Couple of boys got up to no good and jumped a kid. Messed him up pretty good from what I hear. Moe was sending them back to the mainland to face the music. But the ferry broke down. As I said."

Coincidence? Maybe. But Jared wasn't convinced. This was a big one. How "they" pulled it off, he had no idea, but he had no doubt whoever—or whatever—was behind this had disabled the ferry. A few more days provided ample time to spread the infection like wildfire. More people catching it meant more bodies were available to spread it.

Riptide would fall in a few days.

"What about all the people who were scheduled to leave?" Cindy asked.

"They got a free extension to their stay. Yippee for them."

"Thanks," Jared patted the countertop. He moved to the far corner of building, faintly shadowed, and took a seat. He needed to think.

"Seems weird," Cindy said. "Ferry breaking down now."

"Is it possible that someone who is infected got on that ferry and sabotaged the engine?"

Cindy peered out the wall of glass at the ocean, lost in thought. "In most cases I would say no; the doors down to the engine room are locked at all times. But this isn't most cases. Keeping everyone on this island for as long as possible would benefit whatever this is. From the perspective of the infection, hindering the ferry from returning would be paramount for survival."

"My thoughts exactly." Jared added, "What that means is, when the ferry does return, thousands of foreign and domestic citizens are going to return to the mainland—"

"—to spread this thing to the entire planet," Cindy finished, her body going ramrod straight.

Jared had no idea if that theory was literal or figurative. End of the world, doomsday scenarios were a bit dramatic in either case. But the worms that burst from Lawrence's mouth were proof that the infection was real, and it was spreading. Lawrence had been fine the day before. Keith had been dead, arm mangled to the point of almost being severed, and now he was alive and his arm intact, less than twenty-four hours later. The list of known carriers continued to grow and it had only been a day. Imagine what a week would look like.

Imagine this infection unleashed on the global population. Wasn't figurative to Jared.

"We have to find a way to stop it," Jared heard himself say. Brave talk for someone who was quivering inside. He'd almost pissed himself when Lawrence transformed. He'd never backed down from a fight in his life, but goddamnit, this was a fight against an entity he'd never known was real. If he lost a fight in the past, he had simply gotten his ass whipped. If he lost this fight, he'd be spitting tentacles. Lot more at stake.

Cindy started pacing in front of him. "We keep calling this an infection. Right?"

"Right."

"And we call it that because infections can spread."

"I said that because I didn't know what else to call it, but sure."

"Typically, if you get the flu, you go to the doctor, get some medicine, and the medication helps your body fight off the virus."

"Okay. Are you saying we should give Lawrence some penicillin and send him to bed?" Jared knew she was working to a point. He wished she would get there.

"No, what I'm saying is that's simply treating the infection. But I would think the way to stop something like this is to kill the source. To kill the source, we need to *find* the source. Understand?"

Jared hadn't thought of that. They were focused on the soldiers. But what produced those soldiers? Who was the Colonel?

Riptide Island was secluded. The closest body of land was Florida. The next closest was Cuba. The only access to the island was by boat. Larry had mentioned a future project involving the addition of a helicopter pad but that was still in the planning phase with architects and structural engineers.

Either the ferry brought someone infected with the virus to the island or someone with the virus arrived by some other boat. Arriving via the ferry was questionable. And why come to Riptide to infect people if the host was already on the mainland where it could infect millions as it pleased?

The Colonel arrived on this island by a boat other than the ferry. It had to.

"Oh, no," Cindy whispered, pausing her back and forth.

"What's wrong?" Jared asked, following her eyes.

Standing outside, staring at them through the wall of insulated storefront glass, was Lawrence.

And Wes.

Thirty-Three

One guarantee for a waterpark this far south was hot weather 365 days a year. And swimming pools were magnets to people when the sun was popping and the humidity was so high fish were sweating.

Megalodon Waves was crowded and loud. Kids screaming, water splashing, lifeguards shouting at a couple of unruly teenagers who were flashing their butt cracks at girls, and music blaring over the marine speakers hidden in various design pieces like the forty-foot fiberglass shark towering over Pete and Nola as they entered the pool area. *(I've Had) The Time Of My Life* by Bill Medley and Jennifer Warnes was currently playing, and no doubt Pete's mom was singing her heart out along with the track. Pete was not a fan of adult contemporary but he had to admit—not out loud, not to anyone, not *ever*—that the song wasn't too bad. Catchy even.

Pete blocked out the noise and focused on the mission at hand: check in with his parents, tell them he loved them, find Nola's parents so she could do the same, go fight an invisible unspecified foe, probably die.

Pete checked for Keith again but either Pete and Nola had lost the tail or Keith had given up. Giving up seemed a far-fetched fantasy. If he no longer followed them, there had to be a good reason.

Pete flirted with the idea that those who were infected shared thoughts. A hive mind. He'd studied hive mentality in science last year. Mr. Wang had spent a lot of time on it, saying he found the subject interesting, and thought the class would enjoy the lesson as well. Pete had never been less bored at school in his life. Individual bees and ants used the hive mentality to achieve a group goal. Humans used it as well, in sports, in construction, in daily life where each person performed a task to contribute to the team's overall objective. Pete had found it fascinating, though he had never imagined it would be applicable in this type of scenario.

Nola had mentioned that when Pete was on the exam table in the doctor's office, and the sound of footsteps announced the arrival of visitors—Jared and Cindy—Lyla had sucked the legs back in her head, then looked at Keith. She'd said nothing, but Keith had quickly left the room. As if Lyla had spoken aloud and told him to hide. Nola said Lyla had an expression on her face like she was speaking without moving her lips. Nola had even asked Pete if he understood what she meant. Pete had. It was the look his mom had given him many times as a younger, rambunctious kid when she told him to sit down and be quiet without opening her mouth. The widening eyes, the set of the lips, the threatening posture. A clear message sent without a word spoken.

Was Keith's reaction just an automatic understanding that he needed to hide, or was Nola correct and Lyla had spoken to Keith telepathically? Pete wasn't sure, but his instincts said it was telepathic.

It made sense too. The infection needed to spread and it needed host bodies in order to do so. Staying mentally connected ensured a strong bond as the numbers doubled and tripled. The main goal remained the main goal.

And if Pete was right, and the infected were linked together by some invisible phone line, then Keith pulling off following Pete and Nola potentially meant a greater threat had risen somewhere else. The only other humans that knew what was happening was Jared and Cindy.

"I want to say again how sorry I am."

Pete was so lost in thought, he hadn't noticed Johnathon's mom approaching until she was standing in front of him. His feet stuttered under him.

"Um, yeah, thanks," Pete said, tongue imitating feet. His mind was grappling with the fact that she was still here. In the park. *Where's the asshole Johnathon?*

She must've read the question on his face. "Don't worry. That trouble-making son of mine is still in custody here on the island."

"I thought you were leaving last night?" Nola said with an ocean of attitude to spare.

Johnathon's mother—*what was her name?*—smiled grimly. "You haven't heard? The ferry broke down. We get to stay a few more days free of charge. I feel bad for Johnathon being cooped up in that jail cell, but it's like I told him this morning, 'You made your bed, now you gotta lie in it.'"

Pete barely heard anything after "the ferry broke down." All these people trapped. And not even aware of it. His theory about spreading the infection mainland was looking more and more like a reality.

"How did the ferry break down?" Pete asked.

Johnathon's mom frowned. "Not sure. All they said was engine trouble. Had to be towed back to the mainland for repair. Why?"

To Nola, Pete said, "We have to find Jared and Cindy after we check in with our parents." He went around Johnathon's mom and hurried down the length of the pool, eyes flicking across each lounge chair for signs of his mom and dad.

"Pete!" He heard his mom shout. "Over here!"

On the back row, in the middle of a sea of sunbathers, Pete's mom waved a hand. She was wearing a big floppy straw hat Pete had never seen before and the same sunglasses she'd had for years.

"You go check in and meet back at the giant shark in ten," Nola said. "I'll find my parents then we can go."

"What should we tell them?" Pete whispered, leaning close so no one overheard. "They're in danger."

"Say you love them. It might be your last chance." With that grim forecast unleashed, Nola left.

Pete weaved through loud water-dripping children and sat down in the empty chair his mother had saved for him.

"Everything go okay with the doctor?" His mom asked, situating her body for maximum sun exposure. She was an overweight woman who worked forty hours a week and took care of everything for Pete and his dad. She never laid out or took time for herself. It was a sacrifice Pete took for granted. In fact, never considering it until that moment of watching her relax. She sat up, leaned close, raising her sunglasses. "Your eye looks atrocious. I hope that cut doesn't scar."

"Took you a long time," Pete's dad added. He looked half asleep.

It tends to take a while when someone wants to abduct your body and turn you into some sort of tentacled monster, Pete thought. Instead, he said, "Yeah, she wanted to be thorough. Make sure I'm good."

"Are you good?" His mom asked, pushing her shades back in place, relaxing again.

"Yeah, mom, I'm fine." Pete wanted to say more. Something lame like thanking her for being his mom. In the end, he decided to keep it simple. He needed to get going. Time was ticking away. "Mom, I'm going to hang with Nola since this is our last day here. I'll come back later to check in."

His mom smiled. "You like her, huh? What's going to happen when we go back?"

"I don't know, Mom. We'll figure it out." Pete stood, then leaned over, kissed her on a sweaty, sunscreen-lathered cheek. "Love you."

"Love you too, sweetie. Have fun." She added, "And we'll talk about what happened tonight. No if's, and's, or but's."

"Yes, ma'am."

Pete took one more look, a snapshot to save just in case.

Back at the shark, Pete waited for Nola, staying in the shade cast by the giant fiberglass sea predator. The sun was relentless. The wind blowing off the ocean provided only the slightest relief. The people who built this park on an island certainly knew what they were doing. Always hot, almost always sunny. Throw in cold water, cool colors, fun rides, and the perfect people attraction was formed.

Pete wondered what the island had been like before the park was built. He had noticed on the ferry ride in that the southern most section of the island was still wild jungle. The automated voice recording that played over the speakers during the trip to Riptide Island had mentioned that Riptide Rapids used only about half of the island and the other half remained in its natural state, as formed over twenty-five million years ago. Pete had read the brochure on the island the first night at the park. The whole concept of a waterpark on an island formed by volcanic activity intrigued him. The amount of work and resources necessary to take on such an endeavor seemed incredible.

Among the information shared in the brochure was a section dedicated to the history of the island. It said the reason for only half of the island being developed for the park was because the other half was wrought with caves, and rocky slopes and cliffs. It was too costly and time consuming to build anything on that side.

Infecting the citizens on an island was a sound strategy. Isolated. One way on and one way off. Easier to control. But why this island? There were hundreds of islands in the Gulf, the South Atlantic, the Atlantic. What was special about this island?

With any virus, conditions had to be perfect to survive. Abundant food source, favorable climate, ideal geography. Just to name a few. It seemed unlikely this infection accidentally landed on this island. Too many coincidences. He was unsure about a lot of things, but he was confident in the infection's agenda, and to succeed in that agenda, the infection knew Riptide Island would provide the necessary items needed to flourish.

And to know that, the infection had to have some prior knowledge of the island. Otherwise it would have had to be here awhile to gather the information to formulate a world dominance plan. Pete didn't think the infection could survive that long without spreading. If that had happened, the agenda would have occurred before now.

"Hey," Nola said, giving him a kiss. "You good?"

"Yeah," Pete said. "You find your parents?"

"I did. They're good. Mom's already tipsy. Six feet deep in mimosa's at two in the afternoon."

"Good." Pete started walking. "We need to get up with Jared and Cindy. I've been thinking; what if this island has something to do with the infection?"

"How?"

"I don't know," Pete answered honestly. Ideas and theories swirled around like frantic ghosts, wispy and barely visible. "I haven't gotten that far. But, what if this was targeted. Premeditated. Which presents a slew of probabilities. We need to find Jared and Cindy so we can hash it out. See if I'm onto something, or just full of shit."

"Where should we look? They could be anywhere."

"We were all planning to go to the port to catch the ferry. There is no ferry, but we didn't know that until a few minutes ago. Maybe they don't either and went there to wait on us. As good a place to start as any."

Pete tried to ignore the swelling dread creeping along his flesh. The island was almost 700 acres and yet claustrophobia was setting in. He wished he didn't know everyone on the island was trapped. Or that some sinister disease was spreading. He wished to be back in the pool the day before, talking to Nola for the first time. To feel the skittish butterflies in his stomach. Oblivion was bliss.

Thirty-Four

Dave stepped out of the insane October heat into the cool confines of the security office. His shirt was soaked on the back and armpits just from the short walk from the bungalow to this office. Midwest summers had nothing on this place.

The main entrance was like any police station in America. Depressing gray walls, squeaky clean linoleum flooring, minimalist furnishings. Antiseptic at best. Smelled like bleach and coffee. A big mahogany wood grained desk blocked off the entryway from the bullpen which consisted of a few cubicles, a coffee area, some still-new file cabinets. A door to his left was probably the portal back to the rest of the building. No one was at the counter so Dave tapped the shiny steel bell with a placard leaning in front of it that read RING ME. The bell chimed but no one came out.

"Hey! Is someone out there?"

Dave stood on his tip-toes, trying to see past the pre-fab cubicle walls to locate the voice. "Yeah. You security? I need to file a report."

"No, I'm in a cell. The security guard is lying on the floor in the hallway, and ... man, something is very wrong with him."

Dave had no idea what to do. Was this a joke? A ruse by the prisoner—*on an island?*—to trick Dave into helping him escape?

"I'll go for help," Dave said. "I'll be back."

"No! The security guard is shaking and shit's coming out of his mouth. He's gonna die if you don't do something."

Why does this keep happening to me?

Dave wasn't sure if he could watch another person die, or deal with another trauma. But as much as he wanted to drop this problem in someone else's lap, he was here and in a position to help. Besides, once he found someone to assist, that person would simply call the doctor, and Dave knew what happened then.

He tried the door to the bullpen and was surprised to find it unlocked. Through the doorway was a pathway between small, empty cubicle spaces and six four-foot-high tan file cabinets leading to a hallway that disappeared to the back of the building. Dave rounded the corner to the corridor, and, there on the floor, was a seizing guard. He was a big fella, six-foot-three at least, and dressed out at about two-eighty. A clotted, milky liquid that reminded Dave of clam chowder frothed from his mouth. His eyes were rolled back in his head and his arms were clutched to his chest like he was holding a baby. His body trembled as if freezing cold.

"See man, told you."

The voice belonged to a pimple-faced boy of about eighteen or nineteen with the first signs of a mustache. His complexion was erratic, white forehead, red cheeks, splotchy neck. He was inside an actual jail cell, knuckles colorless from a frenzied grip on the bars. Across from him was another cell holding another boy of about the same age. He was watching the guard in wide-eyed terror, silent as a church mouse.

Dave skipped the pleasantries and dropped to a knee beside the guard. The fluid leaking from his mouth was chunky with what appeared to be meat. The steel handcuffs clipped to the guard's side vibrated against the linoleum. Dave had never seen an epileptic seizure but had heard of them. Maybe the guard was prone to these convulsions. Dave tried to sift through his memory for information that might be applicable. He could only remember the part about placing something in the patient's mouth to protect the tongue. The guard's lips were parted, as were his teeth. His mouth almost looked relaxed, especially when compared to the rest of him.

Maybe this isn't an epileptic fit.

What else could it be?

Dave retreated so fast his feet tangled and he fell back. A dawning horror rose like a full moon inside him. This may be how it started with Susan. After meeting with the doctor. Whatever the doctor was, whatever she passed along, this may be how the transformation began. Susan had been a normal human on the porch before going inside. Hours later, she'd become something else. Something alien to planet Earth. A change like that didn't just happen. There had to be a reconfiguration of the body. Organs, muscles, ligaments, tendons, blood vessels, electrical activity, motor skills, bone structure, flesh. Maybe even cellular. Atoms and neutrons. A spoiling of DNA.

"How was he acting when he came back here?" Dave asked. "Just before this happened."

"Weird, spaced out. Sweating really bad. He was walking strange. Like his legs didn't work right. I asked him for water and he stared at me like I was from another planet. Then he grunted, clinched his stomach, and fell to the floor. Started this shit."

"And before that? Earlier today? This morning?"

"Uh, normal, man. I don't know. The same as last night when he arrested me."

He's got it. Same as Susan. Same as the doctor.

Dave could be wrong and, if so, he was putting this man's life at risk, but after what he went through an hour ago, he was taking no chances.

The boys were in danger. Leaving them behind was out of the question. When the guard finished his transformation, they would be the first humans he attacked.

A set of keys hung from his belt loop, jingling like wind chimes. Dave spread his feet and crouched low, crab-walking toward the guard. He leaned forward and stretched his arms, reaching for the keys while maintaining as much distance as possible with his body. His fingers brushed the ring. He needed to get closer. He shimmied his feet, gaining an inch. Now his fingers reached the ring. He fiddled with the carabiner that attached the ring of keys to the guard's belt loop.

Dave could now see the man's name badge: Moe.

Moe, I need you to stay cool buddy.

Dave refocused on the carabiner, squeezing the spring-loaded latch with his thumb and first finger. Two options remained: lift the carabiner and shake the keys loose, or move closer still and remove the keys with his left hand. Shaking the clip seemed like the safer bet. He gave it a rattle and a lift. The keys slipped free and landed on the guard's dark blue pants.

"Watch out!" the pimple-faced kid yelled.

Dave barely registered the words when arms wrapped around his head.

Thirty-Five

"Le conté a una mujer blanca sobre los gringos que vimos ayer," Manuel said to his boss, Javier, while fluffing the pine straw. The flowerbeds were messy after the workers installed all the Halloween decorations. Stomped the straw flat. Unsightly to management.

Javier stared at him like he was stupid. "Why would you do such a thing?"

Javier's English was really good because he spoke it more often than Spanish. Manuel found the dialect clunky and confusing. He preferred the native tongue, but Javier was always busting the workers balls—or vaginas in a few cases—about speaking in English. Being in America and all.

Manuel mentally worked through the words before speaking. "She really worried. One was her man."

Javier shook his head with dramatic flare. Big and sweeping. "No, no, no. You mind your own damn business. I've told all of you many times. Out of sight, out of mind. That's how we fly under the radar." Javier's eyes went glassy as he lowered his voice to repeat his favorite mantra. "The money is good. The cabins are nice. The food is wonderful. And occasionally we get lucky with a stray who is looking for a little exotic. Why fuck with that?"

Manuel could never tell Javier, but he wanted more. What his boss said was true. Manuel had never lived in a nicer place. Or eaten better. His home in Guerrero had been a clapboard hut held together by chicken wire. He'd gone days without a single morsel of food. Slurping water from mud puddles in the street using drug syringes as drinking straws. Wearing the same filthy, stinking clothes for weeks. Only showering—and subsequently washing his clothes, two for one—when it rained.

Those conditions remained fresh in his mind. The memories drove him to become a criminal and sneak into the United States under fear of capture and deportation.

Javier left Guerrero because he was not content to live like that. He wanted more. He took the job Javier offered due to the islands remote location and the opportunity for bigger and better things. He'd work on Riptide for a few years, save his money, and move to Miami. Register with Immigration. Get a green card. Start his own landscaping business. Become a legitimate American so he could sleep soundly at night. Not have to worry about men in dark clothing and guns breaking down the door and hauling his law-breaking ass back to Mexico.

Then he'd be able to afford to pay for his sister to come to America. He'd take care of her.

Manuel dreamed big, but kept those lofty aspirations to himself. His friends and co-workers wouldn't understand. They were content with the daily grind on the island. Happy to have a purpose that put money in their pockets and food in their bellies.

"Go grab Eduardo and make a run for a fresh load of pine straw," Javier clapped at Manuel. "Vámonos. We gotta finish this fast. Lots to do today."

Manuel leaned the rake in the fork of a Bradford Pear and slipped behind the refreshment hut to pull Eduardo from his smoke break. Eduardo grunted as he stubbed out the butt with his booted toe. He knew better than to complain within earshot of the boss so he followed Manuel to the utility vehicle without a word.

Pine straw bales were stored in two landscaping warehouses at the back left corner of the property. Manuel waited until they were well away from the park before he pulled a plastic baggie from his front pocket, and shook out a thick joint.

Eduardo smiled from behind the wheel. "Lindo."

Manuel lit the tip and took two hard pulls, holding the smoke in his chest as long as he could before cracking and releasing the pressure. He handed the joint to Eduardo who took two puffs of his own. Manuel was light on his feet by the time they arrived at the warehouse and backed up to the pine straw bin.

"Tú carga. Me estoy cagando." Manuel instructed.

Eduardo waved Manuel off, and got to work. The main warehouse had men's and women's bathrooms with toilet stalls. This building only had one small restroom in the front corner. Manuel dropped his trousers and squatted, enjoying the rest of the blunt while nature took its course.

Manuel remembered when his sister, Margarita, had first caught him smoking weed. She'd asked why. Why do drugs? Disappointment had been written all over her face, shoulders slumped.

Manuel had just shrugged and took another hit while she marched away, but he had known the reason. Weed had helped him escape. From the anxiety of his condition. From the fear of being a victim of crime which had run rampant around the city. From being recruited by one drug cartel or another and made a servant of the trade.

Weed calmed his nerves, smoothed out the wrinkles, silenced the troubled voices shouting in his head. Why he still smoked the shit.

A commotion echoed through the warehouse that sounded like a dropped shovel.

Dumbass. Such a klutz, Manuel laughed. Eduardo always tripped over something or got hurt performing the most minimal tasks. The guy was an accident waiting to happen.

Manuel took a puff, held it. Shadows appeared at the bottom of the door. Feet.

"Vete a la mierda, Eduardo!"

After a dead silence, knuckles rapped against the door twice, rattling the cheap residential lock against the metal strike.

Manuel slapped the door with his palm. "Vete a la mierda!"

The shadows remained. Manuel angrily tossed the blunt in the toilet, finished his business, and buckled his trousers. *El idiota lo conseguirá.*

He yanked the door open, opened his mouth to admonish his helper, but found the *mujer* from earlier standing there instead.

Manuel gave the utility cart a quick check. A shovel lay on the ground but there was no sign of Eduardo. The woman stood there, staring like she had lost her marbles.

"You okay?"

The woman nodded. "Now I am."

Legs exploded from her face, and Manuel's dreams of bigger and better things came true.

Thirty-Six

Lawrence and Wes stepped inside the building. Wes turned the thumb bolt on the storefront door, locking them inside.

"Hey, you can't do that," Glenda called, stepping from behind the desk and heading straight for the door to unlock it. "What the hell is your problem?"

"Glenda, don't," Cindy said, taking one step forward, throwing her hand up like a bus traffic officer.

"Hold your horses, honey," Glenda said back, feet squeaking on the polished floor as she marched across the waiting room. "I gotta take care of this asshole."

Lawrence kept his eyes locked on Jared and Cindy while Wes went straight at Glenda. Spider-like arms erupted from his head like a grenade explosion and Glenda screamed. But only for a second. Her mouth was instantly clotted with the pulsating worm, and the screams turned to choking, then gulping. She collapsed on the floor. Jared thought she was dead. Or, *hoped* she was dead. But she started shaking violently, feet tapping the floor, bracelets on her right wrist clacking together.

He knew what that meant.

Lawrence smiled. An evil grin, nothing humorous. "The stars await, Jared," Lawrence said. His voice pulled goosebumps from

Jared's flesh like tweezers on blackheads. "You cannot fathom what lies beyond the moon. Infinite darkness ruled by gods of lost creations. In the company of such majesty, you will realize this life you know is minuscule, inadequate. Meaningless. Like a tiny grain of sand on the beach. That is what you are to us. That is what this planet is to us."

"Then why do this?" Jared was sick to his stomach. But he wanted to know. And maybe Lawrence, glowing with egotistical pride, would slip up. Make a mistake and say something he shouldn't.

"Because without each grain of sand, there would be no beach. Without each star there would be no galaxy. On their own, they mean nothing, but together, unified in vision, they create what you call the heavens. We call it our backyard."

Jared was listening with one side of his brain while thinking with the other. Formulating an escape plan.

"Why this island?" Jared asked. Stalling, but also searching.

Thin, scaly, segmented fingers flared out of Lawrence's ears, disappeared. "Something important to our civilization is here. Has been for a very long time. We spent ions searching and finally located it. Here, on this island. We are here to retrieve it."

"Why not just take it and go? Why murder innocent humans?"

Lawrence tried a laugh. Sounded chunky and uncomfortable. "Converting you strengthens us. Increases our numbers." Lawrence swept his arms around, not at the building, but as an indication of everything. "And we cannot leave because planet Earth is a vast improvement over our own declining planet. This galaxy is an upgrade over our own collapsing system. Our dying species can thrive here, grow and prosper. Your atmosphere is very hospitable."

Jared had no idea how any of those answers helped. He searched for something said that provided a weakness, but damned if he saw one. All he could think to do at the moment was get the hell out of here.

He needed a head start. Something to cause hesitation. "You know you made a mistake, right?"

Lawrence tilted his head, brow furrowing. "Really?"

Jared grabbed Cindy's hand and shot to the back of the building where an exit door was located, grabbing a chair on the way. He heard the footfalls of Lawrence and Wes giving chase, closing quicker than expected. He kicked the exit device bar running horizontal across the metal door, then slammed it shut. He frantically wedged the chair underneath the knob handle, successfully blocking the door. Lawrence and Wes bashed against the door a few times before giving up.

"They're heading out the front doors," Cindy said.

Jared grabbed her hand again, and together they ran. He had no idea where he was going. Blind panic gripped him.

"Jared!"

Jared halted and pivoted. Pete and Nola were running toward them.

"I don't have time to explain," Jared said. "We have to hide."

Pete looked around, pointed toward the Riptide Security Office about fifty yards away. "How about that?"

Jared nodded. "Worth a shot."

They darted inside the front door. Jared threw the deadbolt and pushed the button on the lock. That's when he heard the shouting.

Cindy burst through the door leading to the back of the office and Jared followed. Another nightmare awaited.

Moe was one of them. He lay on his back with thin, hairy legs flailing out of his eyes, nose, ears, and mouth. A man hovered over the thing formerly known as Riptide Rapids security officer, his head snagged by the mass of appendages. He pushed against Moe's body with one hand while swiping at the legs with the other. A single tentacle jabbed at his face, trying to find a way into his mouth. Two boys jumped up and down, shouting in cells on either side of the corridor.

"Help! Help!" One shouted.

"It's trying to eat him!" yelled the other.

Jared hesitated, scared to get close, but he couldn't help the man without doing so. He grabbed the fighter around the waist and tried yanking backward. This accomplished nothing except to lift Moe's body off the floor. Something plastic clattered nearby but Jared was too busy to notice.

Cindy jabbed her hand in his face and he was relieved to see what was gripped in her palm: a stun gun.

He released the fighter, snatched the electrified device out of Cindy's hand, and jabbed it against Moe's neck, pushing the red button with his thumb. The effect was instantaneous. Moe shuddered and the tentacles whipped back inside his head in less than a blink. The fighter fell back against the cell bars, and dropped to his butt, gasping for air. Pete and Nola ran to him, dragging him out of harm's way.

Moe looked like he could've been sleeping or ready to place in a coffin. Not a single outward sign of the monster within was present.

"What was that, man?" one of the boys asked. He was pacing in front of the bars, tears dripping down his cheeks.

Jared ignored him. He crouched next to the fighter. "You okay?"

The fighter raised a weary head, eyes sad and lost. "That's the second one I've fought off in the past two hours. So no, I'm not okay."

This guy had survived two attacks? "Who was the first one?"

"A woman named Susan. Long story, but she was with the doctor this morning. She was normal before—"

"—but not after," Jared finished.

The fighter nodded.

"Where is Susan now? How did you get away?"

"I killed her." He thought for a second. "It."

Jared was stunned. Fighter was full of surprises. "You killed her? How?"

Fighter drew in a deep breath. "By accident I assure you. I was just trying to get away from her and we fell into the swimming pool at Tsunami Suites. Her skin turned black and bubbled. She basically melted."

"What—" Jared started but Cindy answered.

"Chlorine!"

Could it be that simple?

There were other chemicals in the pool; algaecide, alkaline balancers, clarifiers. But the strongest, most abundant chemical used in pools was chlorine. It was naturally corrosive. It made sense that such a substance *could* be toxic to an alien life form.

"Now we know how to kill them," Jared said through gritted teeth.

Something bashed the front door like a sledgehammer.

Lawrence and Wes had found them.

Thirty-Seven

Corey couldn't believe it.

"Are you sure?"

Max and Comet stood over Corey, nodding. While Max and Comet had worked on triangulating where the anomaly landed, Corey had begun studying vast amounts of information from all available satellites to track its flight path. After Simon sent the last photo of the so-called anomaly that they now knew was anything but, NASA had opened up their toolbox of high-tech goodies, providing support.

With NASA's help, Max and Comet had narrowed down the "point of impact" to the Gulf of Mexico.

"We don't know exact coordinates," Comet replied, "but it definitely landed in the Gulf."

"Go tell Simon, then get back and help me sift through all this data," Corey instructed. "Let's find out where this thing came from."

Space mapping was time consuming and tedious. But retracing its route and determining point of origin required focus and stubbornness. Both of which was running on short supply. He'd been up over thirty hours. His brain was fried. His body was fatigued. He was operating on coffee and caffeine pills and those were no longer working. The clock was ticking like a nuclear bomb and human lives were at stake. Exhausted and under extreme pressure, Corey wanted to go hide in a closet and sleep. His career at Deep Sky was over. Simon hadn't fired him yet only because he needed Corey to help track this flaming nightmare. Once done, Corey was a goner.

Any other day, Corey would've cared. Greatly. But in that moment, Corey wished Simon would have security walk him out to his car and see him off the property. Remove the elephant sitting on his chest and the weights dragging his eyelids closed.

Funny thing, Corey couldn't do it himself. He wished he had it in him. Get up. Walk out. That simple. But despite the drowsiness and mental fog and stress, Corey wanted to right his wrong. He wanted to answer the questions. He wanted to know.

What was that thing?

He'd studied the picture close. Wondering how it was possible something like that existed. It was a vile damnation of nature. Spat from the perverted womb of a cosmic monstrosity. In direct conflict with everything humans knew and believed about life. Science would be questioned. Religion would be tested. Galactic facts and faiths would be examined. The very fabric of human existence was now suspect. The truth was complex in meaning but simple in fact: we were not alone.

Corey had overheard Simon briefing the White House earlier. He had ascertained from the conversation that the powers-that-be were determined to keep this information buried like an Egyptian mummy. It would be thousands of years before anyone knew anything about it.

Corey understood what that meant: dead men tell no tales.

Despite the end of his career forthcoming in the near future, Corey tossed two more Wide Eyed pills in his mouth. He'd finish what he fucked up. One way or another. What happened afterward happened.

With renewed vigilance, Corey sifted through photos and data streams.

Comet and Max returned.

"Simon called the White House," Max said. "Coast Guard and Florida National Guard are being notified to be ready to respond once we narrow down the location where it crashed."

"Good," Corey said. "You two start with CSMC90 and move laterally along Sector Two."

Neither moved. Corey looked up from the screen to find them both fidgeting, uncomfortable. "What's wrong?"

Comet appeared ready to cry. "We think you're being fired once this is over. We caught Simon saying as much when we walked in to give him the point of impact location."

"Sorry, man," Max said, stared at his feet. "It's my fault. You don't deserve that."

Corey gave them a tight smile. "I know my fate. And I'm okay with it. But right now, I'm here and we're going to find out all we can about this thing. If that helps boots on the ground eliminate the threat and save lives, then it'll be worth it." He swatted Max on the shoulder. "Let's get to it."

Thirty-Eight

Owen strolled down Riptide Avenue, slurping on a slushy. He needed a break from the outlandish—but riveting—story he was writing and decided to get some sun and gawk a little. One big bonus of a water park was all the ladies in bikinis. Owen wore mirrored shades to hide his wandering eyes.

Moms were the majority in the main thoroughfares. Poolside was more suitable to provide what he was seeking. Owen checked the map in his back pocket, found his location, and the direction of the pools. Southwest along Seashell Street.

Everything here was named with cute beach terms: Seashell Street, Tsunami Suites, Coral Cove, Bull Shark Boulevard, Riptide Avenue, blah blah blah. Tourist shit. People ate it up. Wasted money on t-shirts and souvenir cups and fluffy stuffed sharks and hats with shark fins and Riptide Rapid coloring books for the kids and jewelry and trinkets. The list went on and on. Little beach huts built on every corner peddling waterpark wares.

Owen saw it for what it was: commercialism. He despised it, but had to admit, the owners were good at it. The setup was psychologically perfect, luring the visitors in like a fancy saltwater jig. Subliminal messages throughout the park, attendees hypnotized by propaganda without even knowing it.

Owen shook his head, slurped more slushee.

Seashell Street took him under The Reaper that flashed by as he passed, some riders screaming while others held up their arms in some idiotic display of bravery. After the cars were gone, Owen could still feel the vibration of the ride beneath his feet. One thing he was not into was rollercoasters. What was the point? Why were people so interested in safe danger? They wanted to be sent hurling through the air, twisting and turning at incredible speeds, but, oh yeah, strap them down tight with harnesses designed by NASA and used on rocket launches. Scare them but have them smile while they were at it. Because it was *fun.*

Nonsense.

Owen checked his map again to see how much further. Seashell Street took its sweet time meandering in the obnoxious heat before ending at Megalodon Pools, but he noticed a side street, Lanternfish Lane, that offered a straighter shot. And it cut out passing the grotesque abundance of food and souvenir shops. Owen teased his way through the steady flow of traffic, careful not to let his anger at the never-ending tide of bodies bumping into him like a NASCAR race cause him to lash out. He finally reached the mostly-empty Lanternfish Lane and sped up his walk. As he passed Riptide Security office building he noticed two men banging on the entry door. Owen stopped to gawk. He was a reporter always on the lookout for a story, and his internal antenna sensed potential. He stepped back and leaned against a palm tree, waiting. For what he had no idea. That was the beauty of the story. It always happened at its own pace, in its own way. Owen was not one to rush it. He took in the moment, mentally noting the details for later.

Both guys appeared to be park employees. Maintenance wore coveralls, and these two guys were in the same attire. Why would maintenance men need to beat on the door of a security office? Seemed like they would possess a grand master key to the entire park. To open every door. To fix shit when shit needed fixing.

Peripheral movement caught Owen's attention. Box-cut shrubbery surrounded the security building, a tricky attempt to hide it in plain sight. A man and a woman slipped through the shrubs about thirty yards away. They were quickly followed by a teenaged boy and girl who looked like they came straight from a KISS concert, two younger boys, and an adult male. What really caused Owen to salivate was the fact they were crouched low, moving away quickly on soft feet, and constantly checking behind them. Toward the front of the security building. Where the two men banged on the door.

Owen had a decision to make. Follow the group or stay with the two bozos beating on the metal door. It was an easy choice.

He slipped back onto the narrow-paved road named after some random ocean fish and nonchalantly picked up the pace to close the distance between himself and the escapees.

Was that what they were?

Seemed unlikely. The guy who came out of the bushes first wore coveralls like the two banging on the door. He worked at the park. What would he be escaping from and why was he running from his co-workers? With kids following?

Owen's weird-shit-o-meter was chirping like crazy. Something was up.

And he intended to find out what.

Thirty-Nine

Dave followed the group until they were clear of the security office and blending with the enormous crowd. He stepped to the side and stopped. The guy—Dave hadn't had time to get his name—at the front noticed and signaled everyone to regroup.

"You okay?" the guy asked.

"My family is at the pool. I need to get them. We're leaving this place on the next ferry and never coming back."

Dave saw pity in the guys eyes, and knew on some instinctual level what he was going to say.

"The ferry isn't coming. It broke down last night. It's being repaired but they don't know how long before it'll be ready."

Dave's heart sank. A thousand realities crashed down on him. All these people were stuck here while something was attacking island inhabitants. His family was in grave danger.

The man squeezed Dave's shoulder. "I know what you're feeling and thinking. We don't have a firm plan yet, but we're working on it."

Dave had to ask: "What's going on? What's causing this?"

The guy frowned and sighed. "What's your name?"

"Dave." He held out his hand, figuring it was time for formal introductions.

The guy shook. "I'm Jared, I work here. This is Cindy. She works in admin. That is Pete and his girlfriend Nola. They are park guests who met the doctor and barely got away before being turned. I don't know the names of those two—"

"—Johnathon and Fulton," the stocky, pimple-faced kid said. "I'm Johnathon."

"And to answer your question, I don't know exactly," Jared said. "It's alien, I do know that. I don't know how it got here, but I know why it's here, even if it does't make a whole lot of sense right now."

It hit Dave square on the forehead. "The meteor."

Jared looked puzzled. "What meteor?"

"It crashed in the ocean yesterday morning," Dave said. "I was jogging when it happened. I thought it was just a cool thing to see, but that had to be it."

Jared nodded. "Timing is good. This all started yesterday best we can tell."

Dave had another epiphany. "Could that be what disabled the ferry?"

Jared shrugged. "We think it's likely."

"And what does it want? To take over the island?"

Pete jumped in. "To take over the *world*. The island is just the beginning."

Jared nodded. "There's a bit more to it than that, but, essentially, yes, that's want they want."

"Jesus," Dave breathed. The idea was too big to fully grasp, but he could comprehend the ideology of starting small and growing, multiplying. Spreading like a cancer that metastasized from the kidneys to the lungs to the brain. The park was a perfect place to establish a colony of otherworldly lifeforms. Once fully converted, the visitors could board the ferry and debark to parts across the globe. The infestation would be unstoppable.

Dave felt sick to the stomach.

"Because of you, we know chlorine, or the combination of pool chemicals, can kill them. That's our weapon. Good news is the park is full of it. All of the public water attractions use the same chemicals. Different amounts dependent upon the size of the pool, but the same mixture. We have to find a way to use that."

"Water guns," Johnathon said.

"Only a deviant fuck would think of that so quickly," Nola spat.

Dave was surprised by the language. And the hatred behind it. But he read between the lines pretty quick. Pete's face was battered. Nola was his girlfriend. And the two boys had been in jail.

Dave pointed at Pete, spoke to Johnathon. "Are you responsible for that?"

Johnathan looked at his feet.

Jared waved it off. "Whatever happened better not happen again. We don't have time for childishness. Besides, that is a really good idea, deviant or no. All of these stores sell water guns. We go in together and each get one. Put it on your room account. I'm sure if we manage to survive no one will be mad. Then we head over to the pools and fill the guns. This may not kill them, but if it maims and hurts and causes a retreat, then it's worth it."

Dave liked Jared. He took charge and asserted himself in such a way that was sensible. Qualities of a leader.

But Dave still had reservations. His family was here. Protecting them was his first priority. "What should I do about my wife and kids? They may be safer at the bungalow."

"I would leave them by the pool. Right now this thing is spreading in the dark, so to speak. And it wants it that way. The fewer who know about it the better. Them being in public, out in the open in a busy area, is their security blanket. That will change in time, but for now that's the truth. Let's kill these bastards before it gets to that point."

Dave wasn't fond of the idea but with no counter argument, he relented. "Okay. Let's go."

The nearest Souvenir Shack was across Seashell Street. Dave hoisted a super soaker shaped like a machine gun. Like the gun Arnold Schwarzenegger used in *Predator.* A few similarities. He certainly hoped this wasn't a repeat. In that movie, everyone died except the main hero.

He rejoined the group outside the store.

"I think," Jared said, "it would be better to use a pool at one of the hotels to fill these things. Megalodon is packed and we will have unwanted attention there. The hotel pool areas will be empty. Or mostly so."

"What if we go back to Tsunami Suites so you can see what's left of Susan?" Dave offered.

"No good. The staff will be alerted by now and trying to figure out what happened. If we show up, they'll have questions we don't want to waste time answering."

"My hotel then," Pete suggested, holding up his wristband. "I'm at Driftwood Haven."

Jared agreed.

"And what do we do after we fill them?" Nola asked. "What's the plan moving forward?"

"I'm not sure yet," Jared said. "I'm working on it. I'm open to ideas. The water guns are just deterrents. In case they come after us. It's better than the nothing we had ten minutes ago."

Dave felt the eternal guilty tug of doubt hold his feet from moving. He wanted to go to his wife and kids. A wife who was probably cheating on him with his best friend. Except, Dave no longer cared. After witnessing the cosmic insanity of Susan and the security guard, he just wanted to go home. Go to work. Fall into the routine of daily habits. He wanted monotony. He wanted peace and quiet. He welcomed it with open arms.

He had already forgiven Penny. As long as she ended it, he'd be okay. He knew he hadn't been the best husband after Molly had died. He'd made mistakes. Penny had made mistakes. Both of them needed to recognize that and agree to meet in the middle. For the kids. For themselves. For the family.

None of that mattered if these things weren't killed. This alien holocaust had to be stopped.

Forty

Water guns?

Was this some silly game they were playing? A make-believe waterpark version of *Invasion U.S.A.*? Had he been mistaken thinking this was an actual story?

Maybe he should head on to the pool. Better sights to see than this childish activity.

But the group still acted weird. If this was a game, each of them were dead serious about it. No one smiled. No one laughed. Faces grim as death. The leader of the group, the guy in the coveralls, talked with animated hands, movements stern. Owen wanted to hear what he was saying so he mingled with the crowd, slowly moving closer until he cleared the traffic. He used the postcard display carousel just outside the Souvenir Shop as an excuse to be there. Pretending to shop while tuning into what the guy was saying.

Crowds were noisy. Kids shouting, feet popping the pavement, strollers rolling, adults talking, but Owen picked up a few fragments.

"—back to Tsunami Suites so you can see what's left of Susan?"

"—alerted by now and trying to figure out what happened. If we show up, they'll have questions."

"— water guns are just deterrents. In case—after us. It's better—"

What's left of Susan? Did I hear that right? Owen wasn't sure. A kid started crying towards the end. He might've misheard. But that's what it sounded like.

Owen felt it in his bones. A story. All the trademarks were there, especially the tingle. At the nape of his neck. He called it his story sense. That seventh perception. The space between sentences. The gray area. The unspoken words. Phrasing. Innuendo. It all played a part. It was Owen's gift. He'd always had it. It served him in high school when he was lead editor of the *Tiger Times*. It served him in college when he worked his way to lead editor for the *Cavalier Community*. And it continued to serve him to this day. It was why he was one of the highest paid freelancers in the business.

Maybe the story he originally planned was going in the trash bin to be replaced with this potential-to-be-a-blockbuster revelation. Or maybe he'd combine the two stories into one. He envisioned an angle already.

Owen couldn't hear them talking and found they were moving away in a hurry, damn near running.

"Shit," he said to the postcard rack, and followed.

Owen's calves cramped, but he refused to stop. He needed to work more water in his diet. Too much soda and bourbon. He was about to stop when they finally slowed and entered the gate to Driftwood Haven. More proof this story was tailor-made to be his. Owen kept his distance, moving slow to appear as an innocent bystander. And to alleviate the cramp.

The pool area was empty. Completely. Then again, why would anyone be at this lame little pool when a four-hundred-acre waterpark was a few hundred yards away? Owen knew if he walked out in the open he would be noticed. So he crept back into the shadows cast by the six-story stucco building and palm trees. Each of them dropped to their knees and used the pool water to fill the plastic toy guns. Once done, they stood up, and turned back toward Owen. He jumped back and hobbled down the sidewalk and around the corner. He slowed and tried to appear as a casual visitor returning to his hotel.

When he glanced back, hands in pockets, nice and easy and indifferent, the group had stopped near the entry gate, frozen in place. Standing before them were the two guys who had been beating on the security office door. Different now. Their heads a tangled mass spider legs with a single curling tentacle that resembled an octopus arm.

Owen stumbled back and lost his footing, smacking the sidewalk with his full body weight, biting his tongue. He pinched his eyelids closed. *I'm hallucinating.*

He opened them just in time to see everyone in the group raise their water guns and squirt the two maintenance workers with Medusa heads. It was almost comical how silly it looked, but the reaction was no laughing matter. Owen never could have imagined such a horror. The segmented legs shot straight out like arrows and trembled as smoke billowed off their hairy, grey flesh. A grainy, low-pitch screech erupted from the things wide-open, snake-filled mouths and the bodies violently shook as though wracked by seizures. The spider legs suddenly sucked back in their heads and the two guys disappeared through the gate, retreating in pain.

The group looked surprised for a moment, then cheered. High-fiving one another.

"I knew it would work," the guy in coveralls yelled in glee.

"Um, guys," one of the boys said. Owen realized the kid was staring at him.

All eyes found Owen, and Owen stood there, feeling stupid. He was unsure what to do, so he waved.

Coveralls came straight at him in a hard march. "You saw that?"

"Um, yeah. Yeah, I did." Owen was trying to regain his balance. In more ways than one. "I'm a reporter."

That had the desired effect. The guy slowed, his next few steps as tentative as a scared child's first day at pre-school.

"I've been following you guys for thirty minutes. I knew something was up."

To Owen's surprise, the guy smiled. Seemed he, too, had regained his balance. "You're right. Something is up." He pointed toward the gate, where the two escaped. "Those two guys are infected with some sort of virus. Two of a growing army."

"One helluva virus," Owen quipped. "Are there more?" Owen's heart rate sped up. Not out of fear, but excitement. The story was getting better by the minute. Everything clicked into place. Reality and fiction combined and he saw the story like a Hollywood blockbuster. Bigger than Arnold. Bigger than Sly.

"Yes," coveralls nodded. "We don't know how many exactly but we guess more than a dozen."

"Why the pool water?"

"Chlorine. Or a combination of chlorine and other pool chemicals. We're not sure about that either."

"Do you know what they're infected with? This virus?"

"Not exactly. What we have figured out is that something from a place called The Void has made its way back to Earth to retrieve something it lost, and while here it wants to turn everyone in the world into a tentacle-spitting cosmic horror, starting with all of us here on the island. I know it sounds insane, but we've seen it happening."

Owen found it hard to argue after what he had just witnessed. It was unbelievable which meant it was perfect for him and his readers. He had to know more. "How did they get here?"

"We believe by meteor. Crashed in the ocean yesterday morning best we can tell from an eyewitness."

"And your plan is what? Wipe them out with toys?"

But coveralls had a perplexed look on his face. His eyes stared into a distant place of contemplation. Owen knew the look. Was guilty of it himself. He shut his mouth and waited.

Coveralls spun on his heels. "Dave, where did you say that thing crashed again?"

Forty-One

Dread sat on Pete's back like a homicidal gorilla. The weight weakened his knees, exhausted his reserve, and left him lightheaded. They were getting close. He felt it in his gut. When they found "The Colonel" as Jared called it, what then? What were they going to do? Spray it with a water gun?

Jared and Cindy worked on the island, knew the schedule of all the attractions and the specialty activities. Swimming with the dolphins. Swimming with the stingrays. Jet skiing.

And charter fishing.

The charter boat left every morning at six-thirty to fish the Gulf. Leon, the captain, always maintained a northwest heading. Essentially directly towards Louisiana. Leon would have passed over the spot where the meteor crashed. Give or take. Dave wasn't sure of exact coordinates, but was certain of its general vicinity. Dave also remembered Lawrence arriving to work the Haunted Island Festival the night before but had been sent back to his cabin because he was sick. Dave overheard Lawrence tell Brandon that he had been talking to Scuba and blacked out.

The working theory was Leon, Scuba, and the charter mates may have been the first victims. Cindy used the computer inside Driftwood Haven to confirm that a scheduled charter for today was cancelled the night before by Julie, the receptionist. Cindy tried calling the charter office hoping to speak to Julie but only got the answering machine. The charter was a big hit among the male visitors and would never close or cancel without Larry's consent. The operation should be running full speed ahead.

When they arrived to the charter office, the door was locked and the lights were off. Cindy cupped on either side of her face with her hands to block the glare.

"A purse is sitting on the desk by the phone."

Further confirmation their suspicions were not only possible, but probable. At the end of the dock, *Riptide Rebel*, danced on the waves, mooring lines pulling taunt and loosening as the boat was pulled and pushed by the current. The storage building housing all the rods and reels and coolers and bait boxes and freezers and life jackets and various other fisherman paraphernalia was locked up. Not a single sign of use.

Which left the boat.

Jared chose himself, Dave, and Pete as the lucky explorers. The boat wasn't big enough for everyone.

Pete wasn't sure what the other two were feeling, but for him the fear was almost paralyzing. Everything below his neck hardly functioned properly. Even his lungs refused to work, pulling air in and squeezing it back out in lethargic, wheezy contractions. His feet were encased in concrete. Like in those gangster movies where they filled buckets with mortar and let it dry around the enemies feet, then dropped said enemy in the ocean "to swim with the fishes." Pete now understood what that was like. Sensation of drowning.

A humid breeze rolled steadily off the ocean, but it wasn't helping him breathe any better.

"You ready?" Jared asked.

Pete, who was most certainly not ready, nodded.

Jared asked Dave the same question, received the same response.

Nola hooked Pete by the elbow, and kissed him. He could feel her body trembling. “Please be careful,” she said.

Pete planned to be careful, but that depended on what they found aboard that boat.

Riptide Rebel bounced against the cushions on the dock. The weather-treated boards vibrated from the impact. Jared was on first, followed by Dave. Pete was last to climb over the edge. The boat was tidy, nothing out of place as far as Pete could tell. He’d only been on a boat a few times. Some family friends owned a lake house and a pontoon, and invited Pete’s family down several times a year. Pete couldn’t imagine going on one of these fishing charters. Riding out one hundred miles or more, in the middle of the ocean, nothing around but the horizon. Gave him the heebie-jeebies just thinking about it.

“There’s a cabin below,” Jared whispered, pointing to a small half-sized man door. “Pete, you open the door. Dave and I will cover.”

Pete wanted to run. As fast as his scrawny, non-athletic legs would take him. But Nola was standing on the deck biting her nails and bouncing on her toes. His parents were back at the pool, soaking in every ounce of sun before the park closed until nightfall. The park was full of kids in costumes, some already heading back to their rooms in anticipation for the Halloween extravaganza tonight. So many people, living, loving, laughing. Moving through life with oblivious abandon.

And run where anyway?

Pete grabbed the handle on the door, twisted, and yanked it open. Jared and Dave jabbed the water guns forward but nothing lashed out of the opening.

Except a foul odor. Wafting out like fog from a steam room.

Pete pulled his sweaty t-shirt up over his nose. The fabric smelled like armpits but that was better than the stench from the cabin. Jared and Dave covered their noses with their hands, eyes watering.

Jared blinked to clear the tears, and stepped to the door opening. Pete couldn't see much with Jared and Dave blocking the doorway, but he noticed that beyond the frame, darkness prevailed, despite the sun being high in the sky. Jared huffed, then stepped over the ledge and began his descent. Dave was next. When Pete stepped up to the doorway, he was frightened to find Jared and Dave had vanished into the pitch-black darkness. He tilted his head, straining to listen, but all he could hear was the boat creaking and the waves lapping at the hull like an eager puppy.

Hesitation bred cowards, so Pete took the first step without further thought. The steps were smaller than he realized and he almost plummeted to the bottom, but he caught hold of a handrail just before, and was able to stork-walk the remaining steps before reaching solid floor. The boat listed and Pete stutter-stepped before widening his stance. Down in the hole, the darkness was oily, fluid. Flowing shadows shifted and rolled, taking new shapes only to morph into another one. Pete could almost chew on the stench. Raw meat and body waste. A vomit-inducing tandem.

This is what a slaughterhouse smells like, Pete thought.

Pete started to move, wondering where Jared and Dave went, when a fist grabbed his shirt. A quiet *shhh* tickled his ear.

"Listen," Jared whispered.

Pete quieted his mind and tried to ignore the sensory overload. The attempt wasn't completely successful, but an odd sound filtered through. Heavy, raspy breathing. Like a sleeping dragon. Pete picked up nuances in the exhale that sounded like a wet, beefy rattle.

Pete took one step back before the fist grabbed him again. He fought the urge to knock the hand away. Every part of him screamed to get off this boat. The compulsion was overwhelming.

"Calm down," Jared whispered. "As long as you keep your head, we got this. Now, quickly and quietly get the bucket of pool water and bring it back down."

Pete almost choked on the rancid air, but he sucked in a lung-full anyway. He slowly mounted the stairs, careful of the compact treads. On the deck, the salt air tasted like sugar. Even the blistering sun was welcome after the black desolation below. Pete crossed the bow, then froze.

All hell broke loose.

Forty-Two

Once Pete was above-deck retrieving the pool water, Jared tapped Dave on the arm. Hand signals were useless down here. He leaned close and whispered, "I've got a small penlight in my back pocket. I'm going to turn it on pointed at my feet, and slowly raise it to locate the target. Keep your eyes and ears open."

Jared felt Dave nod. He slipped the light out of his pocket. This little light and an all-in-one screwdriver were the two most used tools he owned.

He clicked the butt end where the power button was located and a tiny, but bright beam illuminated his dirty work boots. Jared slowly raised the light along the vinyl flooring until it landed on an oozing, segmented tentacle. The appendage pulsed in unison with the phlegmy wheezing. Jared gulped dry spittle and turned his wrist slowly, raising the beam, unveiling a massive cosmic nightmare of unimaginable proportions.

"Oh. My. God," Dave rasped next to him.

God had nothing to do with this abomination. This thing had been birthed from the perverted womb of Khaos and harvested the raw flesh of Cthulhu. The insectile, prickly body, the dozens of fuzzy, bisected legs, the bulbous head with what appeared to be dozens of lidded, protuberant eyes. Long vertical slits ran along each side of its torso, opening and closing with each breath. Every ten seconds or so, the body would shudder as if experiencing a bad dream. Each arm would shiver, the speared tips of the legs trembling.

Jared wondered how it got down here. The small man-door and narrow, steep stairway seemed hardly big enough. But the thing was doused in a liquid that shimmered off its body like morning dew on spring grass. Maybe its flesh provided lubrication.

Jared glanced up the stairs, seeing nothing but clear blue skies.

Where is he?

"Jared!" Dave cried.

The monster shuddered in rage, rising on its haunches with six main legs that pushed its ovoid head against the low ceiling. Its eyes opened, glowing yellow orbs with parasites swimming inside. It leaned into Jared's light and its maw stretched wide. It roared with fury through jags of four-inch teeth that appeared carved from meteor stone, vibrating in Jared's bones. Jared would've vomited from the rot on its breath had he not been incapacitated with terror.

A leg lashed out, its tip popping Jared in the center of his chest. It felt like he'd been shot. He stumbled back and his ass bone banged against of the sharp edge of the steps. Shock and pain sent a "let's get the fuck outta here" signal to his legs and both finally found life. He scrambled backwards up the stairs, dodging another strike that left a hole in the wooden riser.

Jared was almost to the top when he noticed Dave stopped on the bottom step.

"Dave?" He said, chest tightening as he realized what Dave was thinking.. "Get out of there."

Dave didn't respond, not at first. After the briefest of moments, Dave raised his head. In those blue eyes, Jared saw he was no longer thinking of doing something. He had made a decision.

"Get the bucket and finish the job," Dave said. He turned and disappeared inside the boat.

"NO!" Jared screamed.

Jared scrambled down one step before Dave emerged from the darkness and slapped a hand on the first step. His face and hair were covered in a parasite-filled gelatin. The worms twisted and wiggled down his face. As he attempted to crawl up the stairs, a worm slipped through the tear duct of his left eye. Another used the right tear duct. Some crawled inside his nostrils. Others chose his ears. Dave opened his mouth to speak and Jared saw dozens of the things caught in his teeth. One long and stringy parasite burrowed into his tongue like an earthworm in damp soil.

"Tell my wife and kids," he moaned, each word plopping from his engorged tongue like coagulated milk, "I love them."

He shuddered and leaned back, peered down at his chest. He patted his sternum with trembling hands, then tore his shirt open. Jared stared in horror as Dave's flesh rippled from the parasites swimming in his bloodstream like tadpoles in a creek. Dave's eyes rolled in his head, showing nothing but the whites, now stocked with red, stringy worms.

Jared had no intention of allowing this to happen to himself or anyone else on this island. He clambered to the top, and ran for the bucket of pool water, the cosmic version of Holy Water. He was stunned to see his friends fighting off over a dozen of the things with their colorful plastic toy water guns. Amp was now one of them. Fernando was also one of them. As was Shane. Moe and Barbara. Glenda. His co-workers. Susan's son, the overdosed kid. Transformed. Now controlled by a new entity.

Owen was flat on his back, an older woman standing over him feeding him the disease through her tentacle like fueling a car at the gas pump.

Jared wiped the tears from his eyes. He could cry later. The Colonel was below deck, and he needed to kill it to have any shot at ending this.

Jared leaped from the boat to the dock and grabbed the handle of the bucket. Careful not slosh the contents. He wasn't sure how much he needed to kill that monstrosity but he knew the more the better. He sat the bucket on the edge of the boat and hopped back in, ignoring the shouting and screaming behind him. An ill-timed wave harshly rolled the boat and Jared had to grab hold of the railing to keep his balance. A sudden weight shift caused the bow to rise, then slam back into the water.

The bucket slipped off the side of the boat and landed in the ocean.

Jared watched in horrified despair as the white plastic disappeared below the dock. All hope drained from his heart. Time warped into slow motion, dragging and stretching. Almost in reverse. Jared wondered if he was about to pass out or if this was how the human body reacted when it knew death was approaching, a knowing smile across its skeletal chin. Electrodes firing, circuits readying to be disconnected. Already unplugging nonessential organs.

Jared located Cindy in the mayhem. She was retreating, a grimace of anger—*or fear*—curling her lips, flushing her cheeks. Her water gun must be running low. The same for all of them. The mutants were smoking, flesh black and bubbling, spider appendages in a frenzied tangle, but they held their ground. Refusing to run. Instinctually knowing their master was in trouble and they must protect at all costs. Willing to die if necessary. For the cause. A concept old as time, which the Colonel pre-dated.

A hand clamped onto Jared's bicep, spinning him around.

Dave.

His cheeks were now bumpy with worms. Microscopic tails squirmed from his pores like fine hair. His bloodshot eyes swam with parasites.

This is it.

Forty-Three

Stars were the most prominent features of space. Walk outside on any given night and simply look up. Bright dots twinkled like magic. Some larger than others. Some forming a pattern. Some forming a shape. All masked the abyss that stretched for eons beyond. Phenomena such as the black hole Cygnus X-1 and the supernova SN1987A helped Deep Sky, NASA, and other scientists of the cosmos form a better understanding of space.

The real question everyone within the "space" community, as well as the world, wanted to know was simple: was there life beyond our own?

The secrecy around Area 51 only added to the public perception that aliens existed, and the government knew about it—experimented on specimens even. Crazy stories of alien abductions and sightings were now commonplace on the news and in the tabloids with wide-ranging physical descriptions. No one agreed on whether the third kind more closely resembled *E.T.,* the creatures from *The Thing,* or the zenomorphs in *Alien.* Science suggested humans couldn't accurately imagine how another species would look, or act.

So many factors played a part. The environment being the most crucial component. If the species' planet was like Earth with trees and water and an ozone layer and a sustainable atmosphere, they could look similar to humans. Interacted and communed socially like mankind.

But if a species were born and survived on a planet with harsh conditions, a frail ecosystem, poisonous air, derelict water supply, unhealthy or diminished food supply, adapting to unfathomable conditions, the results were bound to be horrific. Bred and fed a steady diet of darkness and radiation, such a kind was fated to propagate into cosmic mutants.

Very much like the anomaly in the snapshots of the meteorite.

When Corey started the journey here at Deep Sky, he wanted to know if life existed beyond Earth. Many people, specifically the Bible-thumping Christian community, shouted from snow-crested mountaintops that science was wrong about mankind's evolution. The Bible contradicted those scientific discoveries. The Bible also failed to mention other planets or species, therefore, by their accounting, Earth and humans were the only living organisms in this galaxy or any other beyond.

That was a flawed ideology in Corey's estimation. If Earth was capable of sustaining life, and Earth was one planet in what appeared to be an infinite cosmos, it was short-sighted to think no other planet with some form of life could exist.

Now he knew this to be true.

Humans were not alone.

Other species existed.

And one of those were now on Earth.

"Have you narrowed down where this fucking thing came from?" Simon barked. The man was on the warpath. Angry that his team had slipped.

Corey cleared his throat. "Sir, it looks like it entered The Milky Way via the Zone of Avoidance. And because we can't observe that area, we have no way of knowing what's beyond, which means we don't know where it came from."

"That's impossible!" Simon balked. "Do you know the velocity needed for it to jump from galaxy to galaxy?"

"I do, sir, but that's what the data is showing." Corey shifted in his seat. "It came from unobservable space. From a place and time incomprehensible to us. That thing," Corey pointed at the nightmarish image frozen in place on the big screen, "whatever it is, doesn't look like a friendly. It looks like the type of creature that ends our species if we don't get busy finding it. We're wasting valuable time on hypothetical guesses about where it came from. We can do that later. Right now, we should focus our energy on locating its exact whereabouts in the gulf. There are hundreds of islands down there. Cuba is down there. Dominican Republic. You see where I'm going with this?"

Simon was not one to be admonished by an employee like Corey. Corey braced himself for Simon's scathing rebuke. But instead, Simon swallowed the sharp words like a glass of tacks, and said nothing for an uneasy moment.

Simon tapped Corey on the sternum, his fingertip like a ball-peen hammer. "Then get to work finding where it went. And I mean down to the fucking centimeter."

Corey watched Simon storm away. He'd always liked his boss, but he'd also never given the man a reason to direct his rage at Corey. Now that he had joined that small but growing fraternity, he had to admit it sucked.

"Corey," Comet called, waving him over to her desk. Max looked over her shoulder.

"What is it?"

Max pointed at Comet's computer screen. "Based on flight path and trajectory, we think it went down in this area right here." Comet threw the image up on the big screen, and increased its size. A grainy, satellite image of the ocean covered the wall.

"This is about four hundred miles from Cuba," Comet said.

"That's quite a distance from land." Corey had no idea what that thing was but he imagined it would want to get on solid ground as soon as possible.

Unless it's amphibious, he thought and quickly dismissed. If it was amphibious, then traveling millions of miles across the black tundra of space and hopping galaxies for hundreds or thousands of years would surely kill it. There were no water planets along the journey to stop and take a dip like some intergalactic rest area.

"That's what we were thinking," Max said, reeling Corey out of his thoughts.. "So, we looked at what islands are closest to its impact zone."

"There is only one within fifty miles," Comet said, crossing her arms.

"What's the island?" Corey asked, not a fan of the dramatic reveal.

"Riptide Rapids Waterpark," Max said. "On Riptide Island. Comet checked, and they average almost four thousand guests a day. Today is Halloween and they celebrate it by turning the place into a haunted island."

"Four thousand people," Corey repeated, breathless. The island was isolated. Packed with people. A viable potential target.

"I think we have to consider Riptide the most likely," Comet said. "At the very least it should be checked out first."

Corey agreed. "Let's go find Simon."

Forty-Four

The battle was lost, though the fight continued. Pete's water gun was almost empty. He sprayed small squirts just to hold the creatures at bay. The others were trying to conserve as well. This only allowed the things to close the distance small steps at a time, the tentacles lashing closer. Pete took a chance to look for Jared, hoping he had come up with a solution to their problem. But he was too busy fighting off Dave, who was now one of them. Pete stopped spraying to search for the bucket. Under the dock. Along the shoreline.

Nothing.

Panic set in. All around him, natural damnations pushed closer. Emboldened by the weakening defenses. Empowered by the treachery of their existence. Sensing the inevitable. Instinctually knowing that this group was the only thing standing in the way of a monumental galactic victory. The rest of the humans on the island were oblivious to the hostile takeover. Once Pete and his friends were converted, Riptide Island would fall. Within days the population would become hosts. When the ferry returned, the infection would spread to the mainland and the beginning of the end would commence. Evolution would have a new, terrifying architect.

Pete wanted Nola. He wanted to hold her and kiss her one last time. Tell her that somehow, someway, in just one day, he had fallen in love with her. How he loved her little tics; her pouty face, her penetrating stare, her smile, and, most of all, her laugh. He had never been happier than the past twenty-four hours.

He searched for her in the chaos, the shouting, the screaming, the bellowing. But she was gone. His heart stopped in his chest, a full-fledged lockdown. She had somehow been overtaken, and he had failed to save her.

His knees buckled and Pete dropped on the dock. Fear dissipated. Only pain remained. And he wanted the pain to stop. If Nola wasn't here, Pete didn't want to be here either. He wondered if it would hurt. If there would be any of himself left once the other took over. If he would recognize Nola, tentacles bursting from her face. If the love he felt would find its way through. If—

A bashing erupted from the boat, and Pete watched in brain-frozen awe as the deck exploded into the air as if a bomb had detonated. Massive spider legs that looked like some freak monster from one of the old *Godzilla* movies—*Godzilla VS The Mutant Spider from The Void*—danced out of the demolished boat parts, followed by the body to which they were attached. The blazing sun illuminated the silky flesh, highlighting the cursed entity and all its abhorrent appendages. As though it were a dog, its razor-lined maw stretched to an extensive opening, rose to the clear sky, and articulated its rage with a scream the most bone-chilling nightmare was insufficient to properly convey.

The boat rocked violently side to side as the heinous thing moved from its hideout to the top deck. Jared was able to buy a few precious seconds when the boat heaved and Dave lost his grip and footing. Jared twisted his body and rolled over the edge of the boat, dropping to the dock like a fish out of water. He scrambled to his feet and ran to Pete. Together they watched the master of the void, the bringer of the human apocalypse, The Colonel, rise from its slumber to unleash its limitless cosmic hell on Earth.

Jared dropped to his knees next to Pete, resigned to the awaiting fate.

A scream from behind sent a chill down Pete's spine. His friends were out of water and were now being infected. Owen had been the first. Now the rest. Only seconds remained now.

Another scream cut through the noise and Pete realized this was a female scream and it sounded angry, not painful. He jumped to his feet and hunted the owner.

"Nola!"

She had come up behind the creatures on the dock, spraying them with what appeared to be a fully loaded water gun. The creatures were down on their knees, charred skin melting from the bones like wax from a candle. Sitting next to her feet was the white bucket. Pete could see the water sloshing at the brim.

"The bucket," Pete said to Jared, pointing at the bucket.

But Jared was already moving. He dashed across the dock, leaping over the smoldering bodies.

The creature on the boat screeched like a shooting star and advanced over the edge of the boat, its six legs cracking against the dock boards like pistons. Johnathon, Fulton, and Cindy retreated toward Nola who had now turned the water gun on the master. Its skin blistered and smoked but it possessed the strength of ancients. It had survived generations of tortured existence. This was a microscopic discomfort compared to its lifetime of suffering.

Jared heaved the bucket by the handle, then paused. The master closed the distance quickly, surprising in its speed and agility. Its excess limbs jabbed the air like spears, hunting for flesh to impale. One of its tentacles lashed out like a bullwhip and coughed a wad of phlegm at

Nola. It landed short of her, and thankfully so. Writhing in the clear snot were thousands of small parasites that looked like the offspring of a tapeworm and a maggot.

That's what they dump inside the humans they transform, Pete thought, horrified and disgusted by the idea.

Jared allowed the thing to close a few more feet before splashing the five gallons of pool water over the creature. Pete's ears cracked from the insane roar of pain as it flailed on the dock. The limbs were like a den of snakes that had been doused with gasoline and set on fire. Globs of oily slime sprayed from its tentacles, slapping the dock boards, smoking, worms of all shapes and sizes curling and twisting as they died.

Jared snatched the water gun from Nola and emptied the contents into the wide-open jaws of the creature. Its flesh bubbled, yellow eyes popped like water balloons. It heaved backward, fell forward, arms still searching for a body to snatch. Jared dropped the empty water gun, turned and ran to the storage shed. He grabbed a landscaping stone and bashed the padlock off the door, then slipped inside. When he stepped back out into the light, he was carrying a harpoon. Without hesitation, he marched to within ten feet of the dying creature, took aim, and pulled the trigger. The steel bolt blasted from the canister, punching clean through the thing's torso. Jared quickly tied the rope trailing from the harpoon to one of the dock posts. No escape.

Jared handed Nola the empty bucket without saying a word. She nodded and ran away, understanding the assignment.

On the battered boat, Dave floundered, rolling around, appendages flailing in agony. Pete hadn't been sure, but he had hoped that if they killed the master, the minions would be weakened or die. Only time would tell if they died, but it appeared they were at least debilitated.

Nola returned with another bucket of pool water. She shook her head at Jared when he moved to take the bucket from her. She wanted the honors. With eyes on Pete and a menacing smile curling the corner of her lips, she dumped the contents of what was left of the bubbling mass of slimy flesh. The creature quaked, tentacles flopping in lethargic blips, and finally stilled.

The silence was heavy. Each of the survivors experienced the buoy of excitement that they had survived, but the doubt of reality extinguished any idea of celebrating. It was over, but was it *really* over? The thing was dead, yet they each held their breath, thinking maybe it was playing possum. Maybe it would shudder to life and attack with a vengeance.

After what felt like an hour, but was only minutes, Pete dared to believe. They had killed it.

He ran to Nola, careful to give the Colonel's smoldering body a wide berth. She leaped into his arms, and though his ribs ached like a bitch when her legs locked around his waist, Pete didn't flinch. He kissed her, held her tight, whispered in her ear: "I love you."

She whispered back: "I love you, too."

Forty-Five

Jared had to be sure. Dave flopped on the deck until Jared soaked him with chlorinated water. Maybe he would've died on his own. Maybe not. Jared wasn't taking a chance.

"Guys," Jared called, waving them over to where he stood, looking out at the ocean. "We need to confirm they're all dead or dying. If not dead yet, we finish them."

"Once they're all dead, what do we do with the ... you know ... bodies?" Pete asked.

"We'll have to report all of this to the authorities," Jared said. "So, we'll need to gather the bodies and store them somewhere."

"The freezer where we keep all of the meats and ice cream seems the best place," Cindy suggested. The freezer was in the underground facility. It was 5,000 square-foot of storage space. Plenty of room to keep the bodies until someone could recover them. The difficult aspect of rounding up the bodies was not being seen. The upside was being that Halloween would help disguise the reality. Bodies could just be props for the show.

"Doc is not here, so we start at the doctor's office, work our way out from there," Jared instructed. "We check every employee cabin and building. We can use the spare landscaping carts to move the bodies to the cargo elevator. The dollies in storage should be enough to get them to the freezer."

"What do we do with that thing?" Nola asked, pointing at the blob on the dock.

Jared brushed his hair back, shook his head. "I don't know. It's too big for us to move. We leave it for now." He clapped. "Let's get to work."

Jared was weary. Even his bones were tired. This had been the longest day of his life and it was only four-thirty. It would be well into the witching hour before the work was done. What came after tonight was a mystery and one he chose not to try to solve. For now, he focused on the task at hand. One bonus was the park was emptying as patrons headed back to their rooms to allow park employees to prepare for tonight.

He noticed Javier working on one of the flowerbeds.

"Hey Javier," Jared said pleasant enough.

"Hey Jared," Javier said, glancing up from his labor. He gave the group a once over, noticing the water guns but not saying anything.

"Mind if I borrow your cart to take these guys to pick up a few extra carts. Quinten wants more bodies put out this evening. Said he likes how spooky they look. We're going to storage to get more mannequins and sheets to wrap them in."

Javier wiped the sweat from his brow with a dirty rag pulled from his back pocket, checked his cheap Casio watch. "I'm supposed to go over to The Falls in a few minutes but that damn Manuel and Eduardo has not come back yet from getting pine straw. These guys get lost going to take a shit."

Jared shrugged. "I can find them while on the way and tell them to get their ass back here before you skin them alive. By the time your done, I'll be back."

Javier checked his watch again. "Sure, amigo. Tell them to hurry the fuck up. We are running out of light."

The cart was not big enough for all of them but they piled on anyway. The gas engine groaned under the weight, but served its duty.

Jared's first stop was the nearest resort, Bluewater Bay. He and the rest snuck into the pool area using Jared's grand master key, and refilled the water guns. Patrons returning to their rooms gave quizzical glances but no one asked any questions.

Javier was right about the light. Once Jared entered the tree covered paths that ran to the back of the property to all the maintenance and storage buildings, the imminent arrival of dusk became apparent. Much of the work would be done in the dark. Which was good and bad.

"What is that?" Pete asked.

Jared had no idea what he was talking about. There was nothing out here but trees and lurking shadows. "What?"

Pete clinched Jared's arm. "Stop the cart."

Jared stomped on the brake with both feet, knocking all the riders around on the cart. He wanted to ask what Pete saw but Pete held up a hand for silence. The kid was staring at the tree line. At the fence running along the property line. Jared followed his eyes, squinting against the gloom.

The brush shifted. Alive in ways shrubs were not. Normally.

Pete whispered, "It's not over yet. There are more of them."

Jared sighed. He had begun to relax. Thinking they had won. Humanity was safe. The children on the island were rescued.

Wishful thinking.

Pete stepped out of the cart with his water gun, and hunkered low. He moved to a tree and hid behind the trunk. He slipped through the dusk slow and methodical, using the forest to mask his movements.

Jared slid out from behind the wheel and retrieved his water gun from the bed of the cart where Cindy, Johnathon, and Fulton were sitting quietly.

"Stay here," Jared whispered.

Jared crept low, following Pete's path, walking on his toes. Darkness seemed to advance quickly, summoning an army of shadows, masking the movements of Pete and Jared.

Once close enough, Pete burst from behind the last tree near the fence and shouted. The thing hiding in the bushes squawked and its misshapen head erupted into a tumbleweed of tentacles and legs. Pete aimed his gun and sprayed through the chain link fence, dousing the monster with pool water.

The effect was the same as before: screeching, smoking, bubbling flesh, hysteria. It twisted and groaned in the weeds, signs of the dying.

"Where did it come from?" Pete said after a moment of listening to its flesh pop like bacon on a hot griddle.

Where indeed? Jared scanned the fence line and within seconds spotted an opening underneath the chain links. "They tunneled under." Jared pointed at the dugout area.

"I assume that's the part of the island allegedly wrought with underground caves and dangerous jungle?" Pete nodded towards the thick growth of untamed jungle beyond where the thing still fumed.

"Yes. The powers that be decided to wrap the property with a fence to keep anyone from wandering around."

"Sounds like the perfect hiding place," Pete said.

"Why? The rest of them were hiding in plain sight. Converting anyone they could. Why would some be back there?"

Pete seemed to chew on that. Then he had an answer Jared wasn't looking to hear. "Did you notice? That one was different. Everyone we encountered on this side of the fence were still human in appearance.

Hiding in plain sight, like you said. But that thing," Pete jabbed the water gun in the direction of the melted mass of congealed meat, "was not like them. It was like a circus freak. Like the guy in that movie whom everyone called *The Elephant Man*.

"That thing was closer to its natural state of being. It looked like a child of the creature back at the dock. Yellow orbs for eyes. Another set of arms off its back."

"Offspring." Jared tried swallowing but his mouth was dry. "It's having babies."

Forty-Six

Pete chopped at the thick tangle of weird vines and tree limbs with a machete found in the back of the landscaping cart. The water gun bounced on his sweaty back. A toy, but reassuring. Critters and insects croaked and creaked and clicked, nature's soundtrack. Mosquitoes buzzed in his ears. Some night creature yelped and skittered away, dry leaves rustling under paw. The rest of the survivors panted behind him. No one was happy to be here. All resigned to the fact that no one else knew what they knew.

Pete wanted to go home. He wanted life to return to normal. He missed his drums. He missed his friends. It seemed like a year had passed since he last saw them. He really missed Joe, the bass player of the band and his best friend. He'd known Joe since third grade. The two had actually gotten into a fight on the playground while playing kickball. After a trip to the principal's office, they had laughed it off while walking back to class. Since then, best friends.

He won't believe what I've been through, Pete thought, hacking at a thick limb.

What lay ahead was anyone's guess. Jared said he had never been to this side of the island, but he had seen aerial shots, taken back when the land was being surveyed for park placement. He said all he remembered was dense forest then rocky, harsh land. Assuming the surveys had been correct, he guessed the caves and tunnels would be after they cleared the jungle.

Pete had played in the woods as a kid. Commandoes and raiders. The woods where he lived were hospitable. Open, spacious, only dense in small areas. Easy to navigate. The perfect environment to play and run and hide.

This forest was mean as a rattlesnake. It lashed exposed skin, bit his legs, resisting the insurgency of the small band of survivors. Every stick, leaf, vine, foliage, or weed pushed back, leaned into them as if aware of their trespassing, determined to thwart advancement. Pete began to wonder if the woods would ever end when he stepped clear of the tree line.

The sky was a deep purple, darker than an eggplant. A half-moon was already in its place for the night. Stars spread to infinity. After the stuffy confines of the jungle, the salty breeze blowing off the ocean was refreshing.

"Where to?" Pete asked Jared. The ground was a barren, rocky wasteland. Scrub weeds were the only vegetation wild enough to escape the harsh soil. Off to the left the land rose to a jumbled foothill. Straight ahead the grade lowered gradually, and to the right was a wall of windblown rocks.

Jared read the land, pointed straight ahead. "Seems that's the only way forward."

"Guys," Cindy said, "maybe we should wait 'til morning. Do you really want to hunt these things at night?"

"No," Jared answered. "I don't. But we can't wait. We saw one attempting to enter the fence. Others may already be inside the park. We have to stop this tonight if we want any chance of leaving this island as the humans we are now. Tomorrow may be too late."

Cindy's eyes slid closed in weary acceptance, cheeks glistening. She sighed. "Okay. Let's do it."

The terrain was uneven and lumpy. A broken ankle waiting to happen. Pete had no sooner thought it than someone cried out from the back. Cindy was down one knee, hands clamped around her ankle. Her left foot was lodged in a crevice at a weird angle.

"It's stuck," she said. "Jared, give me a hand."

Jared helped Cindy ease the foot free. In the brightening moonlight, Pete didn't notice any swelling.

"Can you put any weight on it?" Jared asked, offering her a hand.

Cindy stood, took small test steps. "Yeah, it's fine. A little sore, but not broken. A slight sprain at worst."

"You good to go," Jared asked.

'Unfortunately," Cindy answered, issuing a small, nervous chuckle.

"Let's get going," Jared said. "Everyone pay attention where you step."

A few hundred yards further they came upon a cliff that overlooked a rocky beach. Ocean waves bashed the slick rocks sending a mist of salt water so high Pete felt it on his face. He leaned over the edge as much as he dared, searching the shore for a cave entrance.

"I think there's a cave below us," he said to Jared. "Bad angle from here, though, so not one hundred percent."

Jared roamed the area, and found a way down. It was steep but it provided the best chance to arrive at the bottom without plummeting to a stony death. Pete let Cindy and Nola go before him, lending a hand to Nola when she lost her balance on a smooth rock.

What had looked like a cave from the top of the cliff was a full-fledged portal to Hell. The black gash in the side of the island was at least thirty feet high and fifty feet wide. Pete was reminded of some old saying he had read years ago and had incorporated into the lyrics of one of his band's original songs: *Beware, ye who enter! Here there be monsters.*

Beyond the crashing waves and howling wind, a silence stretched to the stars. Burdened by the task of one thousand ancient armies, marching into the den of unnatural creatures, Pete allowed the fear and anger and desperation to drape over him like a magical cloak. He had to become a warrior now. He wasn't in possession of a sword like *Conan The Barbarian* but he had the witchcraft of a powerful liquid, tainted with the venom of snakes.

Sounds cooler than pool water, he thought grimly.

Jared nodded without a word, and stepped through the opening. The darkness swallowed them whole and rebuked the intrusion of even the scantest of moonlight.

Inside the cave smelled like a sarcophagus. Rotted flesh and loose bowels. Stench of the walking dead. Long deceased but refusing the summoning of the grave. Jared pulled his trusty penlight out of his pocket and the eager beam gnawed at the blackness like a rat on cheese. Actual rats scurried away from the light, little feet tapping the stone, squeaking in defiance of the trespassers.

"I don't think I can do this," Johnathon whispered from Pete's back.

"So you can jump people from behind for no reason, but you lack the balls to face a challenge head-on?" Nola quipped, voice echoing off the chamber walls. "Yeah, sounds like real tough guy talk."

Johnathon held any further comments to himself, but he didn't flee. Pete was surprised Johnathon was even here. Back in the police station, he had been forced into the situation, but since then he and Fulton could've bailed at any moment. No one was forcing them to tag along. Johnathon and Fulton had just gone along with whatever plan Jared and Pete cooked up. While Pete still thought Johnathon was an asshole of the highest order, he had to admit a certain amount of respect for the kid.

The cavernous "lobby" of the entrance collapsed into a narrow, claustrophobic corridor, the darkness deepening. Jared took the lead. Cindy hooked her fingers in his belt loops to keep him close. Nola reached back and found Pete's hand, squeezing for reassurance.

Jared stopped, and whispered a light, "Shhhh."

Pete's ears tuned in, listening intently. The noise was faint, but Pete could hear an unsettling slithering. His imagination flew into hyperdrive and he saw an enormous black snake, larger than an anaconda, wandering through the cave tunnels, tongue flicking as it tasted the air, now alert to the trespassers and their vile intentions. It advanced toward them, its flesh rippling over the stones. Slow and steady. Predator hunting prey.

Nola tugged his hand, pulling him closer. Pete waited for the snake to strike, though there was no snake. His stressed mind was playing tricks, inventing dangers. But something was definitely out there. That much he knew.

And it's much worse than a mutant snake, he thought.

The air tasted like pennies. Thick enough to chew on. The stench was more acute, drawing moisture from his eyes.

Jared whispered, "Okay."

He took slow steps deeper into the tunnel. Wet squirms grew louder. As did faint groans and grunts. Pete had watched an old porn flick with Joe one time when Joe's parents were out, and there had been a lot of similar grunts and groans and wetness.

I hope I'm not walking in on some cosmic monster orgy, Pete thought. Under different circumstances that would've been funny. Especially with his band buddies. But not now. Not here.

Pete sensed the tight corridor opening before he saw it. Jared's light lost some of its brightness, as if it had happened upon a larger, darker space to illuminate. Jared halted suddenly, causing a traffic jam. Cindy bumped into Jared, Nola bumped into Cindy, Pete rear-ended Nola, and the cycle continued behind Pete. Pete squeezed past Nola and Cindy to stand beside Jared. Now he knew why Jared had slammed on the brakes.

Another chamber had opened from the tunnel, the same size as the entrance cave. Except here, a sickening mass of flesh pulsated like a heart. Writhing tentacles protruded from everywhere. To Pete, it looked like a meshing of bodies. Like multiple individuals had melted together. Amidst the chaos, human legs and arms jutted from red, enflamed skin. A half-exposed face with one distended eyeball hid among the limbs. Jared's light targeted a spot on the abomination close to the stone floor. A throbbing, hairy slash in the creature parted and a sludgy round pod slipped to the floor with a soggy crack. The pod vibrated for a few seconds before segmented arms burst from its side. It scampered to a dark corner of the chamber. Jared followed its movements with the light, and gasped when further horrors were exposed. More than two dozen pods lay in the corner. All in various stages of growth. One was almost the same shape and size as the creature Pete had spotted in the woods. Another was the size of an infant—albeit with grotesque spider-like arms flailing around its tiny body. Still another was in the process of cracking open like a chicken egg, tiny worms jiggling out of the fissures in the slimy shell.

"My god," Cindy whispered.

"God had nothing to do with this," Jared said quietly.

The air in the cave shifted. All movements from the things ceased at once. Silence dangled like a corpse from a rope.

"Oh shit," Pete said.

And he was right.

The pods along the far wall leapt to whatever appendages they had available and dashed toward Jared and Pete. Pete yelped and snatched his water gun off his back. The pool water—*snake venom*—sent the damnable things retreating. Smoke billowed from their wormy, furry bodies.

The mother let out a greasy bellow and rose from her birthing stance. She charged at them, impossibly fast for a creature of such hefty proportions. Tentacles lashed out. One caught Pete's water gun near his hand and knocked it across the room. Jared sprayed her, received a cry of pain and anger, but still she advanced. Pete dove in front of Jared and rolled before returning to his feet and skidding like a baseball player beside his water gun. He brought it up to douse the mother, but something slammed into him and he thumped against the rough rock wall. An almost full-grown mutant lurched at him again, tentacles lashing, mouth-full of pointed teeth gnashing. Pete jabbed the water gun forward like a bayonet. The barrel disappeared inside the things mouth, and Pete squeezed the trigger.

Its torso inflated instantly, bulging until it burst like a gorged pimple. A wet, sticky substance splattered on Pete, a dribble getting in his mouth. He gagged, spit, and raised his gun to spray the rest of the pods who were returning for the fight. Their bodies smoked and blackened as if they had been drenched in napalm. They screeched and scurried in circles, trying to escape the torment. Pete refused to relent. He sprayed until each pod was a melted puddle of viscid fluid.

Mother withdrew to the furthest corner. With Jared, Cindy, Nola, Johnathon, and Fulton fully engaged in the assault, she had nowhere to go. She twisted and screamed, every limb acting—unsuccessfully—as a defense against the acidic chemicals that torched and ate her flesh. Pustules frothed on every inch of her, popping and forming more.

Pete stepped close as he dared and aimed at her gaping mouth. He had seen what happened when it got inside and he wanted to replicate those results.

It worked.

Her torso distended. Swelling as he filled her face with the water. Knowing he was close to running out by the weight of the gun, but emptying it anyway.

She shuddered violently as her body expanded, blackened skin stretching and cracking.

"Back up!" Jared yelled.

They pedaled backward toward the tunnel and was barely clear when she exploded. Meat slapped the stone walls like wet rags, noxious liquid splashed the walls and floor. After a moment, all was quiet except the heavy breathing of the survivors.

"I think I might be vegetarian now," Nola said, breaking the heavy hush.

The levity was needed, and everyone giggled. Then laughed until they were doubled over, tears squirting from their eyes.

Forty-Seven

The calvary arrived at four-thirty a.m. the following morning, November first. The park had closed at midnight and all the citizens had gone to their rooms where they now slept off the hot day of walking and riding rides and getting sunburned, unaware of what had almost happened. The survivors, now bound by shared trauma, spent the night hauling bodies down to the freezer. The park staff had been busy packing up Halloween decorations and assumed the bodies were part of the attraction. None of them would've believed the things were real even if they had touched one of the corpses. It was too outlandish an idea.

Jared heard incoming first. The group sat on the porch of the doctor's office, sweaty, exhausted, but too disturbed by all they had witnessed the past twenty-four hours to want to close their eyes. The subconscious had a way of allowing repressed memories and harrowing circumstances to escape the cages during sleep. None of them were quite ready to run again.

Jared was sipping a beer found in a small refrigerator in the doctor's office when he heard a thumping coming from a distance. It was high in the clear night sky, and tiny lights signaled its approach.

He pointed. "The calvary has arrived."

"Finally," Cindy said, standing and clapping.

Jared was jogging before it crossed his mind to do so. It took ten minutes to reach the marina, and by then he could see that he had been wrong about *a* chopper. Singular. More than a dozen swarmed around the island, looking for somewhere to land. In the water, more lights blinked, flood lights snapped on, revealing five large Coast Guard ships on approach. Along with what looked like a Navy battleship.

Rafts were lowered into the water from the Coast Guard ships and the Navy destroyer and the ocean was suddenly teaming with an army of boats and rescuers heading to the island.

"They know something is up," Pete said. "They wouldn't send all of this if they didn't."

"I guess we'll find out soon enough," Jared said, smiling. He cared less about what they knew than the fact that they knew it and came.

The first boat to dock was long and black and armed with a machine gun. Commandoes wearing black camo and face paint offloaded quickly and efficiently, bearing a shitload of artillery and ready for war. One man headed straight to Jared. His hair was buzzcut, his chin was molded from granite, and he possessed the magnetic air of authority. An alpha male if ever one existed.

"I'm Sergeant Ken Stillwell. We understand there may be a situation unfolding on this island. Can you confirm?"

"I can confirm there *was* a situation unfolding on this island," Jared said with a smirk. He felt a little like a badass at the moment. He and his friends had taken down the enemy with nothing less than water guns before the military could come in with advanced assault weapons and claim victory. "We've neutralized the threat."

Sergeant Stillwell's eyes twinkled. "Really? Completely?"

Jared nodded. "Completely."

"How many casualties?"

"Well over two dozen. That I know of."

"Can you debrief me?"

Jared looked around at the manpower that poured onto the property. "I can, but I'd like a shower first. Maybe some breakfast. It's been a long, dark night."

The sergeant agreed. "That's fine. I'll catch up with you in a bit. In the meantime, can you direct us to where we may want to begin our search?"

Jared nodded grimly. "Start at the boat charter. You'll find the first of what the government will deem top secret and classified. You'll want to transport that thing to Area 51."

Sergeant Stillwell bound toward his men, park map in hand. "Follow me," he barked.

"What now?" Cindy asked.

"Now we get a shower," he answered with a wink.

She blushed. "You're not, you know, too tired?"

"Never."

Jared patted Pete on the shoulder. "What are you going to do?"

"I think I'm going to shower and lay down for a few hours. Hopefully by then there is a ferry or boat waiting to transport us off this rock. And I am never coming back."

"Let's meet back here at seven-thirty. The park won't be opening today, so we'll have a lot of people stranded and confused. We need to get a plan for their departure as well as ours."

Jared and Cindy walked in silence with Pete and Nola until they parted ways to go in their respective directions, seven-thirty meet-up again confirmed. The trip to Cindy's cabin was a dreary haze, but he found his second wind when they stepped into the shower and her body pressed against his own.

Neither took a nap, and only had a bowl of cereal before heading back down to the marina to meet Pete and Nola.

Forty-Eight

The cover-up was massive. The surviving party who went toe-to-toe with the monstrous invaders signed a dozen non-disclosure forms in exchange for a hefty settlement. Right there in the marina before they were allowed to board a ferry to bring them back to Florida. By seven-thirty that morning, Grandiose had a small platoon of lawyers and big-wigs on-site. Everyone involved with the incident were subtly threatened to sign the forms, received a check for their troubles right then and there, and were made to see a doctor who set up a lab inside the Arrival/Departure Building. Doctor Yin examined each person from the survival party thoroughly, even performing x-rays with a mobile military apparatus. State-of-the-art. Once cleared, they were allowed to board a smaller ferry that took them to the mainland, alone. Pete and Jared ruminated "the man" wanted them isolated from the four thousand civilians who were cramming into the marina demanding answers on why they had to leave and when would they receive a refund. Further proof of this guess was granted when Jared asked if he and Cindy could stay and help with the deportation efforts of the stranded patrons and employees, and was quickly turned down.

Standing in the sprawling parking lot outside the Riptide Rapids Arrival/Departure building in Naples, Florida, the survivors enjoyed a moment of goodbyes. Jared and Cindy were heading to their respective homes—Jared to Myrtle Beach, South Carolina and Cindy to Moore, Oklahoma. But it was to be a short visit; Cindy was packing her belongings and moving to Myrtle Beach with Jared.

Before leaving, Jared pulled Pete aside and discreetly showed him a notebook.

"What is it?"

"I found it on Owen when we were moving the bodies. It's his story about the island. He even scribbled notes about the creatures. Their appearance and stuff like that."

"Okay. So—"

"I'm going to send this to his editor. Owen's dead. He didn't sign a nondisclosure form." Jared winked.

Pete winked, and smiled. "That's awesome."

Pete and Nola exchanged hugs with Cindy and Jared. Promised to stay in touch.

Johnathon and Fulton apologized to Pete and Nola for what they had done. Johnathon promised a change in his ways, then climbed in the backseat of his mom's Cadillac Cimarron and headed home.

After everyone was gone, Pete and Nola finally had a moment to say goodbye. But not before planning a meet-up sometime soon. They both had some money now to buy a car. With only eight hours separating them, they could meet halfway for a weekend every few months until they graduated. Maybe the future held a scenario where the two of them were together. Maybe not. Neither knew nor cared. For the moment, they were dating and in love and that was enough.

Forty-Nine

Aliens Return!!

By Owen Newman

There are moments in our history that have defined who we are as a people and a nation. The discovery of America by Christopher Columbus. The Declaration of Independence. The discovery of electricity. George Washington becoming the first U.S. president. The Civil War. Automobiles. World War One and Two. The Vietnam War. The Kennedy assassination. Color television. The Martin Luther King Junior assassination. Landing on the moon. Compact Discs. VHS. MTV. AIDS. The space shuttle Challenger disaster. Computers. And the recent advent of the World Wide Web.

Today, I can assure you another major milestone in American history has transpired and our government wants you to know nothing about it. Deemed TOP SECRET and CLASSIFIED, the evidence of what I'm about to divulge is now in the hands of the scientists of Area 51 to study beneath the auspicious roof of National Security. My very life would be in danger for disclosing such sensitive information, if I had not died fighting for your freedoms. I gave my life because it is imperative that you, the American people, know the truth. It is of the utmost importance that reporters—and citizens—never allow the fist of a government to squash their freedom of speech. To never allow the government to propagandize their words. To never be silent. To speak the truth, no matter the consequences.

This is the truth. I was there. I witnessed it. My sacrifice, and the sacrifice of others, must not be in vain.

I'm sure many of you have heard of or have visited the unassuming waterpark attraction named Riptide Rapids. All sunshine and fun times. Thrilling rides, delicious food, five-star accommodations. Beautiful beaches. A destination vacation spot.

Until, that is, six months ago when our fears and suspicions were realized. When the veil of our nightmares parted to show us worse things exist than a little man pretending to be an all-powerful God. Something came from deep space, invading our planet. Landing near Riptide Island. Hellbent and hungry to reclaim a land visited millions of years ago. This thing was indescribable. The stuff of the twisted. The wretched. The vilest. And I watched it attack humans and mutate living, breathing flesh into cosmic monsters. The plan, as I believe it, was to infect every human on the island—over four thousand souls—and then return to the mainland of America to infect the masses. World dominion. The end of mankind.

Stories have been written, movies produced, and tales told that were only as far-fetched as the author's imagination. H.P. Lovecraft is considered the fictional patriarch of cosmic horrors. Stunning as it may seem, Lovecraft was not peddling cheap wares to scare readers of the macabre. He was, in fact, relaying a truth. And the stories are not nearly as dramatic—or horrifying—as the real thing.

It is with humbling astonishment, that I can announce aliens are real. They exist. And they are not mild-mannered creatures interested in co-existing. They want to annihilate human beings.

It is believed Earth has suffered through five previous mass extinctions. The sixth will likely be under the ruthless bidding of the these abnormal creatures hailing from The Void.

Fifty

Doctor Jack Okun marveled at the grotesque corpse lying before him. He had been waiting for them to arrive for months. A new species to autopsy. The older specimens gathered some thirty years ago had been tested ad nauseam and had no further secrets to reveal. It was exciting to have a new breed to examine.

His first impression was surprise. This creature was an outlandish abomination. Unlike the others who were more civilized in body type, appearance, mass, limb usage, et cetera. The stark difference in physical features and attributes told its own story. There were multiple life-forms stretching to infinity. Their habitat played a huge role in their appearance and their biological desires. The others had arrived in 1958 and peacefully made contact. They had died shortly after landing due to Earth's atmosphere. Like breathing cyanide to humans. Very toxic.

These creatures hailed from a vastly different galaxy. One where the environment perverted the offspring of monsters. This specimen was the exact opposite of civilized. It was malformed and fantastic.

Doctor Okun grinned as he stepped closer, scalpel in latex-gloved hand, blade catching the fluorescent light. His assistant, Carol, stood by his side, ready to pass along whatever tool he required next.

This corpse was the first of over two dozen specimens he was set to autopsy. Some were offspring. Some were converted humans. Some were eggs.

This was the master, its size requiring his staff to push four stainless steel six-by-eight tables together. Tentacles and segmented legs dangled from its body. Doctor Okun leaned over its spherical head and slid the razor along the area above its now blackened eyes. The burned skin flayed apart, exposing a black skull. The skeleton of the older aliens was off-white, thin and fragile. Like the shell of an egg. Doctor Okun had a feeling this creature's skeletal density would rival a slab of granite.

He wiped the fog from inside his face shield and continued. He slipped the blade of the scalpel in the middle of the incision he had just made and pulled the blade along the top of the crown, intending to create flaps which he could use to peel the flesh away from the skull to clear the area for his bone saw.

A hand brushed his leg. He glared at Carol for the lapse in decorum. He had made it clear to her that their personal lives should never interfere with their professional roles. The cameras were rolling, and the world's most powerful eyes would be watching, likely frowning at Okun's assistant's behavior. They might even start questioning whether the two of them should be replaced.

"Let's stay focused, shall we," Doctor Okun said, an edge on his voice.

"Yes sir," Carol answered.

As he dragged the blade to the back of the cranium, a hand tapped his legs again.

"Carol! This is most unprofessional."

Carol appeared shocked. "What did I do?"

Okun lowered his voice, hoping the face mask and quieter tone would not pick up on the cameras. "You keep touching my leg."

Carol leaned closer. "Doctor, that wasn't me."

Okun stiffened. He slowly pivoted. He barely had time to register the problem before a needle pierced his eardrum.

He never heard Carol scream.

****

Okun's assistant, Teddy Harris, watched the doctor from the observation room as he began the autopsy. He leapt from his seat when the creature on the table suddenly became animated, spearing the doctor and his nurse with tentacles.

"Red alert!" he yelled into the red phone next to the monitor. "Red alert in Exam Room 11!"

But already the room was filling with a special chlorine gas. Formulated using the liquid compound from the pool water at Riptide Island. A thick fog clouded the room until Teddy couldn't see anything inside. He waited for the room to clear.

The lone door to the room opened and Vic Page joined Teddy. Vic was head of security for this facility. A job he took with eternal seriousness. Teddy had never seen him crack a smile. His dark face was shrouded by a scowl that appeared etched into his features. Vic was only five-foot-ten but was built like a tank. Shoulders wide, arms thick as tree trunks, legs like machine pistons. The man obviously spent his free time snacking on barbells.

"I thought it was dead," Teddy said. A question and a statement rolled into one.

"We did, too," Vic said. "It hasn't shown a single sign of life in six months and has been stored in a freezer the whole time."

"This means the others might also come back."

Vic nodded grimly. “I’m going to make a call. We have to proceed under the assumption they will all wake up if we thaw them.”

“Will the powers-that-be hold us accountable for what happened to Doctor Okun?”

“Oh no,” Vic said, heading to the door. “They’ll be ecstatic. They wanted living specimens to go along with the object they found buried deep inside Riptide Island."

Teddy's eyes widened in wonder. "What was the object?"

Vic shook his head, and smirked. "I'd tell you, but then I'd have to kill you."

www.ingramcontent.com/pod-product-compliance
Lightning Source LLC
La Vergne TN
LVHW010641110826
845149LV00014B/2909

* 9 7 9 8 9 8 8 7 0 3 9 3 8 *